Codes of Power

Diana Cooper

Codes of Power

HODDER

MOBIUS

Hodder & Stoughton

Copyright © 2003 by Diana Cooper

First published in Great Britain in 2003 by Hodder and Stoughton
A division of Hodder Headline

The right of Diana Cooper to be identified as the Author of the Work has been
asserted by her in accordance with the Copyright, Designs and Patents Act 1988.

A Mobius paperback

1 3 5 7 9 10 8 6 4 2

A CIP catalogue record for this title is available from the British Library

ISBN 0 340 82191 4

Typeset in 12/15pt Sabon by
Phoenix Typesetting, Burley-in-Wharfedale, West Yorkshire

Printed and bound in Great Britain by
Mackays of Chatham Ltd, Chatham, Kent

Hodder and Stoughton
A division of Hodder Headline
338 Euston Road
London NW1 3BH

To my son, Justin, of whom I am immensely
proud, with much love.

Author's Note

I set off to travel round Australia for six months in September 2000, knowing that I would return with information for another book but not knowing what the book was to be about.

When I arrived in Sydney I met three amazing women who took me to an Aborigine birthing site and initiation sites as well as other sacred places. Through them I obtained introductions to Aboriginal elders, settlements and schools in north-east Australia. As I talked to many Aborigines I realised the book was to be a sequel to *The Silent Stones*.

Marcus, Joanna and Helen are once more pitted against the forces of the Elite – the dark brotherhood – who wish to control humanity, and who are now influencing weak men to act on their behalf. This time the Scroll was to bring forward wisdom and information from Lemuria, which has been passed down through the consciousness of the Aborigines. I also became aware that it is only in honouring the best of the Lemurian and Atlantean cultures that this planet can come into balance and harmony. And so *The Codes of Power* was born.

I want to thank all the people in Australia who invited me into their homes and shared their knowledge and inspiration with me. I most particularly want to thank Lynne, Liz, Denise, Cathy, Babette, Juliette, Charles, Doug and Joan. There were many others.

I am indebted to the elders who gave so generously of their time and wisdom, and those who brought me books about their culture when I was staying in the bush.

I also want to thank the universe for providing continuous impeccable synchronicities for my entire six months in Australia. It was for me a fabulous, never-to-be-forgotten journey and I have woven my experiences, together with important esoteric information, into *The Codes of Power*.

As you read this book, you too will undertake your initiation into the Codes of Power. May the wise ancients, the angels and the powers of the light support your journey.

With love,

Diana

Chapter 1

As Marcus strolled through Darling Harbour that December day reflections shimmered in the water like jewels, red, yellow, blue, purple and green, mirroring the vitality of Sydney.

His observant grey eyes missed nothing. He leaped like a cat to catch a child's sunhat, which blew off in a stray gust of wind and was in danger of landing in the water. The stressed and irritable mother was shouting at the unfortunate little girl but Marcus's charm and humour as he restored the hat left her smiling and the child relieved.

'Nice one, mate,' called a burly tattooed Aussie and Marcus acknowledged him with a raised hand and good-humoured grin.

He bought a coffee at a kiosk and stretched out his long legs under a café table, settling back to wait patiently for his woman as many men had done before him.

As he sat, his mind wandered to the extraordinary events of eighteen months ago when he and Joanna had been in Kashmir with her mother, Helen. There they had been given an ancient Atlantean Scroll by a dying Tibetan monk, murdered as he escaped with it from his homeland. With his last breath the old man implored Marcus to reveal the contents of the Scroll to the world.

The Scroll contained such important information about the Great Mysteries of the Earth and special powerful portals on the planet, which could free humanity, that a dark brotherhood called the Elite had tried to kill them in an effort to prevent them from carrying out its instructions.

Finally at Machu Picchu the forces of light had won the first battle against the forces of darkness but Marcus sensed there was another looming.

New translations from the Scroll, which was still being decoded by academics in London, were revealing that the Codes of Power originated in Australia. Just as my work has brought me to Australia! Not really a coincidence, he thought wryly. I guess it's universal synchronicity at play.

It was why he had extended his business trip and persuaded Joanna to come with him for a holiday. Her mother, Helen, had taken the opportunity to fly to Australia with them and was now staying with her old school friend in Cairns, on the north-east coast.

It was a shame Tony could not come too, he thought, for he liked the quiet man, who had played a major part in bringing forward the wisdom of the Scroll. He suspected that Tony and Helen had become very close since they had all fought the forces of darkness at Machu Picchu, but Tony was consumed with finishing his book, the deadline for which was Christmas. Pity, he reflected. They would have enjoyed a holiday here together.

He would not have been so complacent if he had known that the Elite had hacked into the computer from which information about the Codes of Power was to be released. Already the dark forces were planning their next moves.

Unperturbed, he watched the world go by: earnest Japanese students, businessmen in dark suits and polished shoes, mothers pushing toddlers in strollers and every shape and description of tourist. A big white ibis with a long black curved beak and large ungainly feet plodded along in the crowd, ignored as any drab old lady. The bird, sacred in ancient Egypt, stepped sideways and flapped on to a dustbin to forage for scraps. An irony, mused Marcus. From priestess to bag lady!

He jumped as a haughty seagull landed on his table. Its cold yellow eyes were alert, watching for prey. It made him shiver suddenly.

Where was Joanna? Suddenly anxious, he frowned. It was not like her to be late. As if to emphasise his fear a small, scowling cloud scudded across the sun, throwing the world into shadow and deepening his concern.

She said she wanted space this morning to do her own thing. She was eternally independent and he admired it. It was eighteen months since they were at the great portal of light at Machu Picchu in Peru, where she had been stabbed by an agent for the Elite. Now he worried when she was away for too long. As he remembered that day an icy chill ran down his back.

Deliberately he turned his mind to the Codes of Power. This was a new section of the Scroll yet to be translated though he suspected that these Codes would reveal information that could shift the balance of power in the world from greed and corruption to peace and cooperation. His eyes glinted with excitement and he started to drum his fingers on the table. 'The Codes of Power!' he murmured. 'The mystery to be resolved in Australia and we're all here, waiting for instructions! I hope they send translations from the Scroll soon.'

At last he spotted Joanna loping towards him like a colt with her long-limbed upright stride. Her shoulder-length brown hair was swinging under her blue cap, taking years off her age. As she waved a piece of paper triumphantly in the air, she looked like a teenager rather than a woman in her mid twenties. Her brown eyes were lit up by a wide smile that showed her teeth and emphasised her narrow face.

As she threw herself into a chair opposite him, the sun emerged from behind the cloud and drenched her in gold. 'Sorry I'm late. Which do you want first – the good news or the better?' She radiated an aura of excitement and without giving him a chance to reply continued, 'Whew, I'm hot. Get me an iced tea wouldja?' This latter, all in one breath, was delivered with a grin and a slight cock of her head, like a small bird, and was her way of saying 'please'.

Marcus laughed in response to her infectious delight and stood up to get her tea. He knew he would get nothing from her until she had it. 'I'll start with the good,' he called over his shoulder as he strode to the nearby kiosk. A moment later, as he placed her drink in front of her, he reflected that she was irresistible when she was happy.

'Thanks!' She tossed back her hair, fanning her hot

cheeks with the piece of paper. 'The good news is I've got tickets to climb the bridge on Monday!'

'Brilliant!' He had long nurtured a desire to climb Sydney Harbour Bridge but did not think she would want to. 'You're not doing it too, are you?'

'Try to stop me.' She grinned, pleased at his evident delight.

'Great. Well, if that's good, what's better?'

Joanna paused for effect and to allow a raucous mob of bright green lorikeets to fly past. Her voice rose slightly with excitement. 'I popped back to the hotel to check the e-mail. This one's from Mum. She's in Cooktown and she's got an intro to an Aboriginal elder who may know about the Codes of Power!'

Startled, Marcus repeated in a whisper, 'The Codes of Power?' Then he glanced automatically over his shoulder.

'Sorry!' Joanna dropped her voice. Her stomach clenched in sudden fear and she too looked round to check that no one was listening. 'I forgot for a second. Surely they can't still be following us?'

'I'm sure it's all right here. I'm probably paranoid.' Marcus squeezed her hand, sorry to see her jubilation quenched, but he spoke in a low voice, remembering how relentlessly the evil band of the Elite, who wanted control and power on Earth, had tried to kill them for the information in the Scroll. They could be following them still. He knew they played a long game. 'What does your mum say? Has she heard from London? Does that mean she knows what the Codes of Power are? And why should an

Aboriginal elder know about the Codes?' He was buzzing with questions.

'Here, read it.' Her dark eyes were alight once more. You couldn't knock Joanna's spirit for long. She stopped fanning her face and handed him the print-out of Helen's e-mail.

Thursday

Hi there, you two,

Am leaving Sylvie's today and flying to Cooktown! That's a little place right at the top of Australia on the east coast, where Sylvie has a contact who knows an elder called Uncle George. I'm going to meet him! I'm certain the Aboriginal people hold the key to the Codes of Power! And I've got a gut feeling Uncle George knows something!

Scientists believed that the Aborigines have been guardians of the land in Australia for 60,000 years but now they are beginning to prove it is more like 150,000 years! It's the only continuous culture to have survived for so long. They must know something we don't.

I'll keep in touch. In the meantime, Sylvie says why don't you fly up to Cairns and do some diving on the Great Barrier Reef. You're welcome to stay with her! Then you could hire a car and drive up to Cooktown – I'm told it's an interesting trip, though I didn't fancy driving all the way on my own. It's just a suggestion but looking forward to seeing you soon.

Love, Mum

P.S. Sylvie wants to meet you both. She sends her love.

Marcus looked into the swirling excitement in Joanna's eyes. 'Yes!' he exclaimed. 'Yes! Yes! Yes! To all of it!'

'Thought you'd be pleased.' She laughed.

'Your mum's a star,' said Marcus. 'She's as independent as you are and just as resourceful. I wonder how she'll get on in Cooktown.'

Joanna laughed. 'She'll be fine. But be honest,' she teased, 'we've been nothing but trouble for you since we met, though we do have advantages like getting you diving trips on the Great Barrier Reef.'

As it transpired fate had other plans.

Chapter 2

Helen had survived a slightly choppy flight to Cooktown in a plane the size of a gnat and had slipped easily into the slow, quiet rhythm of the place since her arrival the day before.

Cooktown is a small town, originally founded on gold, which has long since run out, and famed because Captain Cook's boat was shipwrecked on the reef there. Depending on who you talk to, he was either helped or hindered by the local Aboriginal tribe. It is so far from civilisation that it is 'beyond the bitumen', for the main road peters into a dirt track forty miles before the town.

Helen was staying in the Sea View Motel, where she had an upstairs room, clean, simple and more than adequate. A wooden verandah, really a covered way, ran round the building at first-floor level, shading the rooms from the sun or offering shelter from rain. Here, tables and chairs set outside each room made it an idyllic place to relax and watch the view.

A wide, patched road meandered in front of the motel and a mango tree dripped small unripe fruit on to it. Palm trees, bearing prolific bunches of green coconuts, fringed her view as she looked out over the wide estuary with its grass-clad sandbanks and quiet jetty.

Today the water spread like a grey-blue sheet, shot with silver, and a handful of boats were scattered in the harbour, all facing in the same direction like soldiers. Apparently they would turn towards the hotel at high tide and then Sally from the café on the wharf would feed the fish, huge mullet, which swarmed in for the feast. In the distance layers of hills, like cardboard cut-outs, faded into the misty distance.

Helen sat on the verandah outside her room quietly watching it all, as she had done much of the time since her arrival, and felt contented.

A guest, walking past her to his room, registered her as a slim, self-contained woman in her fifties, with a pleasant smile and gracious manner. Her dark, slightly slanted eyes and high cheekbones prompted him to wonder if her ancestry contained an Asian element. But no. Helen was pure Celt, half Welsh, half Irish. She had inherited an interesting combination of mystic intuition and sturdy common sense.

Like so many of her sex and generation brought up to be self-effacing, Helen's greatest enemy was self-doubt. She judged harshly her character defects and discounted to herself the many acts of kindness she performed. Yet she was wise and constantly strove to do the right thing and see the other person's perspective in all situations.

She glanced at the grizzly clouds, wondering whether they would clear or mass and darken into rain-clouds. Cramming her umbrella and her sunhat into her bag, she decided that December in Queensland was as changeable as March in England, just hotter.

This morning she intended to explore Cooktown. Not that there was much to see, just a wide street lined with shops, which looked as if they came from a cowboy set, and the museum and botanic gardens.

On her way out she asked at reception if they had a safe for her passport and money.

The manager's wife replied, laughing, 'You don't need one here. There's no crime in Cooktown. Court meets once a month to deal with someone driving without a seat belt or who's perhaps indulged in a little pot. Everything's safe here!'

Helen felt an easing of pressure in her mind, a kind of alignment in the order of things. She loved this quiet place. She hummed to herself as she picked up the Cooktown guide from a pile on the reception desk and flipped through it.

She read: 'Finch Bay is a popular swimming beach despite the crocodile warning signs. Locals swim at the northern end of the beach only. At the bend in the creek a two-metre estuarine crocodile is seen on a regular basis. This crocodile is not regarded as a threat but wading in the creek is not advisable. Warning: Sea Stingers. These jellyfish are seasonal, December–March and contact may fatal.'

Her euphoria vanished and the back of her neck felt tight. It was unsettling how easily her mood could be affected in this strange place so far from home. She shook her head as if to shake off a sense of danger. It reminded her of the feeling she'd had when the Elite was chasing them. But that's over now, she told herself firmly. We haven't had a sense of them for a long time.

The rain was falling soft and warm. She paused to chat to the manager as he came up the path.

'Mind the snakes,' he warned. 'Someone saw a taipan in the ditch by the road just now.'

'A taipan!' Her eyes widened. They were the most deadly and aggressive snakes in Australia.

He nodded. 'Don't walk in any long grass, will you?'

Helen felt her stomach tense. Australia! If it wasn't snakes, it was spiders, sharks or stingers. And crocodiles as well. For an instant she wished she was back in safe old clement England, where the sea was cold but safe, spiders did not bite and the only poisonous snakes were adders. And in all her life she had never seen one.

It seemed every Australian delighted in telling her of a friend who had trodden on a deadly snake, which had whipped up and bitten them.

The manager was watching her with the concerned look that hardy Australians reserve for their delicate European cousins. She suppressed a shiver and tried to smile urbanely. 'I'll take care.'

Out in the street she put on her glasses to examine every innocent twig before she passed it and stamped her feet in their stout shoes to warn any snakes of her approach.

On Sunday she was meeting Uncle George, the Aboriginal elder. I can't wait, she thought happily and walked more upright, forgetting the dangers of the country as she wondered what he was like and, even more important, what he knew. She was convinced he would be able to tell her something of significance about the Codes of Power.

She did not know that the meeting would plunge her into the greatest challenge of her life.

Chapter 3

There was not a breath of air in Sydney when Joanna and Marcus went sightseeing on Saturday morning. Fierce heat bounced from the buildings and pavements, creating an oven in which the intrepid tourists cooked. A dropped ice cream melted into a sticky puddle in moments.

'That'll be me soon,' Joanna moaned to Marcus, half laughing. 'And you'll mourn the woman you loved, who liquefied before your eyes.'

Marcus chuckled as he looked at her perspiring scarlet face. 'I'd say you look more like a volcano about to erupt into flames! Bear up. Just two more blocks and we're at the hotel.'

They sprinted from one patch of shade to the next until they reached the palm-lined, air-conditioned foyer of their hotel.

In their room, the chilled air was sheer bliss and a cool shower soon restored them, though Joanna insisted that her brains had been cooked and she would never be able to think again.

Then she sobered. 'I think we ought to tell the universe clearly that we want the information about the Codes of Power,' she said with an air of determination. 'We've been talking about it constantly for the last few days.'

'Oh, so your brains weren't cooked then!' Marcus teased.

'Silly, I'm serious!'

'I know you are. You're right. We should focus our clear intent, so that the universe responds to the energy we send out.'

Joanna pondered a moment. 'We want to be led to the Codes of Power and be given the qualities needed to use the information and power wisely.'

'Sounds great.' Marcus was already sitting cross-legged on the bed. 'I think we ought to put your mum in too. She's bound to be part of it.'

'Oh yes! I agree with that.' Joanna lit a candle and then sat beside Marcus, closing her eyes and breathing herself into a deep space. They projected out their intentions clearly to the universe. There was utter silence. Afterwards they sat in silence for a moment.

'Now let's see what happens,' Joanna said quietly. She opened her eyes and smiled at Marcus, who leaned forward and ran a hand sensuously down her arm, kissing her with soft lips so that she fell unresisting on to the bed. She wasn't wearing a bra and one of his hands stroked the warm curve of her breast, feeling her nipple hardening in response through her T-shirt. He was pulling it off when his mobile rang.

'Leave it,' murmured Joanna, running her hand down his chest, but he shook his head firmly.

'No. We've asked the universe to lead us to the Codes of Power. Now we must be alert for responses. That has to come first.'

Why do you always have to be so noble, thought Joanna irritably as she listened to his side of the conversation.

'Hello. Oh hello, Stephen. How are you doing?' He listened, then said, 'Sure, that would be great. We'd love to!'

Joanna tickled him, trying to distract him. 'Who is it?' she whispered, curiosity overcoming her annoyance. 'What would we love to do?'

Marcus waved his free hand to quiet her but, knowing his vulnerability, she doubled her tickle attack.

'That's very good of you. What time?' Marcus was squirming, trying to fend her off and trying not to laugh. 'We'll be there . . . Great. See you later. Bye.' He put the phone down, playfully threatening Joanna with his finger.

'That was short and sweet. Who's Stephen? What did he want?' She smiled innocently.

'I've a good mind not to tell you now, you minx.'

And she giggled, knowing he would.

'Stephen's a bloke I met through the contract I was working on. Nice fellow. Suggests we meet for dinner tonight.'

Joanna was instantly serious and Marcus replied to the unspoken question in her eyes.

'We've got to assume he can give us a clue about the Codes of Power.'

She nodded in agreement.

'Now where were we?' Marcus murmured as he pulled her close. 'Have I told you recently you're beautiful, Jo?'

'Not recently enough,' she responded, smiling deep into his eyes, her pupils enormous.

They reached the restaurant before Stephen and found a table in a quiet corner. The room was fresh and airy with small white-clothed tables, softened with little posies of pink flowers. Marcus ordered a beer and Joanna a mineral water.

While they waited for Stephen, Marcus tried to fill Joanna in on him. 'He's quiet, dedicated, hard-working. Looks Italian but he's got an Aussie accent. I don't know much about him except that he knows his stuff work-wise and,' he added with a shrug, 'he seems a nice guy. But why he should ask us to dinner I have no idea.'

'Oh well, the universe works in peculiar ways,' she responded sagely. 'Cheers!' She clinked her glass with his. 'Here's to the Codes of Power.'

Stephen arrived a few minutes later and Joanna agreed he looked like a middle-aged Italian in his white shirt and neat dark trousers. He was stocky with short grey curly hair. She thought he had the face of a man who had suffered.

Marcus introduced them. As Joanna looked into his blue-grey eyes, softened by thick dark lashes, she was intrigued to find he was scrutinising her, not as a woman but as a soul.

They chatted inconsequentially, ordered their meals and let the conversation meander over a wide range of subjects. It was pleasant but not earth-shattering. Joanna glanced at Marcus. She could tell he was equally puzzled. What was the point in the meeting?

As if on cue, Stephen put down his knife and fork. 'I don't really know why I phoned you,' he said hesitantly. 'I just had a sudden strong impression I must contact you.' He shrugged slightly. A clock chimed and none of them heard it.

Marcus sat forward, his eyes firmly fixed on Stephen's face. 'Now we have to find out why we're meeting like this.'

Joanna noticed that the taut lines round Stephen's eyes had relaxed. He signalled the waiter for more drinks, then sat back. 'I suspect I've been sent to help you with something.' He paused and his voice dropped. 'Something beyond ourselves, of importance to the world.' He looked at them with all-seeing eyes and at that moment they both knew he could help them in their quest for the Codes of Power. They would have to trust him.

Marcus raised his eyebrows in silent question to Joanna and she nodded imperceptibly. He touched his chin for a moment of thought, then decided to start at the beginning and tell Stephen about the Scroll.

'It's an ancient document from Atlantis. That's a culture from another age, before our recorded history,' he explained.

Stephen indicated that he knew about Atlantis.

Marcus continued, 'Oh, so you know that the Atlanteans developed their left brain, their intellectual mind, with an emphasis on science and technology but they lost their spirituality?'

The older man nodded.

'In the end evil dominated and by divine decree the continent was flooded. You know that?'

Stephen nodded again, watching him with an impenetrable expression.

Marcus continued, surprised at the depth of Stephen's knowledge. 'However, certain untainted Atlanteans who escaped the flood took a Scroll, containing the wisdom of Atlantis, to Tibet, where it was held in sacred trust until it was time to reveal the contents – at a time when Earth was in crisis. I feel that's now, when we could move into a new Golden Age, or we might destroy ourselves again. We have to get the information out urgently.'

Stephen's eyes were bright as he looked from one of them to the other. 'The Scroll of Atlantis? I thought it was a myth.'

Joanna leaned forward. 'The Scroll was made of material we don't have any more because the Atlanteans had superior technology. It was pliable and didn't fade so the information was preserved.'

Marcus added softly, 'Most of the Scroll was destroyed in a fire and now we've only got the microfilm.' He vividly remembered the horror of the night when the temple in India where they had taken the Scroll was attacked and set on fire. He and Helen had escaped with the microfilm and a few pieces of the original material. The monks were not so lucky. Most of them died in the massacre. He shivered.

The older man was listening intently and Marcus went on. 'Among other things the Scroll reminds us about human illusions and the Great Mysteries of the planet. Also about ley lines and portals, which have to be kept clear so that we humans can communicate directly with Source or God. It gives specific instructions about tones and symbols, which can be used to do this.'

Marcus wondered whether to talk about the Codes of Power, which were mentioned in the Scroll, but Stephen had withdrawn his attention. He was sitting back slightly, with a faraway look in his eyes as if contemplating something distant. At last he said, 'My people understand these things. It has been our sacred task to honour our Mother Earth and keep the ley lines and portals pure and open. Only we call them song lines and sacred sites.' He paused, noticing that his guests had glanced at each other in surprise.

'Your people?' queried Marcus.

'Yes,' he replied with infinite pride. 'I am an Aborigine.' Stephen smiled at the politely veiled astonishment of his guests 'My father was Italian. My mother Aborigine.'

'But you look totally European!' exclaimed Joanna. 'I mean Australian.'

'The Aboriginal gene is recessive,' explained Stephen. 'But, you know, nothing can take away the fact that I am Aborigine.' Unmistakable pride reverberated in his voice and he spoke with slow dignity. 'Just as the Nazi attempts to exterminate the Jews did not succeed, the white genocide of our people will not succeed.'

Joanna shuddered. Genocide was a strong word. Was it really true? she wondered.

Marcus too was shaken. He found the horrifying words

spoken in such a sage-like manner profoundly disturbing. He thought, I've got a lot to learn from this man.

Stephen broke the awkward pause. There was a strange light in his eyes as he said, 'And now, what information do I have for you, I wonder?'

They looked at him expectantly and his face creased in thought. Slowly, deliberately, he pulled a red crystal from his pocket and examined it as if it were a precious stone. Coloured the red of the earth, it was roughly triangular in shape and about three inches long. One side was curiously rounded. It seemed to glow.

'This came from Uluru – Ayers Rock – and there's a story behind it which will interest you. But first perhaps I should tell you a little about our culture?'

He placed the crystal on the table. It lay, pregnant with promise in front of them. Marcus and Joanna could not take their eyes off it.

Chapter 4

Stephen stared at the red crystal lying in the centre of the table, shimmering in the candlelight.

'Our culture is very ancient,' he began. 'The oldest in the world. It's unique and very spiritual. It's true that we couldn't read or write and developed nothing techno-logical but in other ways we were incredibly evolved. I guess that within our Aborigine wisdom lies many answers.' He hesitated, speaking modestly, shyly even. 'I believe we hold the key to the future of the planet.'

Joanna stared at him intently, her face flushed with concentration. 'Do you mean the answers are in your Dreamtime?'

'Mmm,' he considered. 'Our Dreamtime is the uni-versal consciousness where all knowledge is held.'

'I'd love to know more about the myths of your Dreamtime,' responded Joanna.

'You must meet my daughter, Tamsin. She knows much more than I do about the Dreaming stories.'

'We'd love to, wouldn't we, Marcus?'

He nodded. 'But could you tell us a bit about totems?'

'Of course,' he replied. 'We believe that Great Spirit put all creatures and aspects of nature on Earth. Each person and tribe looked after an animal or plant or rock. This was his totem. But you don't just look after your totem animal. You identify with it and emulate its qualities because it is part of Great Spirit. You certainly don't eat it, or you only eat certain parts of it.'

He stopped abruptly as the waiter dimmed the lights and they realised that they were the only people left in the restaurant. It broke the mood of the discussion. Stephen beckoned for the bill. 'I think we need to talk further. Perhaps we could meet tomorrow? It's important.'

He glanced at Joanna with a smile. 'I'll explain our Dreamtime and . . .' He picked up the red stone from the table and weighed it in his hand. 'Something that's important for all of us.'

They burned to know what it was. Both wanted to say, 'Tell us now,' but something in his mien prevented them. He would say nothing more on the subject tonight. They looked at each other in resigned excitement.

As they all left the restaurant Marcus said, 'One thing puzzles me. I was saying to Joanna, I haven't seen a single Aborigine in Sydney. Why not?'

Stephen paused for a second. 'There are some things you may not understand.' His voice became dangerously soft. 'When the Whites settled on our land here, they brought diseases against which my people had no immunity, diseases like smallpox, syphilis, measles, influenza and even the common cold. We died in our hundreds.' He was silent for a long time. A bus rumbled past and a car hooted. 'They shot the rest in cold blood.'

They fell into step, one on either side of the Aborigine,

walking briskly along the late-night pavement. Stephen spoke crisply. 'The Westerners arrived with guns believing it was their right to take our lands. So they appropriated our traditional hunting grounds. Their cattle and sheep needed vast quantities of water and drank many of our water holes dry. That meant we could no longer go walkabout as we had always done.'

He eyed them gravely. 'Our walkabouts are ritual journeys in which we follow the footsteps of our ancestors. We sing the ancestors' songs exactly and in this way we re-create the creation.'

'Oh!' Joanna broke in. 'And Christians are taught that the Seraphim constantly sing round the throne of God to maintain the power of creation! It's the same thing, isn't it?'

Stephen smiled at her. 'I think so,' he agreed.

'So what's a song line?' Joanna persisted. 'Is that a ley line? Is that the route of your walkabouts?'

'So many questions!' Stephen smiled broadly, showing largish white teeth, which made him look softer and more boyish suddenly. 'A song is a map. It gives detailed and intimate directions. And yes, those are the routes our ancestors took. And yes, of course, they formed the ley lines of Australia and were the basis of the sacred journeys we undertook on walkabout.'

'Most people think of walkabouts as skiving off,' commented Marcus.

'Indeed not. They were pilgrimages, sacred duties. Rituals and ceremonies were performed in certain places and at special times. They were holy travels.'

'I wonder if we have ever tried to understand your culture,' murmured Joanna.

'You said the imported cattle drank the water holes dry?' Marcus repeated, aware that they had deflected Stephen from the subject.

'Yes they did. And as the water holes became dry we had nowhere to live or hunt. Wherever the Whites lived, they thought our traditional foods like kangaroos were theirs and called it poaching if an Aborigine took one.'

He sighed. 'We could no longer survive in the bush. Our clans were forced on to the missions or stations, where we worked without pay for white man's handouts. This was white flour, white sugar, alcohol and tobacco, food with no nutritional value. Our bodies were used to bush tucker. We couldn't metabolise that stuff. Worse still, they broke our spirits by deriding our beliefs, telling us we were wrong and desecrating our sacred sites.'

Joanna touched his arm in a gesture of sympathy.

He shrugged. 'You will find the broken remnants of my people in the slums of Sydney. Like all dispossessed they are angry. But broken spirits can and must mend. Torn roots eventually reach deep into Mother Earth for sustenance again.' He breathed in the night air deeply. 'We must all learn from this.' Then he squared his shoulders and changed the subject abruptly.

'Do you know,' he said, to their surprise, 'that the Aboriginal people descend directly from Lemuria? That's the great civilisation before Atlantis. We are very ancient and I believe there has to be a higher purpose for everything that has happened to our culture. I am sure there must be a future we can all share. Perhaps we seek the key together.'

As he pulled the piece of red crystal from his pocket, cradling it gently in both hands as if it were delicate china, he said, 'This crystal holds the key to that which you seek. But first there are things you must understand and experience.'

Marcus and Joanna looked at each other, holding their breaths in the hope he would continue.

'Tomorrow!' he said firmly.

Chapter 5

Rather early next morning Joanna rang her mother. 'Hi, Mum! It's me! Did I get you out of bed?'

'It's Sunday!' protested Helen. 'You sound very chirpy for this hour of the morning!'

'Listen, Mum. What do you know about Lemuria?'

'Lemuria? Not a lot. It was the civilisation that preceded Atlantis. At first they were very ethereal and spiritual. More so even than early Atlantis but they never developed technology and were Stone Age people.' She stifled a yawn. 'Why do you want to know?'

'One more question, then I'll tell you. How and why did Lemuria end?'

'As far as I know the people forgot their purpose and got heavily into black magic. Eventually the age was terminated.'

'Just like the end of Atlantis?'

'Similar. I think there was a great explosion and then a flood.'

'Where was Lemuria?'

'In the Pacific Islands and Australia I think. And some parts were saved from the flood. That's all I know. Now tell me what it's all about.'

Joanna told her mother about their meeting with Stephen. 'He had a strange red crystal which he wouldn't let us touch. I've never seen a crystal that colour before. He said it was part of the key we seek and was quite enigmatic about it. It was odd. But he's going to tell us more later today.'

'How intriguing!' Helen's mind was whirling with possibilities. 'Something's definitely starting to happen. What else did he say?'

'He said the Aboriginal people had descended from Lemuria and held the key to the future of the planet.'

'That's fascinating! Well, I told you, scientists are now saying carbon dating on the Great Barrier Reef shows Aborigines were here one hundred and fifty thousand years ago; but to be here since Lemuria, that's something else! To have survived the end times and to have developed totally separately from the Atlanteans. That's amazing!'

'Mum, do you think the Aborigines hold the key to the future of the planet?'

'I wouldn't be surprised. Their myths are as ancient as time and were handed down as a sacred trust. They must be full of esoteric information.'

'And their lives have always been dedicated to looking after the planet.'

'That's true. I think they've got to have a link with the Codes of Power because the Scroll says the universal energy pushes people to be in the right place at the right time. And we're here in Australia looking for information. It's got to be.'

Joanna was nodding though her mother couldn't see. 'We should hear some more about the Scroll soon. There hasn't been a translation for ages. Have you heard anything from Tony?'

Helen blushed slightly at the mention of Tony. When he looked after her at Machu Picchu they became good friends, slightly more than good friends, though she scarcely acknowledged it to herself, let alone her daughter. She thought of him more often than she cared to admit.

'Just a short e-mail. I picked it up yesterday,' she murmured vaguely. 'Bits and pieces of gossip. His daughter's expecting a baby. It seems to have brought them together a bit. And the book's progressing well.'

'That's good. About time,' said Joanna, smiling to herself. So her mother was communicating with Tony!

'I'll e-mail him to ask if there's anything new from the Scroll.'

'Yes, do that,' agreed Joanna. But they both knew they would have heard immediately if there were anything to report.

Helen showered and dressed, then set off for the internet shop. After yesterday's rain, today was scorching and the puddles in the wide patched road were steaming. A dog lay panting in the shade of a wall and a bunch of pink galahs were quarrelling like irritable children. Helen picked up one of their feathers, which floated down to her feet. She smiled and decided it was a lucky sign. She had a feeling there would be news today. It's time for something to break, she decided. But to her annoyance the internet shop was closed. Damn, it's Sunday, she realised.

Languidly she retraced her steps past the police station, half hidden by a strangler fig and a vast mango tree. Next door, the courthouse, with its comfortable unused look, was painted cream and was fronted by palms. Dozens of green and red lorikeets flew noisily round a huge frangipani, white with blossom, while violent patches of purple bougainvillea splashed over whitewashed walls.

She passed the motel and meandered down to the quay, where a drunkenly swaying notice reminded that estuarine crocodiles are dangerous. Nervously, she glanced about to check that there wasn't one lurking anywhere and frowned at a suspicious-looking log. Locals had warned her that crocodiles came on to land and could run faster than humans! Everything seemed clear, however, and she felt relieved. No one looked bothered but then they wouldn't, would they, she thought. It was part of life to them.

Fanning her hot face with her hand she strolled to the beach café where she could sit in the shade, indulge in an iced tea and forget about dangerous creatures. Life felt slow and harmonious. 'I like it here.' She sighed with pleasure as she watched a black and white stork standing patiently in the water on one red leg. Its long black beak was poised like a spear waiting to be thrust into an unsuspecting fish.

*

When Helen returned to the motel there was an urgent message for her to phone Joanna.

Hooray, she thought, racing up the steps despite the heat and picking up the phone in her room.

Chapter 6

Marcus answered the phone.

'Hello! It's me!' said Helen.

'Helen! How're you doing?'

Helen chortled. 'You sound completely Aussified! But I got an urgent message from Joanna to call.'

He laughed. 'Joanna's just slipped out for a few minutes. I take it you didn't access your e-mail.'

'No. It's Sunday. The internet place was closed.'

'Thought it might be. Guess what! They've released a bit more of the Scroll. It's quite extraordinary.' The excitement in his voice sent a little shiver of anticipation through her.

'Go on then! Read it!' she exclaimed eagerly.

'Okay.' Marcus was pleased with her reaction. Helen was usually so calm and steady that he did not always know how she felt. 'It's headed "Preamble to the Codes of Power". Just listen to this: "For the Golden Age of Lemuria, which preceded Atlantis, the Source of All That Is created a Garden of Abundance in rich red earth, with soft weather and a cornucopia of plant and animal forms to provide all that was needed."'

'It must mean Australia!' interrupted Helen. 'But not the weather surely? You could never call it soft.'

'Just a moment,' answered Marcus. 'Let me go on!'

'Sorry.'

' "The first Lemurians living in the Garden of Abundance were pure in heart and mind. These luminous beings knew that they were custodians of Mother Earth, thus they nurtured and cared for the natural world as an act of service and dedication.

' "Through constant ritual and ceremony they connected with the Source of All That Is and kept the Earth, its animals and plants sacred.

' "Once again, as in previous Golden Ages, the purity was defiled and tarnished by those who believed they were separate from the Spirit of One. This led to a desire to control other people and life forms. It is the cause of all war and disease.

' "In late Lemuria the use of black magic became widespread. Electromagnetic waves of evil from the black magic caused chaotic weather conditions and Lemuria experienced violent storms and floods and fires. But still humans went their wayward way until the waves of darkness penetrated the very earth, causing terrible earthquakes and volcanoes. Finally a cataclysmic explosion rent a vast crater in the centre of Lemuria. Noxious gases poured out over the continent, forming a suffocating blanket, which smothered most life forms.

' "By Divine Decree the experiment of Lemuria was terminated and great floods, in reality the tears of Mother Earth, engulfed the Garden of Abundance." '

'My God! That's horrific!'

'I know. I hope we're not heading that way now.'

'That's why we're seeking the Codes of Power to bring light back to Earth!'

'I know, though sometimes I despair.' Marcus sighed, then added, 'There's quite a bit more.'

'Go on!'

He resumed. ' "By grace of the Source of All That Is, a few pure and wise souls who held faith with the light were saved from the cataclysm to continue the divine experiment in a limited way." '

'The Aborigines!' Helen exclaimed.

Marcus read on as if she had not spoken. ' "The explosion and flood at the fall of Lemuria shifted the axis of the Earth, which changed the climate of the lands. The gentle climate became harsh but still, in divine mercy, the Source of All That Is provided all the needs of those who survived. These souls continued their spiritual path and created an enduring culture based on sharing, cooperation and trust.

' "However, their tradition was oral and information was passed on through song, rhythm and dance. They did not learn to scribe. Nor did they develop their intellect." Oh, hang on a sec. Joanna's just come back.'

Helen could hear the door shutting in the background and Marcus saying, 'Hi. I'm just telling your mum about the latest information from the Scroll.' Then Joanna shouted cheerfully in the background, 'Hello, Mum!'

'Say hello back!' Helen told Marcus.

'Your mum says hello back. Now where was I? Oh, this is interesting!' He continued where he left off: ' "The world of Lemuria and the world of Atlantis only met but once. Three Lemurian wise men or karadji were directed by angels to cross the ocean to the continent of Atlantis. The angels guided them to the Great Cathedral in the Sacred Heights in Atlantis. This is a measure of their evolved stature, for only the purest and most powerful can gain access.

' "Here they revealed orally this history and much Lemurian wisdom. It was recorded by the scribes of the High Priest of Atlantis and was later incorporated into the Scroll, for the elucidation of future Ages." '

'That's incredible,' Helen could not help bursting out.

'I know. It's mind-blowing, isn't it.'

'And to think it's being revealed now. It's awesome.'

'Yes it is.'

'Carry on, please!' she begged.

'Okay. It goes on: "We, the Wise Ones of Atlantis, remind you that the Scroll will only be released at the start of the Golden Age of Aquarius if it is necessary.

' "Humanity must reach a certain level of consciousness for the Golden Age to blossom. It can only take place when the wisdom and love of Lemuria and the technology and intellect of Atlantis are combined and balanced by all. These qualities must be equally honoured and valued.

' "When this happens the galaxies and universes will herald the seventh Golden Age. The last and most glorious Golden Age on Earth. The Age of Aquarius. Legions of angels will mass on Earth to help the transition." '

'How wonderful,' breathed Helen and she could hear Joanna agreeing in the background.

'And now we're really coming to it,' said Marcus. 'Listen to this! "For this to happen, certain information must be revealed." And now there's a heading, "**The Codes of Power**", in bold letters.' Marcus spoke more slowly and lowered his voice as if to add impact to his words. ' "We believe that humans will have discovered that information can be stored in quartz crystal. Therefore you will understand what is now revealed, though it is not known in what way humanity will develop this. However we trust it will be for the benefit of all." '

'It means computers – silicone chips, we assume,' Joanna yelled so that her mother could hear.

'Of course!' Helen exclaimed.

'This is the really important bit. Listen to this. "Before Lemuria sank, the blueprint for this planet was encoded and stored in a giant keeper crystal, known as Uluru." '

'You mean Uluru – Ayers Rock? It's a vast crystal coded with information? Good heavens!'

'I know,' agreed Marcus. 'Amazing, isn't it! And there's more about the Codes of Power. Listen! "The Codes of Power is a sacred initiation to be undertaken at the start of the Golden Age by certain souls. As the initiatory tests are passed the divine curriculum of the planet will be revealed, for Earth is a University of Light." What does that mean?'

Helen shrugged. 'We're here to gain a degree in spiritual information and knowledge and we'll be given the course details, I guess.'

' "Whoever attempts the initiation of the Codes of

Power will experience severe challenges and hardships. All must be surrendered, even life itself. The brave souls who undertake this initiation will be guided by the Universal Forces."'

'Why are we receiving this information?' Helen sounded nervous.

She admired Marcus for the quiet firmness of his voice as he replied, 'I think you know that, Helen. I presume we are to undertake this initiation of the Codes of Power.'

Part of Helen thought, Help. I'm nowhere near good enough. Yet another part of her was exulting.

'What an opportunity!' rejoiced Marcus.

Helen could hear paper rustling as he turned another page. 'There's more?' she asked.

'Just a bit. Here it is. "Much of the information for the Codes of Power is also held by the Original Ones, but they too have lost part of the key."'

'The Original Ones! Who are they?' asked Helen.

Joanna shouted, 'Aborigines, of course. *Ab origine* is Latin for "from the beginning".'

Of course, thought Helen, summoning Latin lessons from the recesses of her mind.

'It was you who commented that the Aborigines must have been the pure ones who were saved at the time of destruction,' said Marcus. 'Possibly the Westerners who named them knew intuitively that they were the first people in Australia. We can't wait to see you, Helen, to talk it all over.'

'Me too!'

'We'll let you know what Stephen says and Tamsin, his daughter, hopefully.'

Helen wished she was with them now. She'd love to meet Stephen and Tamsin. But she was seeing Uncle George this afternoon. 'Are you coming to Cairns to dive at the Great Barrier Reef?'

'Yes. We've spoken to Sylvie. On Monday morning we're climbing the Sydney Harbour Bridge and we fly up after that.'

'Great. I'm glad you're meeting her. We were really good friends at school. We kept in touch even when she emigrated here and when I stayed with her in Cairns she hadn't changed a bit.'

The automatic voice broke in to say that the phone card was nearly finished.

Joanna grabbed the receiver. 'See you next week, Mum and love you lots.'

'Love you too.'

Helen put down the phone, her head in a whirl of excited thoughts. It was as well that she did not know what lay ahead.

Chapter 7

Helen was collected from the motel by Jane, an acquaintance of her old friend Sylvie. She was to introduce her to Uncle George, the local elder. Jane was a thin, energetic little woman with short, defiantly curly hair and a hard Australian twang. Helen already knew that she had worked side by side with her husband to build up their trucking business and had expected someone bigger and beefier, possibly more formidable. Jane's husband, Ferdy, was generally 'big' in the area.

You'd never know it, Helen thought, amused, as she hauled herself into the old, very muddy working truck.

There was no actual want of friendliness on Jane's part, more a reserve and clear sense that she was doing Helen a favour because Sylvie had asked it of her. She gave the impression that she was incredibly busy and this was time away from her business. At the same time she was pleasant and offered to be at Helen's service, but always with the underlying sense that it was a duty.

When Helen asked about her husband, she replied that he had taken a truck to Cairns and could not get back to Cooktown because the creek was flooded. 'It'll probably go down tomorrow,' she added with an indifferent shrug.

'It's always like this in the rainy season. Sometimes we're cut off for days or even weeks but he should get through in the four-wheel drive.' She explained that the water ran very fast in the creeks when they were flooded and it would be easy for the vehicle to be swept away. 'And the crocodiles come upriver!' she added.

Without saying a word, Jane implied she thought Helen odd to seek out an Aborigine, even one of George's calibre. As they drove into the blocks of houses behind the main street, Helen asked if her husband employed any Aborigines.

Jane shook her head. 'Nope. Too unreliable. They go walkabout without a word and sometimes never come back. They're nomads.'

'I thought they were great stockmen?'

'Yes, excellent stockmen. They were good on the stations,' conceded Jane. 'But you'd better talk to my husband. Some of the ones he was at school with are elders now. Here we are. This is George's house.'

As they clambered down, she remarked, 'George is special. You won't find the other elders like him. I'm sure he'll be able to answer all your questions.'

Uncle George's house was a small, single-storey concrete building, with a garden neatly laid to lawn and bushes. A purple bougainvillea struggled in a pot under the window. On the fence sat a solitary kookaburra, uttering its strange lingering laugh. The front door stood wide open and welcoming.

Helen was relieved. She had dreaded that he might

live in a dingy house, surrounded by rusty cans and litter. Don't be so judgemental, Helen! she thought crossly.

At the front door she was met by a pungent smell of sweat and coffee. Then a short, slightly stooped man with grey hair thinning on top came out to greet her. His nose was broad and flat in a chubby face and he was very black.

As Jane introduced them, Helen was aware of Uncle George's unfathomable, dark ancient eyes looking full into hers, searching her soul, and his almost angelic smile. The impact on her was so striking that it was some moments before she noticed in her Virgoan way that there was a button missing on his short-sleeved, striped shirt, which left a gap over his stomach, and that his grey trousers were very old. He had bare feet.

Introductions performed, Jane left them almost immediately and Helen followed Uncle George into the lounge, which contained a small sofa, a dining table covered in papers, two hard chairs and a computer work-station. The kitchen was separated from the living area by a counter.

She commented on the computer and Uncle George replied that one of the greatest things his people had to thank the Whites for was teaching them how to record accurately. 'Until your people came to our land, we had no writing or maths. Everything was passed on by song.' He smiled gently.

A born reconciler, thought Helen.

Faced by this extraordinarily dignified and wise man,

Helen perched self-consciously on one of the hard chairs and wondered what on earth she was doing there. What could she talk to him about? Jane had told her that he represented the Aboriginal people on several councils and that he was a highly respected negotiator and leader. He flew all over the country and was presumably very busy. She was taking up this man's precious time!

Helen was rarely at a loss for words but this was one of those moments. She was longing to ask if he knew about the Codes of Power. How could she broach it? She covered her unaccustomed diffidence with smiles and nods. Uncle George seemed at no loss, however. She soon learned that he was a self-deprecating man of generous spirit and forgiving heart.

He was also an old man in Aboriginal terms, for he told her that he was nearly seventy, a great age when the average life expectancy of an Aborigine is a good twenty years less than that of a white Australian.

He started to outline a land claim issue he had been working on. 'We looked after the land for thousands of years and the land looked after us,' he reminded her. 'We believe we cannot own it, for the land owns us. It is our sacred trust to care for it. Generation after generation, we passed the secrets on through our stories and we maintained the spirit of the sacred places with corroborees.' He paused and added by way of explanation, 'They're our celebrations and ceremonies.'

Helen nodded.

'Then Europeans came. We greeted them and helped them, as it is our culture to share and be friendly but they shot our people and took our land. They desecrated our sacred sites thoughtlessly, not even realising what they were, and refused us access. It would be considered sacrilege if someone did that to your churches.'

She nodded again.

'They called the land "Terra nullius" – that's Latin for empty land – though we spent our lives travelling from place to place honouring the land. Now two hundred years later, to claim our rights as traditional owners, we have to prove that we own the land under our Aboriginal land laws. We also have to show that the descendants have had a continuous association with it.'

'How far back?'

'Since 1788!'

Helen's forehead wrinkled in concentration. 'And can you do that?'

Uncle George replied quietly, 'We have done so, despite what happened in 1941.'

She motioned for him to continue.

'I was seven years old,' the old man started, 'living with my parents and brothers and sisters on the Lutheran mission. We had to live there because we couldn't get food. It wasn't safe to go into the bush. Too many of our people were hunted and shot there. So we lived like refugees, given our rations and a blanket. We had no vote and apartheid was strictly enforced by the conquerors. Our beliefs and our culture were derided.'

He paused and said in a gentle tone, 'I don't want to make it all sound bad. Life for me was good in the mission. As a child I ran barefoot when I could and played with other boys in a paperbark canoe in the creek. We learned to be watchful of crocodiles.' He chuckled at her expression.

What an unimaginable horror! she thought.

The old man was rambling on. 'And we rode horses bareback! Oh and we fished. I can tell you if I caught a barramundi I smiled for a week. We stalked goannas and hunted for sugarbag.'

'Did you go to school?'

He nodded. 'Reluctantly as any small boy whose parents can't read and write and who think that school work is a waste of time.'

'But you're an educated man!' exclaimed Helen. He spoke excellent English.

'No!' he replied with his self-effacing smile. 'I had little education apart from watching people and listening.'

'Sorry, I didn't mean to interrupt you.'

'Not at all,' he replied, ever courteous. 'Back to when I was seven. One night trucks rumbled up to the mission in the middle of the night. No one knew what was happening. White men pulled us from our beds and we were crammed into the big lorries. We were very frightened.' Even as he talked about it, his eyes rolled as if he were reliving the terror. 'I remember my mother was crying. That made me more afraid, for she was always happy and singing. I held my little sister.

'Everyone was taken. The trucks pulled out. My uncle asks where are we going. A white man snarls, "Be quiet," and kicks him so hard we can hear the thud of his boot on my uncle's leg. Then everyone is quiet.'

Helen noticed how he had moved into the present tense as if it were happening right now.

'It is the dry season, very hot, baking, fearsome heat. They keep us in that truck without water or food for two days . . . Two days in that heat! No water.' The old man turned to Helen. 'Can you imagine?'

She shook her head in disbelief and it broke the spell.

He took a deep breath and returned to the story. 'Two babies died. They transport cattle in the same way even now. Western people do not understand the spirit of an animal or a person.

'They took us south. My mob could not cope with the climate. It was cold and we weren't used to it. We couldn't cope with the different diseases. Many died.

'My little sister, Elena, she died in my arms. My nephew, one brother, my aunt, four of my uncles – all succumbed. Over a quarter of my people died.' His voice was emotionless like one who has come to terms with the incomprehensible.

A quarter of your family killed, thought Helen. It's inconceivable. The horror of it silenced her for a moment. She did not even notice the hairy spider, which crawled under her chair past her foot.

'Why? Why did they take you?' Helen asked at last.

Uncle George continued. 'War had broken out. Our minister on the mission was German, so they took us. As if we knew anything about war! Or him! He was a good man. A man of God. He had the welfare of the Aborigines at heart.'

'You must feel very angry!'

He shook his head gently. 'No! It's past. Anger doesn't help. I have long since forgiven. Now we must learn from each other and reconcile our differences. We must look at what we have in common, not what separates us.'

Helen nodded humbly.

While they had been talking a man and a woman had walked into the house. Uncle George waved distractedly to them and said, 'Help yourself.' To Helen he explained, 'We share everything. It's our culture.'

The couple continued to stare and Uncle George repeated, 'Go on. Take what you want. Have a shower or some tea, but you can see I'm busy.'

Very slowly the pair took whatever they needed from the kitchen and left reluctantly. Moments later another woman ambled in, a huge woman, very black, with a low brow, small eyes, large fleshy lips, bare feet and wearing a dirty shapeless dress. She said she wanted sugar but really she was curious to see his visitor. Uncle George murmured, 'My niece.' And dutifully went to help her.

'Why, when Captain Cook landed at Cooktown did the Aborigines offer to help?' Helen asked, when he sat down again.

'We have a deeply ingrained culture of sharing,' he replied. 'We believe the Great Spirit and Mother Earth provide enough for all. Nothing in our culture prepared us for people who wanted to kill and take our land. All our stories are about sharing and our children are praised when they share.'

Helen nodded and the old man continued. 'Our culture was structured so that everyone was looked after. An uncle must look after his maternal nephews and take important decisions for them, like who they marry. What was his was theirs, canoes, boomerang, spear, anything. And naturally each clan was happy to share food and shelter. Do you know there's no word in our language for ownership?'

There was a moment of silence as Helen digested this. At last she asked, 'Would you tell me a little of your Dreamtime?'

Uncle George said he would be happy to do so and Helen sat back in anticipation.

Chapter 8

Uncle George leaned his elbows on the table and placed his fingertips together in what seemed to Helen a very European gesture. Perhaps it was universal. He had strong, firm hands with short fingers. He thought for a moment before he started to speak slowly.

'We believe that the Great Spirit or Wawu is in everything. Another name for God is Timbarral, or Biame. It means everything. Wawu, the Great Spirit, belongs to the One Time, beyond the Dreamtime. Great Spirit is creation, is father sky, is Mother Earth, is grandfather sun, is grandmother moon, is black, is white, is red, is everything. Great Spirit is the stars and the blackness between the stars. From Wawu everything emerges. To Wawu everything returns.'

Wow, thought Helen. That's oneness with God.

The old man's eyes had glazed slightly as he spoke. Now he snapped into perfect focus and looked at Helen with his deep seer's eyes, as if assessing her readiness to hear and understand. After a moment, satisfied, he continued. 'Our dances honour the earth, elders, sky, animals, trees, rocks, sacred sites – everything. Our ritual dances remind us that we are all one.'

Helen nodded, thinking that this was the genuine

spiritual essence of all religions before human interference.

'We help the ancestral spirits look after the sacred sites. There we do ceremony and dance. This enables everyone to understand their place on Earth. We are not alone. We were created to be part of the great design. Sacred ritual helps us to understand the union between life and death.'

Helen could hear a bird screeching outside.

He added simply, 'The land and the Aborigines are one.'

Helen sighed. 'You have a wonderful connection with the divine.'

'Yes. We Aborigines are very sensitive to the sacred, which enables us to tune in to the Dreamtime or universal energy. Thus we are able to have mystical experiences.

'We express things in symbols. We believe that the landscape was formed by the actions of sky heroes at the time of the Dreaming.' His eyes glinted with humour. 'You have a big bang theory but we have visionary geography.'

'Visionary geography,' repeated Helen. 'What a wonderful expression!'

Uncle George chuckled. 'It is, isn't it? Because we hold a deep reverence for our tribal country, we understand the mystical and metaphysical origin.'

'It's so different from our Western perspective, which is limited to the physical. Few Westerners would understand your vision.'

'True. You understand me but many wouldn't.'

'So would you say your Dreamtime myths are stories with a meaning?'

'The way we see the world draws together the visible and invisible realms and our Dreaming is a way of explaining this. But our myths can also be considered moral tales and every child is taught with stories. I'll give you an example.'

His eyes twinkled suddenly and Helen realised he loved to tell stories.

'This is a story my mother used to tell my sisters, and I remember it well. "In the Dreaming, which is the same as your 'Once upon a time', there lived a gentle, harmless fisherman.

' "When he was initiated the elders gave him a wife who was pretty, a good cook and never let the firesticks go out. But . . . and it was a big but, she nagged and criticised all the time. Her husband was so good-tempered he put up with her, even when she threw things at him.

' "At last he decided he'd had enough. When his wife went out hunting for yams, he loaded their canoe with grass meal cakes and, grabbing his stone axe and spear, he pushed off into the sea.

' "His wife heard him paddle away and dashed to the beach. In rage she grabbed handfuls of leaves from a stinging plant." ' The old man paused and warned, 'Be careful of that one. The hairs on the leaves can irritate so much that they can kill you. It's bad.'

Helen winced.

' "The nasty wife threw the leaves into the wind which was blowing towards her husband as he escaped in the canoe. But wind was a good spirit and decided to help the man who had been so patient, so he changed direction and carried the leaves back to the beach where he created a little willie willie or whirlwind to surround the wife.

' "As they touched her, the leaves were torn into shreds and each became a vicious flying, stinging insect. They were the first mosquitoes." '

Helen laughed. 'That's lovely. One little story contains so much.'

'Yes,' he agreed.

'Can I ask you another question?' She pointed to a framed picture of two cockatoos, one black and the other white, facing each other. 'Is that your totem?' She knew that every Aborigine had a totem animal or plant, which they believed they were connected to and must protect.

Uncle George nodded, picking up the picture, and looked at it proudly.

'Could you tell me about it?'

The old man smiled. 'These are my totem. The black and white cockatoo.'

'Is there a story attached to them?' Helen wanted to know.

'Oh yes! In the Dreamtime there were two cockatoos, one black, one white. They were brothers. The black one hated his father because he made him black. He planned to get even with him and plotted against him. But the white one helped his brother to understand that black and white are equally important. He bridged the gap and made him feel all right.'

Again Helen was drawn into his dark wise eyes as he looked at her. 'That's my task. I must express my totem qualities. The cockatoo and I are one.'

Helen ran her hand through her hair to disguise that she felt so moved by his words. She nodded.

'The elders stand for reconciliation,' he added.

She observed the shadowy shape of a lanky young man slip through the door into the kitchen. His clothing was faded and torn and he walked with attitude. Without a word, he helped himself to food from the cupboard and disappeared into the back of the house. Helen registered this with vague unease.

Uncle George had noticed too and his lips tightened. 'Dirk!' he called, sounding irritated. 'Please take whatever you want and leave us.'

Dirk reappeared, a tall, very dark and wild-looking youth with long untidy hair. He swayed slightly and gazed at Helen with small, angry eyes. She wondered if he had been drinking. He frowned and she shivered suddenly as goose-pimples stood up on her arms.

The youth moved provocatively, very slowly, eyeing Helen with something akin to malice. He helped himself to a cake from a tin and burped.

'Go!' commanded Uncle George, clearly reining in his anger. As the young man lurched out, Uncle George explained, 'He's my sister's grandson, Dirk. Under our laws all that is mine is his. That's how it is.'

Helen remained tactfully silent. The old man had already told her that he did not allow drink or drugs in his home. She suspected that, as in many families, he did not see what he did not want to see.

'Like so many of my people, my nephew, or you would say great-nephew but I call him my nephew, has lost his connection to Great Spirit. Many feel powerless and drink.' The old man sighed.

Perhaps he did notice, she thought.

She realised that Uncle George was not going to mention the Codes of Power, if indeed he knew about them, so she said, 'I wonder if you know anything about the Codes of Power?'

He closed his eyes and the expression on his face became calm and infinitely wise, as if he were attuned to the universal consciousness. The room was still. He seemed to grow bigger and she was sure his aura expanded.

At last the old man opened his eyes and scrutinised her, not just her face, but every level of her energy fields. She felt alarmed at the intensity of the exploration, believing she could not pass such an examination.

'Are you ready?'

She nodded. Just then they heard the sound of Jane's truck. Damn! Damn! Oh, why didn't I ask earlier? she cursed silently.

He read her mind and responded quietly, 'It was not the right time earlier.'

She flushed at her transparency. 'Thank you so much. I'll have to go. I've taken up too much of your time.'

'Can you come again, my dear?' asked Uncle George in his normal voice. 'It's been a pleasure talking to you. And we have things to discuss if you seek the Codes of Power.'

He rose stiffly from his chair and fetched a triangular red crystal from a shelf. As he placed it on the table in front of her, he said, 'This was given to me by my grandfather and his father gave it to him. It's from Uluru. Before he died he said to me, "One day you will pass this on to someone from far away. Tell that person, 'Humans are caretakers of Mother Earth.'"' He faced her and looked into her eyes. 'I believe that person is you.'

He ran his hands lovingly over the crystal, which was strangely smooth and curved on one side only and glowing red on the other. He handed it to Helen and she accepted it with reverence. Her mind was whirling. Why me? What's it to do with the Codes of Power? And was this like the red crystal Stephen had shown Joanna and Marcus? She felt a warm surge of love and awe for this wise and generous man.

'Thank you.'

He smiled. 'Come again soon. I have much more to tell you. Next time we talk about the Codes of Power.'

As they rose and walked to the door to greet Jane neither of them saw Dirk, who had been lurking behind the front door, move away quickly and disappear into the bushes. He had heard something that excited him and he interpreted it as he wished to. The Gold of Power! He repeated it to himself. 'The Gold of Power.' He stumbled down the side of the house, muttering, 'I'll get that out of the white bitch.'

Nor did they notice the black car, which was parked a few doors along the road. As Helen got into Jane's truck, the driver moved smoothly into gear and glided after them. Agents of the Elite were watching.

Chapter 9

As Jane drove her back to the motel Helen talked to her about the Aborigine culture of sharing.

'There's a downside,' warned Jane. 'Of course, it wasn't a problem until we arrived because they didn't have any possessions. Men carried spears, a woomera, that's a spear thrower, a shield and a boomerang. Women a coolamon and a digging stick.'

'What's a coolamon?'

'A piece of curved wood which can be used as a basket, a baby carrier, to dig with, almost anything.'

'I see. And the downside?'

'Have you heard of the famous Aboriginal painter, Albert Namatjira?'

Helen shook her head.

'Well, he was an Aranda artist. When he sold his paintings he became rich by their standards. Then clan members he never even knew existed turned up in droves to sponge on him. Of course, according to their culture he had to share all that he had with them.

'First they wanted a truck for communal use. At that time no native had ever owned a truck. To all accounts they raced round everywhere in it and had no idea how it worked. That's always happening. They get some

54

money and buy a vehicle but don't bother to put oil in it or look after it, so they dump it. Easy come easy go.'

'Not too good,' murmured Helen.

'There was worse to come. Namatjira was made a citizen, which meant he could buy alcohol and vote.'

'You mean he couldn't before that?'

'No. The Aborigines became citizens and got the vote in 1967. Until then they were wards of the government and not considered able to manage their own affairs. They still can't if you ask me. Just look at them. It's a disgrace to pass a pub on dole day. They're lurching round the streets.'

Helen felt irritated. I'd probably be an alcoholic if I'd been abused, lost my family and home and told that my culture and spiritual beliefs were wrong. But she did not voice her thoughts. There seemed no point in pursuing it with Jane, the die-hard Queenslander. 'Go on about the artist.'

'The rest of his mob weren't allowed liquor. We call clans mobs here.' Helen knew that so she nodded. 'It was illegal to provide an Aborigine with alcohol. The penalty was prison – minimum six months.'

'Six months for drinking alcohol! That's horrific.'

'Meant to be a deterrent.' Jane shrugged and continued, 'Under traditional Aboriginal law, Namatjira had to provide his clan with anything they asked for. They demanded beer and so of course he was obliged to buy it for them. He didn't really have any option.

'The man was in an impossible position, of course. The

white laws versus traditional law, and I can tell you their traditions are very powerful. He was caught and sent to prison. They say his prison sentence shattered him and he died of a broken heart.'

Helen thought about this man, sacrificed to a cultural conflict and sighed, feeling helpless.

'Another thing,' threw in Jane for good measure, 'they can't even do something simple like measure up a window without help.'

Helen sat back and pulled her seat belt a little tighter as she contemplated Jane's words. Why couldn't the Aboriginal people do something like measure up a window? Yet their ability to find their way in the bush without landmarks was legendary. Why hadn't they developed writing yet they had such an incredible grasp of symbolism in their creative work? Even the relatively modern dot paintings were original creative master-pieces, with their helicopter symbolism. And although the bush Aborigines didn't grasp the concept of reading, their memories must have been incredible to retain and hand down all the myths and songs and legends.

Why is it, she wondered, that they had such a long-lasting peaceful culture and were so in tune with the metaphysical world and yet had no concept of technology or science?

As she considered this she realised it was because the Aborigines had exclusively developed their right brain, which is responsible for creativity, imagination and artistic ability, also rhythm, rhyme and song. That would account for their method of communication through creative dance, song and storytelling, she mused. And the right brain governs the feminine qualities of sharing, trusting, nurturing, being open-hearted and inclusive. In their cooperative society the Aborigines developed all these qualities to create a peaceful, long-lasting culture. Of course, development of the right brain also accounted for their highly evolved mystical and spiritual understanding of life.

Suddenly things made sense to Helen. The Europeans who came from Atlantis were left brain dominated, she reflected. Hence they developed rational, logical minds, which advanced technology and science, writing and reading. They were able to create structure and order, measure things and be numerate.

She continued to consider this as the truck rattled down the main street. And, inevitably, when you value the logic of the left brain more than the wisdom and love of the right, it results in disconnection from feelings and spirit. The consequence of this is the formation of religions with a focus on limitation and exclusivity rather than a spiritual perspective, which is why so much cruelty was perpetrated in the name of Christianity.

Her thoughts flowed. Disconnection from spirit results in power struggle, conflict, repression and efforts to control others. It results in patriarchal societies, in which governments are constantly being destroyed or overthrown or replaced. There's a constant striving for more, without the stabilising effect of the feminine energy.

Her contemplation was cut short as they pulled up outside the motel. 'Well, here we are,' announced Jane.

'And, assuming Ferdy manages to negotiate the creek, you'll meet him soon. He was at school with several of the elders. He'll tell you plenty.'

'I'll look forward to it,' said Helen, clambering out into the sticky heat. 'Thanks for the introduction to Uncle George and for the lift.'

'That's okay. I'll take you to see another elder called Philip tomorrow.' She called out of the truck window, 'The Abos were stuck in the Stone Age, you know. We rescued them and brought them into the twenty-first century.'

'See you tomorrow,' said Helen, waving. Somehow, she thought, we have to learn from each other and merge the best of our cultures. We've got to balance yin and yang, right and left brain, black and white, East and West. Acceptance and balance. That's got to be the way forward.

As she passed through reception she was surprised when the charming young manager handed her something wrapped in a tattered, dirty strip of cloth.

'An old Aborigine I've never seen before left you this. He's not from around these parts. He said it was very important.' The young man was looking at her with a question mark in his eyes but Helen was equally puzzled.

She took the cloth bundle to her room and unwound it gingerly. At last the rag dropped away and in her hand pulsed a vibrant red crystal about three inches long with one smooth curved side. Her eyes alight with excitement, she unfolded a grubby piece of paper, which had been pushed into the folds of cloth. On it was scrawled one word: BALANCE.

Quickly she took from her bag the crystal that Uncle George had given her. They fitted into each other like a jigsaw.

Chapter 10

On Sunday morning Marcus and Joanna were waiting impatiently in the hotel lobby for Stephen to collect them. Stephen's step had more spring in it than the night before and he looked younger and more cheerful than Marcus had ever seen him. He was wearing old clothes as if he had moved into a world where clothes did not matter. He had already hinted to them in his gentle way that for his people clothes were a symbol of European dominance, of little relevance to the essence of life in a hot climate.

Once they were in the car and bowling out of Sydney, he explained that he was taking them to the Central Coast about an hour distant. 'Marcus, I want to take you to a men's site. And, Joanna, my daughter Tamsin will take you to a different site for women's business. We'll stop to pick her up on the way and I hope my sister Martha will go too. She's a full blood and had a different father from me. She and Tamsin know the women's Dreamings.'

Joanna felt a thrill of delight, tinged with regret that her mother was not here. Mum'd love that, she thought.

An hour later they stopped outside a faded and shabby little house, where they were greeted with radiant smiles by several Aboriginal children, who tumbled out as they arrived. They all have beautiful luminous eyes, thought Joanna.

Marcus had not expected to see children. He stood back for a moment watching them jumping and dancing round 'Uncle Stephen'. Clearly they adored him and he them. Ragged and probably dirty by European standards, they radiated a joyous quality, missing in so many children he knew.

Within moments they had been drawn inside to wait for Martha, who had popped down to the shop. The family was noisy and full of laughter. Marcus touched a didgeridoo leaning against a wall. Instantly a young teenager with short frizzy hair picked it up and handed it to him.

'You play!' he commanded, with a huge toothy grin.

Marcus laughed good-humouredly and muttered, 'I'm hopeless at anything like this.' The children crowded round him as he blew down the tube, producing a few rude noises, which rendered them convulsive with laughter. Stephen watched with an expression of unaffected pleasure.

Then the boy took the didgeridoo back and put it to his lips. They were all silent as the extraordinary rhythm throbbed through the room. Joanna could feel her head nodding and her body responding to the deep evocative sounds. She wanted it to continue for ever and when she caught Marcus's eye, they exchanged a glance of mutual delight.

*

Some time later a woman, who was evidently Stephen's sister Martha, walked in carrying several shopping bags. She was very black, heavily built, with wild hair and bare feet and incongruously dressed in a grubby pink T-shirt and torn, red flowered skirt.

She dropped the bags with a sigh, seeming ill at ease to see the visitors. Abruptly the boy stopped playing. The entranced children came back to reality. Then, sensing her discomfort, they fidgeted and started to bicker.

Martha lowered her eyes when Stephen introduced her to Marcus and Joanna. She held out a limp hand. 'Bin shopping. Shoulders little bit ache,' she grunted in response to their greeting. She chided the children in a grumbling voice to unpack the groceries. Evidently she had not had the advantage of education like her brother and they wondered why not.

In an effort to dispel the discomfort in the room Marcus made polite conversation with Stephen. The children looked sullen as they put away the shopping. A girl found a packet of chocolate biscuits in the bag and harassed her mother for one.

The awkwardness dissolved, however, as soon as Stephen's daughter arrived. Tamsin was medium height and slim, coffee-coloured with neat brown hair and a beautiful smile. She had a degree in Aboriginal studies and spoke impeccable English. She looked them full in the eye when she spoke to them and had a chirpy self-confidence, which was very appealing. She's Westernised, realised Joanna and that makes a connection easier.

Feeling immediately comfortable, Joanna noted her

tendency to judge people by their tidiness, cleanliness and fluency in English. She reminded herself that English was probably Martha's fifth or sixth language, while her own second language, French, was atrocious.

It was not as if each Aboriginal language was simple. She knew that their many languages had complicated syntax and a varied vocabulary so that the people could explore and express deep subjects. Yet she still felt a barrier. Much later when this broke down she discovered that Martha possessed a rich vein of knowledge and wisdom, but it had to be carefully mined.

Rather to their surprise Martha decided she would accompany Tamsin and Joanna to the women's site. 'I come. Sit alonga backa car. You talk talk,' she announced.

Because Martha had some chores to finish, Marcus and Stephen left first. As they drove off the main highway, down narrow roads lined with silver-green eucalypts, Marcus leaned out of the window and breathed deeply. He loved the space, the distant mountains, the clear sky and the feeling of freedom.

'Tell me about the sites,' he said at last, bringing his head in.

'There's one by the ocean where all the clans gathered for corroboree and exchange. We'll go there first.'

'A corroboree is a gathering or party, right?' checked Marcus.

'Right. Clans came from a wide area, walking for days, weeks sometimes, to be there. They met their friends and relatives, and danced of course. Food was bartered and uncles arranged wives for their nephews.'

'Uncles arranged marriages!'

Stephen smiled. 'We Aboriginal people lived under very tight social structures, so that everyone was cared for. No one was ever alone or had to fend for themselves. Women had their place and men had theirs. A man's duty was to arrange the initiation of his sister's sons and find brides from the right skin.'

'What does that mean?'

'I'll try to explain but it's quite complex,' Stephen warned him. 'Because we were few in number it was of paramount importance that breeding was correct. For instance a man could only marry a woman from certain clans and often only from certain totems. Their children must marry from specified different clans. It was all regulated in order to ensure the highest quality of genetic inheritance.'

'So you couldn't choose your partner?' Marcus questioned.

'Absolutely not. Very often your partner was chosen at birth because of the right skin combination.'

'But you could have sex before you were married?'

Stephen roared with laughter. 'We do not have your Victorian attitudes to love and sex! Girls and boys have many sexual partners, but once they marry they must remain with their husband or wife, unless there was a fertility rite, of course.'

'A fertility rite?'

'Yes. Then there was a mass exchange of partners to

ensure the continuation of nature and to allow a little freedom. We know that when rules become too rigid, people break them. This way expression takes place within the laws. The missionaries stamped them out, of course.'

Of course they would, Marcus thought. They wouldn't understand how people could be so happy, yet have such different customs. Once again he marvelled at the Aborigines' pragmatic interpretation of rules.

He asked curiously, 'What about children then? Those that are not the husband's.'

Again Stephen laughed. 'Our whole concept is different. Very few tribes even now will accept the genetic link between the baby and the father. They regard the baby as a spirit, who has chosen to come in to the mother.'

'Well, I agree with that! But I also accept physical paternity.'

'We do not have the complication of the physical. A child's spirit comes to the mother and the child belongs to everyone. It's a gift to the clan. Everyone loves and protects it and all the uncles care for it. Our family groups are very child-centred. We believe in kinship.'

'There must be a wonderful feeling of belonging.' Marcus could not help thinking of his isolated childhood, with one jealous sister, who made his life difficult, and an authoritarian father.

'Yes,' agreed Stephen. 'All Aboriginal people who lived in the traditional way felt totally loved and nurtured. They belonged. Everyone was kin. There was a sense of confidence. People were always laughing and happy.'

'Does their birth tie in with their totem?' asked Marcus.

'Not their birth but their conception or quickening. The mother will remember an animal or plant that was around at that time. She realises that the sky hero who showed himself as that animal in the time of the Dreaming has come to say the child will carry its message and energy.' He paused and changed gear noisily as he drove round a tight bend. 'Sorry, I'm not explaining very well.'

'Yes you are!' Marcus encouraged him. 'The child will carry the energy of the totem animal?'

'Yes. He identifies totally with the animal. Metaphysically they are one. During his initiation he's made privy to certain information which belongs to him as a birthright. He learns the chants and responsibilities, which are now his. They also bind him to a particular piece of land and he is now its custodian and must perform rituals there to keep it sacred.' He paused for thought and automatically slowed down. 'We've always known that when the rituals stop, the animals leave, the birds fly away and there's sickness in the plants. Now in places where our custodianship has been usurped, this is clear to see. Terrible things are happening to our land.' He sighed and Marcus did not know what to say.

They drove in rather sad silence for another mile or so and then all at once the blue sea unfurled before their eyes. Stephen stopped the car by a low wall and they clambered down to a vast area of flat rock. Giant waves crashed onto it, exploding in a shimmer of white. Seabirds wheeled and squealed in the breeze.

Marcus took off his trainers and walked in bare feet on the rock, bracing himself against the wind. It felt primeval, the cool stone under his feet, the surging seas and the rock, worn smooth but uneven into an enormous primitive dance floor.

'Just imagine,' said Stephen, 'hundreds of our people arriving here. Some of them had walked for a week or more in the heat and dust. They came here, straight as arrows, through endless miles of bush. Our people always knew the way.

'All the men were carrying spears and shields. Women with babies on their backs carried only a digging stick and coolamon for food they collected. They were supremely fit as they trailed in from every direction. Dozens of tribes. People eager and excited, greeting their extended families, showing off their new babies, cooking the fish and wallabies, the snakes and goannas that were available over campfires.'

He swept an arm to encompass the whole area. 'See them sitting in family groups, toddlers, children playing games, teenagers laughing and teasing. Older boys copying uncles and fathers. Girls helping the women collect bush tucker and prepare the food.'

Somehow Marcus could hear the chatter of voices and smell the flesh roasting over the smoke. He could feel the air of festivity and sense of occasion. No wonder they had a feeling of belonging, when everyone journeyed to meet together once or twice a year, he reflected.

And then his mind took him on a tangent to his own family. I haven't seen my cousins on my father's side for years. And I've got nothing in common with my other cousin. Most of my friends hardly keep in touch with their siblings let alone their extended families. It's not surprising there's a sense of fragmentation and isolation in the West. And to think we forced it on to the Aborigines by displacing the families and dishonouring their traditions.'

He sighed. Stephen was watching him silently.

'I was just thinking about extended families meeting regularly and everyone belonging.'

'Indeed every Aboriginal person knew his place or role in the clan. Every single person was an important part of the family and knew it,' replied Stephen. 'It's unbelievable how it's been shattered.'

'In the name of progress,' said Marcus.

'In the name of civilisation,' added Stephen. He paused in thought for a moment, watching the movement of the eternally powerful sea. 'And the traditional people had such a sense of purpose.' Idly he chewed a piece of grass, his mind far away.

'Sense of purpose?' Marcus repeated, inviting him to continue.

Instead, Stephen touched his arm. 'Come. Follow me,' he said mysteriously. 'It is time for you to understand something special.'

And he turned and loped across the rocks back to the car.

Chapter 11

Marcus followed Stephen across the rocks. The older man had an air of determination about him and he had evidently decided to show him something important. Unexpectedly Marcus felt his heart thump in his ribs.

'I'll take you to a men's site,' said Stephen, jumping into the car.

'An initiation site?' asked Marcus hopefully.

'It was for more than just initiations. At the men's site there was a place for men to grieve with other men, a place to rest alone in peace, a place for them to celebrate – and, of course, the initiations too.'

They were soon on a dry, dusty track, which twisted through the grey-green bush. A thin brown twig draped across the road came alive and streaked to safety. Huge rocks strewed the countryside as if scattered by giant hands, and white butterflies fluttered in rising spirals above them. For half an hour they jolted along until the lane widened into a parking place, where they left the car. Marcus followed Stephen through the bush until they reached a flat rocky escarpment where animals and hunter figures were etched into the stone.

Stephen pointed out the faint outline of a kangaroo and a goanna. 'These pictures explain that one could hunt kangaroo and goanna here, while those marks represent the footprints and indicate the best direction to track them.'

Marcus could just make out the faded figures.

'Yes, yes. This was rich hunting grounds,' added Stephen. 'Come, follow me.'

They walked through a valley of stone, with scraggy bushes sprouting from every earth-filled crack. Suddenly it opened out into a huge rocky arena.

'This,' announced Stephen, 'was an initiation site.'

They stood in silence looking with awe at the primitive stones – a sacred, hallowed place. It was like being in a church, Marcus thought. Yet very different.

A blue butterfly spun around him, distracting him for an instant. A dry twig snapped under his feet and made him start. This was primeval. Extraordinary.

Marcus sat down on a rocky outcrop and Stephen perched beside him.

'Let me tell you about my grandfather.' Stephen settled himself and thought for a while before he began.

'My grandfather, Barnabas Ngulati, of the goanna totem, was an elder, a wise man. He was a very knowledgeable and proud man. Born in this land. His land.' The older man paused and his gaze swept the countryside, his countryside. 'He had two older sisters. All are equally welcome but the first boy is important. He ensures the continuance of the clan. There was much rejoicing and feasting. His father killed a wallaby in the hunt that day and they dug a pit and roasted it. The women pulled up lily roots and gathered wild berries.

'He had a childhood of fun and laughter, climbing trees, swimming in water holes, walking with his family to do their special work at the next sacred site. He copied his father and learned to hunt with tiny spears, encouraged by the men and the women. Life was happy. There was much celebration, singing and dancing. And at night they all huddled round the fire with the dingoes and each other for warmth and company.

'And then when he was nine his boisterous and carefree childhood ended abruptly. It was time for his initiation.'

Stephen sat silently for a moment. Marcus wondered if he too had been through initiation. In answer to his thought, Stephen said, 'You see I don't know about my father. I can't tell you about his initiation nor did I experience a traditional initiation. My father was white. My mother was given to him in exchange for tobacco. This was quite common. Women were traded for alcohol or tobacco after the Whites came. I have never seen him. I am told he was Italian and worked on the station.

'But a half-white boy was not welcome in the family. My mother had to work hard to keep me alive. I was called "that whitefellow baby". Once she left her sisters to look after me, because she was sick and needed to lie down. Apparently my aunts watched me toddle to the water's edge. As I fell in they did not move to stop me. My mother must have sensed something happening because she woke up and ran to the edge of the water hole. She managed to get me out and got me breathing again. The aunts just shrugged and said, "Whitefellow baby. Him better dead!"'

Stephen told the story without expression, so Marcus could only guess at his feelings.

'When I was six my father, that is the man I called my father, took me to the mission and left me. There was a lot of pressure on him to do this and I don't suppose my mother had any choice.'

They remained for perhaps five minutes in silence. Then Stephen said slowly, 'Forgive me. I rarely talk about this. But life at the mission was horrific for a small Aboriginal boy used to a free way of life. But they did give me schooling, without which I would not be where I am today.'

He gazed into the blue distance. 'I do believe my soul chose this experience before I was born. I must be black and white, traditional and modern. In some way I must learn to be a bridge between the cultures and help to bring understanding to each. Rather than consider myself to be disadvantaged, belonging to neither culture, I believe I have the advantage and honour of being Aborigine. At the same time I have been brought up to understand in some small way the Western mind.

'Both my birth father and the father who brought me up for the first six years were instrumental in bringing about my destiny.'

Marcus marvelled yet again at the Aborigine's incredible capacity for spiritual understanding and forgiveness.

At that moment a long fat goanna plodded, like a contented old man, across the path below the rock. 'My grandfather would say, "Him juicy fellow!"' Stephen grinned, breaking the silence. 'Back to my grandfather's initiation. That's what you want to know about, isn't it?'

'Well, yes, I suppose so,' replied Marcus. 'But how do you know about it?'

'Good question. When I was older I managed to trace my family. My mother – I must not name her other than to call her the Dead Woman as her passing is too recent – was looking after my grandfather, Barnabas Ngulati. He was very old then. But I sat with him for many hours talking. I wanted to understand my ancestry and he told me many stories.'

'Why can't you name your mother?'

'When someone has died their name must not be mentioned for at least ten years after their death. No one wishes to call back their spirit inadvertently.'

Marcus nodded. 'I see.'

'When my grandfather was nine he had no material possessions, had never seen money or had any idea what it was about. Nor did he know that his idyllic childhood was about to end.

'One day his brother-in-law captured him and told him the Elders now decreed it was time to become a man. For a traditional Aboriginal boy this is a time to dread. A time of banishment and silence, of self-denial and cruelty. There was also ritual humiliation and blood-letting and pain.

'My grandfather Barnabas told me he never knew such fear before or since, and he had to hide it. It must not be shown.

'He knew he would be circumcised and this was done with a razor blade without antiseptics or anaesthetic and dressed with a lump of wet clay from the river edge.' Both men winced. 'That sounds bad enough,' said Stephen. 'But his father was circumcised with a sharp stone.'

They shuddered together.

'What else did initiation entail?'

'He was not allowed to speak to certain of his tribal relatives, including his mother, for two years. Some foods he was not allowed to eat for the same two years and others were banned permanently. His humiliation was to sleep with his sisters-in-law, a loose term, without talking.'

'So much self-discipline and denial!' commented Marcus.

'Unimaginable. At that age it must seem like for ever. And when you think the clans were so small, not to talk to your nearest and dearest must be intolerable, but its purpose was to inculcate self-control and to command total discipline. And it certainly did that. They emerged as men.

'There was more. The young boys were put through three days of fear and sometimes exhilaration by the old men. They were also taught the secret language of initiates and must address any Elder they met in this language.

'In a state of fear, hunger, thirst, lack of sleep, a boy was taught the secrets of his tribe. They learned of their history, myths and culture in song and chants. Verse after verse had to be memorised. When these were all learned, only then was the secret name of God revealed to the novice. The elders kept this secret to the very last. The boy's childhood was severed and he was thrust into manhood.'

Marcus listened, enthralled.

'Barnabas Ngulati was then presented with his churinga, an oval-shaped piece of wood taken from his totem area and fashioned by his father's father. It was inscribed with esoteric markings, pertinent to the boy alone. Each male member of the tribe held the churinga to his breast to symbolise his belonging to the whole.

'The meaning of the symbols, which were his connection to the Dreaming, was then explained to the boy by his father. My great-grandfather said something like this to his son.' Stephen's eyes glazed and his voice became sing-song.

'This is your own body from which you have been reborn. It is the true body of the Great Spirit Goanna. The stones which cover him are the bodies of the goanna men who once lived at the sacred mountain. You are the Great Spirit Goanna himself. Today you learn this truth and from now you are the chief of the totemic site. All the sacred churinga are entrusted to you for safe-keeping. Protect them, guard the home of your fathers, honour the traditions of your people. We have more verses, greater and more secret ceremonies to make known to you. They are your heritage. We have kept them in trust for you. Now we are getting old we pass them on to you. Keep them secret until you are growing old and weak and then, if no other young men of the goanna totem are living, pass them on to other tried men from our clan, who may keep alive the traditions of our forefathers, until another chief be born.'

The older man paused, as if overawed by the power of

his heritage. 'The initiation ended with a men's corroboree. The men were painted and so were the boys being initiated. They learned the sacred dances, which honoured the animals and the sites. They were charged from henceforth with their safe-keeping.'

'No wonder you are so proud of being Aborigine,' said Marcus.

Stephen smiled. 'I am. And may I somehow be instrumental in allowing the culture to continue or,' he added, 'at least allowing the wisdom of the culture to continue.'

Marcus looked round at the flat rocks and marvelled at the history and knowledge they contained; a memory of the longest surviving culture on the planet.

Stephen paused for a moment in deliberation. Then he took off a pouch which hung round his neck. He opened it and carefully, gently pulled out a piece of red crystal, with one rounded smooth side. 'This comes from Uluru. I showed it to you in the restaurant. My grandfather was given this by his father, who received it from his father. He told me to give this to someone and I'd know when I met him. I've carried it for many years and it is yours. I am to tell you, "Life is corroboree."'

He handed the stone to Marcus, who accepted it reverently, conscious of the great honour bestowed on him. He did not yet know what Helen had received.

'Life is corroboree?' he repeated carefully.

Stephen nodded. 'You say "Life is a celebration." In other words enjoy and honour it. Join together to offer thanks to the Great Spirit. Ceremonies raise the energy of the natural world and enable spiritual intervention to take place. They are a way of connecting to the ancestors and the creator Gods. They are essential to life.'

'Thank you. I'll remember.' Marcus cupped the crystal in his hand and stared at it as if willing it to reveal its secrets.

Chapter 12

Joanna sat next to Tamsin in the front of the car enjoying the wide, open roads and the sense of vastness and space. A couple of huge magpies paraded along the verge in their uncompromising black and white coats. They were so much bigger than English ones. Everything here is larger than life, she thought and, as if to emphasise this, an enormous black raven reluctantly abandoned its roadkill and flapped off disdainfully. After the pastel blues, pinks and greens of England, the rich, strident and vivid colours of Australia filled her with excitement.

Tamsin turned the car off to the left, along a narrow road. Here the bush straggled to the edge of the track and the slender eucalyptus trees, which looked so close together from a distance, seemed far apart.

Joanna glanced at Tamsin's neat small hands on the steering wheel. They were firm yet relaxed and clearly she was a competent and assured driver. She relaxed with a small sigh.

Some few miles later Tamsin announced, 'We're going to a female birthing site first. It was used for hundreds, probably thousands of years. I think you'll find it fascinating.'

'I'm sure I will,' agreed Joanna, wondering what it must have been like to give birth out here in the middle of nowhere, without medical facilities. One thing was certain, women had done it for millions of years but the idea was scary.

When they parked the car Tamsin warned her to be careful of snakes. 'I'll go in front and there'll be no problem but stamp your feet slightly. They'll feel the movement and slip away.'

Martha had been totally silent in the car and Joanna felt she had been uncomfortable. Now Tamsin spoke to her aunt in their local dialect and the big black woman gave a beaming smile.

'I told her she was in charge of teaching you bush lore,' Tamsin said to Joanna with a laugh, before plunging through the scrub.

Aunt Martha ambled behind them, now clearly in her element. 'Find good bush tucker here.' Her eyes lit up. 'Hey,' she panted, after a few strenuous minutes. 'No good racing. Hot hot. Here nice berries . . . good eat.' She stuck out her tongue and indicated to Joanna to pick and eat a small dark blue berry. For a moment Joanna looked doubtful and Martha sensed her reluctance.

'Me eat first.' She picked a berry and ate it with much smacking of her fleshy lips. Joanna laughed and followed suit. It tasted bland, not sweet as she had imagined. Tamsin flourished a name she could not remember and said it was full of vitamin C.

There was no shade and the air seemed to shimmer as it does when it is blazing hot. Joanna pulled her sunhat off for a moment to let her prickling scalp breathe. A thorny bush caught her bare leg and she could see the scratch oozing blood, which looked like tar through her sunglasses.

Martha pointed to a grassy mound from which protruded a tall spiky stem, rather like a bulrush. 'White man call him Blackboy.' She laughed heartily as if this were a good joke. 'Him make good spear.' Sweat was pouring down her plump face. She clearly wore no bra under her T-shirt and the nipples of her huge sagging breasts stood out, for her top was wet with perspiration.

. Tamsin led them another fifty yards through the clinging, scratchy bushes and they emerged in a clearing. Ahead the rocks were enormous, set on the ridge of a hill. This birthing site had been established by Aborigines of old with a clear view of the surrounding countryside, so that they could see any impending danger.

Martha pointed to the central rock, which naturally formed a slight dip where a mother could squat with some support to give birth. Joanna shuddered inwardly at the thought. There was something to be said for hospitals and technology.

There were grooves in the rocks, which were made by sharpening stones to make tools for such uses as cutting the umbilical. Another hollow in a rock, filled with water, acted as a bath and ceremonial baptism font for the baby.

Tamsin pointed out with some asperity that the purpose of a baptism to them was to thank the Great

Spirit for the child. 'We do not have to bring a baby to God. That implies there can be separation.' She continued, 'In your Christian baptisms the priest puts a cross on the third eye of the baby. This closes the spiritual connection, so the child must go through an intermediary to connect with the divine. The white man's way literally turns people into a flock who have no option but to follow the priest. In our traditional way everyone is connected to the Great Spirit.'

Martha was sitting on the rock pointing to three round holes in a row, each about six inches in diameter and eight inches deep. They had clearly been chiselled out of the rock. The big black woman touched one of the holes. 'Clay mixed good with herbs. Help pain. Stop blood. Him good.' She made a rubbing motion on her tummy.

'We knew a great deal about herbs and their use in pain relief,' Tamsin clarified this statement. 'Mixed with clay and water, it was an excellent antiseptic too.'

Joanna nodded.

Martha continued as she touched the next hole. 'Him fill water. Put hot stones. Zzzz.' She made a sizzling sound and they all laughed.

Tamsin elaborated, 'The small stones were heated on the fire and added to the water in the hole. Then flints and any other implements were put into the water to be sterilised. It's strange. We're always accredited with having no idea of hygiene, and it's true, our understanding was rudimentary but obviously we must have known it was important in childbirth.'

'And the third hole?' Joanna asked, intrigued.

'First remember we were traditionally nomads. Because of this the babies were all born in the birthing season, a period of eight to twelve weeks.'

'How did they manage that?' Joanna asked in amazement.

'In traditional times there were sacred love ceremonies. Of course, intercourse took place at other times, but because of the power of the ceremony, the men and women were at their most potent and fertile, so there was a big chance of conception.' She paused. 'Also there was discipline. My ancestors were in touch with nature. We understood and worked with the animals and plants. If the kangaroos did not become pregnant one year, no one mated, for it meant there would be a lean year ahead.'

'That's really taking responsibility,' said Joanna. 'Nowadays people expect the state to look after their babies if they can't. We hand over a lump of money in taxes and with it we delegate charge of the children's health, education and often housing too.' She shrugged. 'But it isn't satisfactory. There's no challenge and no responsibility.'

Tamsin grimaced. 'The nanny state! We have it too. Well, it couldn't have been more different in traditional times. At the end of the eight to twelve weeks the mother and child must be fit and well, ready to walk on to the next hunting ground.

'In many clans if the baby was too weak or defective, it was given a sleeping draught, made from berries, returned with reverence to the spirit world and invited to return later.'

Joanna thought of a friend of hers whose grossly disabled baby was serially operated on until she died at the age of ten months. The little mite had endured a short life of agony. She had a niggling recurring thought, which upset her greatly, that the operations might have taken place in the name of research. She put that thought away. 'And if the baby was well?'

'Oh, the mother holds the newborn baby up to the Great Spirit to thank for a safe delivery.'

'What if it was raining? Or cold? It's not always hot here. How did the baby keep warm?'

'If it was cold or raining, it was wrapped in the bark of the paperbark tree. It's soft and waterproof. It's used for canoes, roofs, lining cradles – all sorts of things.'

Martha lumbered over to a nearby tree and pulled off a piece of bark. 'See. Feel him. Warm soft.' She stroked it against her cheek to indicate its softness, then handed it to Joanna. It felt like chamois leather.

Martha declared, 'Number one brother born here. At piccaninny daylight. That one rock. Big soft one with leaves. Many midwives. Quick push push out. Bit cold day.' She shivered to demonstrate. 'Him wrapped round round.' She pointed to the paperbark tree and continued, 'Uncles, father, all men guard place. Stay bottom hill. No come near.' She laughed as if the thought of a man being near the birth site was a preposterous idea. 'Him fine, strong baby. Him big lungs.'

Tamsin said, 'He would have been breastfed by his mother and often by his aunts. There was plenty to go round.'

'How do you wean a child between breast and meat?' Joanna wondered.

Martha laughed uproariously. 'Watch bird. She know.'

For a second Joanna was baffled. Then Tamsin explained. 'Mothers masticated food for toddlers too big for the breast and fed it to them, mouth to mouth. Simple and clean. No need for a liquidiser or a tin.'

'Of course! Nature supplies all the answers, doesn't it?' She couldn't help comparing the traditional family, all sharing in the bringing up of a baby, with the isolated boxes in which modern women coped alone. 'You had wonderful traditions,' she said gravely.

Martha grunted and patted the rock to indicate to Joanna to sit down. 'White man got no Dreaming. Him go 'nother way. We got Dreaming. Ancestor spirits give name. Give breathing to all.' She pointed round her at the rocks, the trees, the sky and a lizard, lying on the rock. 'All need all.' She interlaced her fingers in a symbolic gesture.

Tamsin was nodding in agreement with her aunt. 'The Western cultures have no sustaining spiritual vision. Our ancestor spirits named and breathed life into everything – into plants, animals, stars, everything. And all are interdependent. Our ancestors live in the sacred places and we can tap their spiritual power through ritual. In traditional culture, the clan walked from place to place practising ritual and ceremony and drawing in the power of the mystical.'

Martha made a face suddenly. 'Walk walk talk talk sing sing.' She grinned. 'Happy peoples. Sore feet. Happy land.'

Chapter 13

'Come!' said Martha. 'See animal spirit in rock. We bin show something special.'

Once more Joanna walked between the two women clambering uphill through the bush. Martha stopped to point out a huge dinosaur fern with its giant pineapple-like fruit. 'Him here beginning time. White man eat – is poison. Want now now. No! Must soak longa time. Then cooking.'

Tamsin elaborated, 'It has to be soaked for at least three weeks. We used to wedge them into the flowing river to wash all the toxins out. The dinosaur ferns got a bad reputation because the Westerners ate them immediately and were desperately sick.' Martha nodded vigorously.

Joanna tried to imagine what it must have been like for those early settlers to arrive in this strange and hostile land with snakes and unfamiliar poisonous fruits. What a nightmare!

Martha panted. ' Looka rock there!'

She pointed to a dinosaur-shaped monolith ahead and was evidently delighted when Joanna exclaimed, 'Oh, it's a dinosaur.' She looked round. 'And there's a crocodile.'

Tamsin said, 'Got it in one. And there's a snake. Can

you see it? The rocks took on the shapes of the animal spirits and were honoured as such.'

Joanna found the snake difficult to see but could make out a bear's head in another rock. By the time they had examined all the rocks, they had reached the top and were high above the gum trees, which were coming into flower. A rooftop of white blossoms floated below them and beyond was the shimmering blue sea. They had climbed on to a baking flat rock where butterflies fluttered all round them.

An eagle soared in the azure sky above them and Tamsin explained that in their culture they represented flying to wholeness or healing.

Joanna noticed that Martha still dropped her eyes when she looked full at her. She decided to ask her why she did this. Summoning up all her diplomacy she put it to her.

Martha grunted, 'I bin learn avoid trouble. Looka whitefellow in eye and he bin take children.'

Tamsin nodded. 'The older generation have lived through terrible times. Whites could whip you for looking at them, saying it was defiance. That happened to your father, didn't it, Aunt Martha?'

She looked at her aunt who nodded and said, 'He bin pretty quick learn keep head down. No looka whitefellow. Walk behind. Only way keep safe.'

'White people expected the Aboriginal people to be inferior and they browbeat them to surrender. That's why our older generation won't look a white person in the eye. It's a matter of collective survival. And the feeling of subordination was inherited and passed down the generations. It'll take time to regain our confidence but it's beginning to happen.'

'Yes,' agreed Joanna, looking at Martha with new eyes. 'It's beginning to happen.'

As the three women sat on the rock and gazed at the sea, their walls and feelings of separation tumbled down. Martha put out her big black hand on to Joanna's shoulder in a companionable gesture. She wafted her other arm in an arc encompassing the entire countryside.

'Mother go good!' Her voice reflected her love of the Earth, her mother.

The big wise woman told her that they always encouraged concern and compassion towards all creatures as well as loyalty and responsibility to their kin and the group as a whole.

Tamsin added thoughtfully, 'Research shows that there's more peace and continuity in cultures that honour these aspects. But when the excessive masculine qualities are present the social structure becomes power-based and hierarchical.'

'And that equals struggle and often war, I suppose?'

'Oh yes. And it seems evident that when the universal feminine qualities are present, the—'

'Such as what?' interrupted Joanna.

'Oh, receptivity to spirit, empathy, intuition, togetherness, things like that; and symbols and myths, of course.'

'Right.' Joanna nodded.

'Family too,' added Martha, who had tried to follow

the conversation and her niece touched her to acknowledge her contribution.

'What was I saying? Oh yes. When the feminine qualities are accepted then the masculine characteristics like order and structure are balanced.'

'That makes sense.'

Martha surprised them by saying that in many clans it was only when a man has obtained the highest degree of male initiation that they become eligible for initiation into women's law.

Even Tamsin was surprised. 'I didn't realise that but I'm not surprised!' she exclaimed.

Martha grinned. 'Man having bag – him putting sacred objects there. Woman having womb. Wisdom here here.' She pointed to her uterus. 'No need initiation. Have anyway. Bleeding, pain, babies.'

'You know,' said Tamsin, 'our Dreamtime stories are the oldest myths on the planet.'

Martha said, 'We sing him, dance him stories. We paint, we tell him stories. No write.' She shook her head as if writing were bad.

Tamsin picked it up. 'Traditionally the Dreamtime stories were sung or chanted and danced, often in deep trance. This enabled the hidden message of the myth to surface to consciousness and to be passed down the generations both consciously and unconsciously.'

'In a way that writing couldn't?'

'Writing is a left-brain activity. It has its place. It helps to keep records and to pass on facts. But I do believe the reason our culture remained so strong for so long was because we had this oral tradition which enabled the spirit of the story to be passed on.'

'So the essence of the message was received in the subconscious and the detail in the conscious,' said Joanna thoughtfully. 'I never thought of that.'

'Interestingly,' added Tamsin, 'the word legend comes from the Greek *legein* or *logos*, which translates into such words as language, law and light.'

'And light contains spiritual knowledge and information. Fascinating. So the traditional way comes from a deep well of unconsciously understood law, which is respected and honoured.'

'Yes.'

'And the modern laws have been formed from the rational mind, which is in opposition to the natural law. It results in organisations and governments that are constantly being overthrown because people intrinsically know it is wrong, so there's a constant search for something better.'

'Which can never be found because it is out of balance.'

Joanna stared at the hot, flat rock, wondering hopelessly if humanity would ever learn.

After a pause Tamsin reflected, 'You know, all humanity has a desire for immortality or continuity of some sort. That's why people so desperately want children. They have to continue the line. In your culture people want to acquire wealth and power to pass it on to their children.

'Our traditional culture simply does not have that.

There are no personal possessions and one person being dominant is not acceptable, so we promote sharing. The desire for continuity has become a collective responsibility for the continuation of the culture. Each clan is bound to pass on the traditions.'

'It's like having a reason for living that is greater than the individual,' agreed Joanna, feeling better.

'It is.'

Martha moved away from them to a crevice in the rock. She crooned softly to an injured lizard. Every fibre of her being was empathising with the hurt animal. There was a tangible sense of love and caring emanating from her. Joanna had a lump in her throat as she watched them.

The lizard made no attempt to move. Martha placed a few cool, healing leaves over it. At last she returned to sit by them on the rock and said, 'Him spirit go ancestors now.'

The big woman reached behind her head and undid a piece of string. To it was attached a small cloth bag which hung between her pendulous breasts. She undid the drawstring of the bag and pulled out a piece of glowing red crystal, similar to the one Stephen had shown them in the restaurant. Joanna stared at it.

Martha turned and spoke quickly to Tamsin and urged her, 'Go go you speak.'

Tamsin explained. 'Aunt Martha was given this stone by her grandmother, who was her mother's mother. It's been passed down the family for generations and is very sacred. It comes from Uluru. The story is that one day it is to be given to someone who will know what to do with it. Aunt Martha feels it is for you. The message it carries is to maintain harmony between humans and the natural world.'

Martha held the stone in her cupped hands and closed her eyes for a moment. Then she handed it to Joanna, who felt overwhelmed. What a sacred honour!

She cradled the precious piece of crystal in her hands and whispered, 'To maintain harmony between humans and the natural world.'

Chapter 14

Helen never ceased to be fascinated by the changing sky in the wet season. This morning it was painted alternate patches of pale and dark grey, while occasional blue teased through. By midday it was happy with scarcely a cloud to trouble it.

Seagulls were crouching in separate mobs on the shore. Occasionally one rose to stretch a leg or a wing before settling down again.

She enjoyed a leisurely morning at the beach café where she'd pampered herself with hot chocolate and scrambled eggs while chatting to Sally and her husband, Bob. He liked to talk and told her all about his life and his children, his boat and how he met Sally, who was his second wife. Helen dearly loved a romance, so she had a contented morning.

No sooner had she returned to the motel than the phone rang. It was Tony and she felt a surge of pleasure when she heard his voice.

'Tony. How are you? I'm so glad you rang. I've got so much to tell you.'

'Fire away,' he said cheerfully and she remembered warmly that he always listened to her. She had virtually given up on men because the ones she attracted always seemed to want to do all the talking. She was happy to listen but she also wanted to be heard. Not only did Tony listen but he had a knack of drawing her out. It felt good.

She told him how she had received the two red crystals from Uluru and how they fitted together. He sounded intensely excited and fired several questions. She replied as best she could but then she asked, 'Why? Why do you want to know?'

'Look, Helen. I think each of those pieces represents part of the blueprint of the planet. I've got something to tell you too. A bit more of the Codes of Power has been translated.'

'Oh fantastic! Tell me. Does it say something about the crystals? Go on.'

'Okay.' He laughed. 'It's fascinating. You know it said before that Uluru, that's Ayers Rock, is a giant keeper crystal where the blueprint for the planet is encoded.'

'Yes.'

'Well, apparently when Lemuria sank during the great upheaval, Uluru itself fell sideways and is no longer upright. More than half of it is below the surface.'

'Really?'

'According to the Scroll, flood water boiled and bubbled over the plains and crashed around the great keeper crystal. Everything was covered in swirling mist. And, here's the interesting bit. It says: "Before Uluru fell a crystal ball from its centre shot into the air.

' "At the beginning times of the Golden Age of Lemuria, the Source of All That Is had placed in the crystal ball the

Codes for maintaining the continent as the Garden of Eden. He then charged it with power. Anyone who held the ball received some of this power. Many quested for this power and went through an initiation to test that they were ready to use it appropriately.

' "It was intended that each new initiate should touch the crystal ball and pass it on to the next, using its power to guide the planet with wisdom. No one was to keep the ball. Initiates were expected to honour the Codes of Power and help others to live by them.

' "However in accordance with the duality of planet Earth, power can be used for good or bad. In the end times of Lemuria, Satanaku, the evil one, leader of the dark forces, seized the crystal ball by magic. He refused to pass it on but kept all the power to himself and controlled the planet by evil means. He used the power of the crystal ball to energise and empower black witchcraft, which eventually led to the downfall of Lemuria.

' "When all was lost and downfall inevitable, Satanaku attempted to win mercy by returning the crystal ball containing the Codes of Power to Uluru. It was in vain, for his heart was too impure and the evil he had perpetrated was too calculated.

' "As Uluru, the mighty keeper crystal of the planet fell, the crystal ball shot into the air. It shattered into eleven pieces, which landed all over the continent.

' "Over centuries Wise Ones, the mystics, the seers and Knowing Ones were drawn to the pieces and retrieved them from where they fell. Each knew that the piece he or she held was sacred and represented an aspect of the

Codes of Power for the planet. Each kept the crystal in trust and passed it down through the generations.

' "The time will come when the eleven pieces of the crystal are brought together. Whoever does this will go through their own initiation as he or she reintegrates the ball and is offered certain powers. The power must never again be held in one person's hand. When the crystal ball is complete again it must be returned to Uluru. Only then can the blueprint of our sacred planet Earth be activated." '

'My God, that's amazing! And you think these pieces of crystal could be from that ball?'

'I don't know. But they could be!'

'But why were they given to me? It's crazy.'

'I don't know, Helen, but—'

She was not listening. Her voice had risen in excitement. 'Tony, when Uncle George gave me the first one he said, "Humans are the caretakers of Mother Earth". Could that be part of the blueprint – one of the Codes?'

'Could be! The Scroll indicates that Source has provided enough for all and it's our task to husband the resources wisely.'

Helen calmed the excitement that was bubbling inside her. 'I agree. We should only take enough for our needs and instead of taking more than our fair share, we ought to help all species to develop and evolve in harmony.'

'I agree. Hold on.' Helen could hear paper rustling. 'Yes, it says here: "Humans must honour the Earth, plants and all living creatures spiritually as well as physically." '

'Does that mean never interfering genetically or decimating a species for our own gain?'

'It's common sense really, but for the true blueprint of the planet to be activated we have to make sure everyone honours it.'

'Yes. Easier said than done. Many of the old Atlanteans have reincarnated now and are replaying their old pattern. They're taking from Earth and experimenting on everything.'

'Something must be done,' Tony agreed. 'But I've got something else to tell you.'

Chapter 15

'What have you got to tell me?' Helen demanded eagerly.

'I'll tell you in a sec. First, what do you think the second piece of crystal represents?' Tony asked.

'I told you the paper with it said, BALANCE. More than that I've no idea. But it does fit the first crystal perfectly and they obviously form part of a ball. Oh, it's so exciting!'

'What were you talking about or thinking about just before you were given it?'

'That's the funny thing. I was in Jane's truck thinking that we all had to come to balance for the world to move forward.'

'Go on!'

'Well, she told me how an Aborigine in the bush can't measure things and I got to thinking about them being exclusively right brain and us being too left brain. And how really we all need to learn from each other and be balanced.'

'Indeed! Look, I've got some bits of translation here. I think what you've said is right. Part of the blueprint of the planet is this thing about balance.'

'Come on. Stop holding out on me. What have you got there?'

Tony laughed and she realised that his laugh had become more relaxed and infectious in the year that she had known him. 'Very little and it's fragmented. There's something about male and female being equal and complementary, created to express different aspects of the divine.'

'That's not just men and women. We know they're equal.' It was Helen's turn to laugh and Tony chuckled. 'It's balancing all the male and female aspects, presumably in individuals and cultures.'

'Like what?'

'Well, logic and intuition; being active and passive.' She paused for thought. 'Would you agree black and white are complementary?'

'I suppose so. It's yin and yang.'

'Exactly. And there is good and bad in both black and white, isn't there?'

'Sure.'

'Well, the colour black symbolises the feminine. The little black dress suggests feminine and mysterious. On the negative side of black you have black magic.'

'I think I follow you.'

'I'm going on a bit of a tangent here but interestingly Aboriginal cultures have a deep fear of black magic and they're also very superstitious. One reason for this is because they're psychically receptive to the spirit world but don't have the masculine power to handle it.'

'So it's back to an imbalance of masculine and feminine power?'

'Sure. In the West we tend to dismiss the power of black

magic – and the dark forces as a whole. We underestimate it because we're disconnected from the psychic and spirit world. The balance would be to stay connected and acknowledge the dark but use the masculine power of light to deal with it.'

'I agree. And presumably part of their fear of black magic is the devastating effect it had on Lemuria. That must be coded somewhere deep in their psyche.'

'I'm sure it must be.'

'So let's go back to the masculine and feminine energies,' prompted Tony.

'Okay,' agreed Helen. 'The female has babies and then nurtures and cares for them, creates a home etc. And metaphysically the feminine energy conceives new ideas and looks after them until they are ready to come to fruition. Wisdom, creativity and nurturing energy are also feminine.'

'And the masculine?'

'Well, the male is strong and protective. He finds food for the family and is out there hunting so he has a wider picture of the area. So metaphysically the masculine expands horizons, takes ideas and carries them through, seeks knowledge, is logical.'

'So the aim for individuals and cultures is to develop both qualities equally to find a sense of peace and safety.'

'Of course. So the West is too masculine, acquisitive, aggressive and logical. The good side is we've used the left brain to expand technology and science and develop communications. We've just shut down the creative, compassionate and spiritual side.'

'Right.'

'And the Aborigines are too feminine-orientated, which has led to stagnation. They have kept their connection to the spiritual and creative realms but haven't expanded and developed their potential.'

'It makes sense.'

'That's how I see it. Do you think the balance will happen automatically when the blueprint of the planet is activated?'

Tony cleared his throat. 'The Scroll indicates that when certain people are ready they will take the initiation to the Codes of Power by bringing together the pieces of the crystal ball. When this is done, then many more will undertake initiation.'

'A bit like the hundredth monkey?'

'Yes.'

'Do you think I'm one of those undertaking the initiation? An initiation to help everyone.'

'Probably. Just don't forget it will be dangerous.'

Her stomach flipped. Of course it would be dangerous. 'I know.'

'Maybe all the pieces of the crystal will come to you. Perhaps that's all you've got to do.'

'I hope you're right.' Helen laughed shakily. She was aware that initiations test your greatest fears and challenge you even to death itself. She wanted to believe what Tony said but she didn't really, not for a moment.

Chapter 16

On Monday morning Joanna and Marcus were standing under the Sydney Harbour Bridge, where it straddled and dominated the estuary like a giant piece of Meccano.

Joanna gulped. She was about to climb up that! She could see small groups of climbers clinging to the structure like truncated columns of grey ants. Beyond it the sky was a flat blue plain on which fought tumbling, grey clouds.

Marcus laughed in delight. He had always been strong and agile, with a good head for heights, and was looking forward to climbing the bridge. 'Mum used to say I was like a monkey without a tail,' he told Joanna.

'Maybe a gorilla then?' she responded quickly and he grinned widely. He loved her repartee.

Half an hour later they were in the waiting room with their group of ten fellow climbers and Craig, their bronzed and handsome leader. He gave them a safety talk and then reminded them to go to the toilet as if they were children going on an outing. Such is the power of suggestion almost everyone headed for the cloakrooms.

As Craig kept up a constant flow of quips, which made them laugh and relax, they were breathalysed one by one. They had to place all their belongings into lockers, including tissues, hankies, money and watches. 'If a 20 cent piece is dropped from the top of the bridge it can crack a motorcycle helmet!' Craig told them. 'Imagine what something bigger would do.'

He handed out grey boiler suits.

'Why grey?' asked one of the group.

'Because it's the colour of the bridge and doesn't distract drivers when you emerge between the fast lanes of traffic on the highway up there.'

Joanna felt a clutch of tension behind her shoulders and tried to shake it off. She accepted a handkerchief with elastic sewn on to it to put round her wrist. Their sunglasses were held on with elastic threaded through special loops in their climbing suits.

By the time they had gone through the metal detector and had radio mikes and strong metal safety chains fitted, they all felt ready for a space walk. Then Craig made them practise climbing vertical ladders with their safety harnesses until they could all manage as a team.

Eventually they clambered one behind the other on to the catwalk and up ladders and were soon high above the busy roads where they could see but not hear the whizzing traffic. Above them trains roared, so that the bridge shook and vibrated. Higher than that was the highway.

They scrambled up and up, stopping only occasionally for photos. What had been a gentle breeze at ground level had whipped up into a gale and buffeted them relentlessly. The fierce clouds were now twisting and snarling in the shrieking wind.

When a middle-aged man expressed alarm Craig

laughed and shrugged with the insouciance of youth. 'Try coming up when it's really windy.' Joanna held tight to the frame of the bridge, her knuckles white.

Marcus loved it. 'Fantastic,' he shouted when they stopped at the summit. He spread his arms to include the entire vista of a lilliput Sydney: miniature high-rise blocks, matchbox vehicles in wide streets, the blue-grey waters of the estuary teeming with tiny ferries, catamarans, motor boats and yachts. And gracing it all the Opera House like a majestic shimmering swan.

Stephen had told them, 'Climbing that bridge changes your life because your unconscious starts to see the bigger picture.' Joanna was contemplating these words when suddenly she felt a punch in her solar plexus, like a blow from a sledgehammer. Hit by a dreadful premonition, she cried out and the colour drained from her face. She staggered slightly.

Marcus whirled round and was shocked. He thought she was going to faint with vertigo. Grabbing her firmly, he shouted, 'Hold on, Jo. It's okay. You'll be fine.' Her hand was tiny and ice-cold in his big warm one.

'Oh, Marcus. It's not the height. It's Mum. I've just had an awful feeling she's in danger.' She gulped, her eyes unseeing, like glass. A seagull cried in the distance.

'No!' Marcus no longer doubted Joanna's premonitions, or Helen's for that matter. A cold shiver ran down his back. He felt helpless but he had to say something to reassure her. 'We'll phone as soon as we get down. It'll be all right. I'm sure it'll be all right.'

She nodded, knowing there was nothing either of them

could do. And then Craig was beside them checking what was the matter.

'It's okay. I'm fine.' She managed a ghost of a smile in response to his queries but he was not convinced. He insisted she descend next to him and so in silence, with shaking legs and an impenetrable feeling of doom, she started the descent.

Through her foggy mind she tried to visualise her mother in a ball of gold light. The instruction in the Scroll was to hold a person who was in danger in white or gold light. Then the angelic forces could help to protect them. She knew that Marcus too would be picturing Helen in a protective bubble.

'Last time I spoke to her I told her about the crystal Martha gave me and she was so excited,' Joanna murmured to Marcus at their next stop. 'She said to me the adventure had begun and we must be very careful.'

Marcus squeezed her hand. 'It'll be all right. You know she can take care of herself.'

'I hope so. Oh, I do hope so!'

As soon as they collected the mobile from the locker, they phoned Helen in Cooktown. The girl on reception told them she had gone out an hour ago and not returned.

'Oh, why doesn't she have a mobile,' groaned Joanna. 'Where's she gone? Marcus, I've still got that awful feeling. Something's going to happen.'

It was several hours before Joanna, shrivelled with anxiety, managed to speak to her mother.

'Mum. I've been trying to get you for ages. Are you all right?'

Surprised, Helen reassured her that she was fine. 'Why? What makes you think anything's wrong?'

Joanna told her of her experience. Her mother was concerned but did not let it show. She knew only too well that psychic impressions are often picked up out of time. 'I'll be careful,' she promised. Very careful, she thought.

With every ounce of discipline at her command, she persuaded Joanna not to worry. 'I'm just off with Jane to meet another elder, called Philip. You go off to Cairns and enjoy yourself. Sylvie is looking forward to meeting you both. Have a great time diving on the Barrier Reef and I'll see you next week.'

'Right you are, Mum.' Joanna felt immensely relieved. 'But take care of yourself.'

Helen looked out of the window and thought about Joanna's premonition. She had no doubt her daughter had picked up impending danger.

The boats on the estuary were still, their reflections clear, as if they had been placed on a blue mirror. A thin boy on a bicycle and the laughing dog running beside him brought the tableau to life, while a huge black and white butterfly landed casually on the balcony beside her, then languidly fluttered into the trees. It all looked so benign, so peaceful, but every nerve in her body was screaming. Her mind flew back to her visit to Uncle George's house. She remembered the look of hatred in his nephew Dirk's eyes and suddenly she shivered, the hairs on the back of her neck prickling as an intangible fear clutched her.

As if on cue a slightly unsteady young man with a bottle

in his hand swayed down the dusty road. Today's Monday, she found herself thinking. The danger's on Thursday. Dole day. The day when they all get drunk. The thought of Dirk very drunk was suddenly terrifying. Be careful, especially on Thursday, she thought.

She sat down limply on the edge of the bed, her heart thumping wildly.

Chapter 17

Jane picked Helen up on time.

'This elder's called Philip,' she shouted over the roar of the truck. 'And,' she warned, 'he's nothing like George.'

She was right. Philip was lounging in the decrepit fly-infested lean-to of his bungalow waiting for them. He looked wild, rough and unshaven. His black, curly hair was dishevelled, his clothes torn and dirty. Two mangy dogs barked but he yelled at them to shut up and they slunk into the shade where they panted noisily.

Helen's heart sank. Jane introduced them and Helen said politely, 'It's very good of you to see me.'

His responding leer showed a mouth full of broken and ugly teeth. 'Naw problem.'

'Okay if I come back for Helen in an hour?' asked Jane.

'No worries. I'll take her back to her hotel.'

Helen could not help glancing at the pile of rust in the guise of a car on the drive and shuddered mentally.

'Thanks, Philip. Bye, Helen!' Jane left and Helen abandoned all hopes of finding out about the Codes of Power. She wondered what on earth she could talk to Philip about but it was not a problem. He loved to talk. Very soon, despite the sweat trickling down her back and a number of persistent flies, she found herself fascinated.

'I was a stockman for years, 'bout seventeen years, working twelve hours a day and receiving no pay. They never thought of paying us and we never thought of asking. We got a pair of trousers and dampers, sugar and tobacco.'

'No meat or veges?'

'Nothing like that. The old men dug the vegetable garden for the white man family.'

No wonder their teeth are so bad, Helen thought. And that diabetes and heart disease are endemic. Their immune systems must have been shot.

'Anyway,' continued Philip, with a shrug and a noisy drag on his cigarette. 'Now the government's bringing in compensation. About time.'

She waved away a couple of flies, buzzing round her red and perspiring face and the elder returned to his favourite subject, his life as a stockman. 'We were up at the crack of dawn and in the saddle till dusk. Yeah, it was dangerous. You'd gallop beside a bull, lean over and grab its tail, then flip it over and brand it. Hooves'd be thrashing and the bull'd be in a terrified rage as the branding iron burned into it. It's a miracle there weren't more accidents.'

He was on a roll. 'I think they should give us money for a cattle station for Aborigines. There are plenty of successful ones and we could soon make a go of it. After all we practically ran the stations for the Whites for years. They made their money on our backs, so it's time we got paid.'

Philip's mobile rang and he answered it, clearly proud

that she was listening. He talked loudly and enthusiastically. 'That was Billy, one of my nephews,' he told her. 'He wants me to choose a car with him. He's got compensation money to spend.'

It was on the tip of her tongue to ask, 'Compensation for what?' but something stopped her. As far as she could tell there was compensation for just about everything. Guilt money.

'Does he know how to look after it?'

Philip shrugged and laughed with a strange hissing sound through his broken teeth. 'You know what kids are like. They get a car. No idea how it runs. Forget to fill it with oil and dump it. But I can show him.'

A huge black woman waddled out of the kitchen to the rusty old washing machine, which was plumbed in under the car port. She did not speak to or even glance at Helen as she loaded the machine and switched on a very noisy washing cycle.

As the woman plodded back to the kitchen, Helen ventured a tentative, 'Hello,' but there was no response or sign that she had heard.

'My daughter,' explained Philip. He winked knowingly. 'Good party last night.'

Philip talked on inconsequentially for a while and Helen wondered whether she should leave. Then without preamble he began to tell her of his childhood. She never knew what triggered it. 'I had two older brothers, John and Peter. They both had white fathers. Different fathers.

'At that time there was a compulsory expulsion order from reserves for mixed-blood kids. Applied to any kid over fourteen, sometimes twelve. If the local cops thought they were of mixed blood, they could come in and chuck the kids out.'

Suddenly he was angry. 'What the hell did they know anyway? No one trusted the cops. We'd all run into the bush when they arrived and we were scared, I can tell you. We'd hide day and night until they left.

'This time John had a bad leg and couldn't run fast. My other brother, Pete, tried to help him but the cop got them and chucked them out of the reserve. John was thirteen. We could hear him screaming as they dragged him away. My mother . . . Well, she went crazy. She knew she'd never see them again.'

Helen felt sick and her heart was thumping. She thought of Joanna at thirteen. She was still a child then and certainly couldn't fend for herself. She had read that those kids expelled from the reserves eked out an existence in the perimeters. What was it about a so-called civilisation that could do such things?

Stupid question, she thought gloomily. The West was and still is led by damaged men, whose hearts are split from their heads. Hurt people can't feel their own pain or that of others. Traditionally the ruling classes in our culture have always sent their children to boarding school at pathetically young ages, designed to cut off their feelings. Then they're trained to be politicians, military commanders, business leaders and even missionaries. No wonder they order people to do incredibly cruel things and make decisions based on logic not humanity or even common sense. We've got to change soon.

Philip was looking at her as if waiting for an answer. She shook her head blindly. 'It was terrible,' she said quietly and stood up. 'Unbelievable.'

Suddenly a suicidal lizard ran across the concrete floor near the dogs. Instantly they were awake, barking and pouncing. In the mêlée the lizard darted through Philip's legs and up the wall.

The elder's mood changed and he was like a teenager, excited, animated, shouting derisively at the dogs. He was grinning broadly. 'You have to be quicker'n that, boys,' he yelled.

Helen moved towards the car. Philip's driving was as wild as his looks. He drove erratically, hooting and waving to all his friends on the way and stopped in front of the motel with a squeal of brakes in a flourish of dust.

Once more she failed to notice the black car, parked down the road, in which a stranger was sitting. He watched Helen walk into the motel, then started the engine and followed Philip back to his house.

She did not know that this man was an agent of Sturov, who was head of the Elite and the most evil man in the world. And this agent was now talking to Philip. It does not take much persuasion to induce a weak and angry man to work with the forces of darkness.

Chapter 18

Helen's friend Sylvie met Joanna and Marcus at Cairns airport. She was watching out for them as they entered the reception area, a big-boned, bulky woman with long hair tied back, careless of the fact that she was bursting out of her shorts and T-shirt.

She recognised them immediately from Helen's photographs and descriptions and greeted them in a booming voice. They soon learned that she had one volume – loud. She also proved, like many Australians, to have a heart of gold.

Soft, warm rain fell ceaselessly from glowering grey clouds. The new arrivals stared in bleak dismay. 'Shouldn't be rains this early,' Sylvie apologised, clearly feeling personally responsible. 'It'll be better soon. I promise.'

Marcus laughed. It was so English to apologise for the weather.

'It rained when Helen was here and she called it "decidedly inclement", but I told her it was bloody awful,' said Sylvie.

Joanna chuckled. She could just hear her mother reframing this wall of rain as 'decidedly inclement'.

As they left the airport and headed for Cairns, they

peered through the downpour at the blurred mountains and sodden roads. Half an hour later they turned off the main highway and entered a neat world of widely spaced, elegant, wood-fronted bungalows, manicured lawns and tended palm trees. The rain had paused.

A safe conventional world, thought Joanna, reassured. Marcus sensed her relief and squeezed her hand. He knew that since the premonition of her mother being in danger she had felt generally apprehensive.

Sylvie parked in the car port and Marcus grabbed the cases from the boot of the car. Joanna walked ahead up the drive. She stopped suddenly, frozen. A very long green and blue snake was draped across the path like a carelessly dropped hose and apparently oblivious of her presence. She dared not move.

Sylvie came up behind her and stamped her feet. The snake uncoiled and slithered off at the speed of lightning, disappearing under a straggly bush by the path.

'Well,' said Sylvie, surprised, 'just a harmless tree snake but I've never seen one in the garden before, nor in this weather. It's really unusual.'

It's an omen, thought Joanna uneasily. The feeling of dread returned and settled in her stomach.

The next day Sylvie had some shopping to do in Cairns. She drove her guests into the town centre in rain as depressing as any England could offer. 'Be careful of the Aborigines. They're angry round here,' she warned. 'And I wouldn't book a diving trip for tomorrow if I were you.

Weather's not going to clear yet. Okay if I meet you here in a couple of hours?'

'Sure.' They thanked her for the lift and she hurried off under her umbrella, leaving them staring at wet pavements.

Joanna wanted to buy a book about Aborigine Dreaming and soon found one, which explained the Dreaming symbols. She would have been content to sit in a café and read but Marcus looked downhearted.

'Come on. Let's go and see what trips are on offer,' Joanna coaxed. She could hear her hearty tone and hated herself for it, especially as she could sense Marcus shrivelling. So they headed for the harbour where the boats were moored to find out about diving on the reef. Here their visions of diving in azure seas in sunlit, colourful reefs finally evaporated. There were few people about on the rain-swept piers. All they could make out of the Great Barrier Reef was desolate moaning sea overseen by a sulky sky.

Joanna could see how disappointed Marcus was. 'We could still book a dive for tomorrow,' she ventured gamely, but he shook his head.

'No point really. Come on, let's walk down the esplanade. Something else will turn up.'

He took her hand and they ambled along in the mist, so heavy with rain that they were never truly sure if it was raining or not.

The path edged the sand flats, where the mud was alive with movement. Muddy skippers, creatures up to one foot long, looking like mini snakes with antennae, were leaping right into the air. A passer-by told them, 'It's the only creature that can live in water and on land.'

They paused to watch them run, jump, burrow and swim. 'They're quite extraordinary!' exclaimed Marcus.

As they walked further, the mud became firmer and crabs stood like stationary arches in rows or in clusters. Whenever Joanna crept closer to take a photo they would sidle sideways in unison or silently submerge. She was frustrated and amused at the same time.

'They must be extraordinarily sensitive to sound and movement,' she observed at last with a resigned laugh, when for the tenth time she had inched herself forward on tiptoe and all crabs had immediately and simultaneously vanished.

Marcus chuckled in sympathy. 'Hey, look.' He indicated a curlew who had caught a crab and was running off with it, a gull in hot pursuit. From time to time the curlew put down the crab and squawked at the gull in a display of bravado. The harassment continued in a quasigentlemanly way until the gull's patience snapped. Then it attacked with determined ferocity and the victim relinquished its prize with a wail.

The tide had started to seep in and as the water rose above the mud, the sea was teeming with birds: egrets, ever alert and watchful, ready to spear their prey, redbeaked cormorants, sandpipers, oyster-catchers and the inevitable bullying gulls. Three huge black and white pelicans stretched and preened. They worked in unison to chase fish, then formed a triangle and expertly ladled up their bounty.

Once they had released their expectations, it became an enchanting afternoon and Joanna relaxed and forgot her sense of danger for a while.

Chapter 19

Later, when they returned to Sylvie's bungalow, they received a wholly unexpected call from Tony, who had evidently tried in vain to phone Helen.

'I've e-mailed you but I really wanted to talk to someone about it,' he confessed. 'The Scroll has revealed more information about Lemuria and the Codes of Power. It's quite extraordinary.'

Instantly they were one hundred per cent alert. 'Go on,' urged Joanna, while Marcus dashed to pick up the other extension. 'What does it say?'

Tony cleared his throat.

It's his one really annoying habit, thought Joanna. He must be nervous.

'Well, this came through this morning from Professor Smith. It's about life in the time of early Lemuria.'

Joanna and Marcus listened eagerly at the other end of the phone as Tony told them about the latest translation from the Scroll. 'It's obviously passed on by one of the pure priests of Lemuria and he's telling it as if it is happening right now. I suppose in those times there was only now.'

'What does it say?'

He smiled and read: ' "In this glorious time of Lemuria

all is differentiated and yet all is one. If you see a flower, you do not merely touch it and smell it, you merge your consciousness with it. Therefore you experience what it is to be a flower." '

'How wonderful,' breathed Joanna.

' "As we become one with that flower, through it we interconnect our consciousness with everyone or everything. We reach out and immerse ourselves in each tree or animal or human until we feel its joy and pain and know it intimately." '

'That must be awesome!' exclaimed Marcus.

'Almost unimaginable,' agreed Tony. 'And the next part is a natural consequence of it. Listen. The Scroll says: "Therefore we cannot harm anything because it is part of self. There is no killing or need to kill. Everything is evolving perfectly in love and peace and joy. We grow through love." '

'Yes, I suppose killing something would seem like chopping off your own arm.'

Joanna said thoughtfully, 'Mystics who have merged with the Oneness, report the same feeling.'

'Shall I go on?'

'Please!'

'It says: "We communicate by consciousness transference, which is a kind of telepathy. All is open. There are no secrets. How can there be when two consciousnesses can merge? No one can hide anything or would want to." '

'So there's no crime or cheating or lying? Wouldn't that make life so much easier?'

'Lawyers would be out of work,' quipped Marcus.

'And politicians,' added Tony.

'A life of total transparency,' Joanna mused. 'Go on, Tony.'

' "We instantly become one with everything in the universe and truly experience ourselves as part of All That Is. We are one with the beauty and awe of the Creator.

' "Our only purpose is to understand all creation and expand our consciousness. Therefore we practise experiencing being all." ' He paused and emphasised: ' "We never desire to change anything, for we know all is divine. To try to change the natural world is control. It comes from the ego." '

'That's true. If we humans want the structure of plants and animals to change or be different, we are trying to control God's creation.'

'Hang on,' argued Marcus. 'Without the urge to evolve, there would still be smallpox! Surely it's part of the human task to try to improve our lot.'

'I don't feel it's talking about change with the intention of helping the natural world to its true state of wholeness. I think it means experimentation to change the essence of a plant or animal. Genetic modification for one, and cloning and even the use of toxic chemicals.'

'And introducing animals into a new environment as predators, like the cane toad. Presumably in the original Garden of Abundance before humans did start interfering, these weren't necessary.'

'I guess the intention is important too,' suggested Tony,

the tone of his voice implying he wished to move on. 'Just listen: "At any time we can leave the physical and enter our light bodies. We can move consciously between one and the other. This vibrational shift is easy for us. Therefore, we do not need physical transport." Now what do you make of that?'

Marcus frowned. 'Were they even more evolved than the Atlanteans, who used crystals to power their vehicles?'

'It's true the Atlanteans were more technically advanced,' responded Joanna, 'but Mum said that the Lemurians were more ethereal. Their vibrations were lighter, so they could come in and out of their physical bodies more easily.'

'I'm sure Helen will have more to say about it,' Tony said to stop their discussion. 'There is a little more.'

'Sorry!' they replied as one.

' "Here there is no ownership. All is shared. Our only aim is to grow and experience spiritually. We have no need or desire for belongings. We feel that these can only cause separation. We choose cooperation and community. Community is where people meet to share ideas to expand the divine.

' "When a new soul enters, all in the community welcome and support it. There is only love.

' "Our education is about drawing out the wisdom in each soul and allowing it to understand the nature of the universe. Every child is empowered to think and know for itself and to connect to the light of Source." '

Tony paused and cleared his throat again. 'That's pretty extraordinary, I think, don't you?'

'Wow!' said Joanna. 'It sounds like Shambala.'

'Perhaps it was.'

'Shambala? Isn't that a mythical place?' asked Tony.

Joanna chuckled. 'It's a mystical place in the Himalayas where people lived a perfect life for hundreds of years.'

'I thought it was more than that?' queried Marcus. 'Didn't your mum say that it was a place in the inner planes above the Himalayas where the greatest Ascended Masters meet?'

'You're right!' agreed Joanna. 'It is.'

'Hey, you've lost me. What's the inner planes?'

'Poor Tony!' Joanna laughed. 'The physical life is the outer planes. There is also a spiritual life, which affects the physical, and it's invisible to us. That's the inner planes.'

'Right,' said Tony.

'It seems they lived in their daily lives what we aspire to,' added Marcus.

'Well, I agree with that,' responded Tony. 'I'd really love to share this with Helen. She'd be so thrilled.'

'She'll be mind-blown,' agreed Joanna. 'Try her tomorrow. She'd love to hear it from you.'

'I'll give her a ring.'

'Thanks for ringing. It's lovely to hear from you. I'll get on my laptop now and pick up the e-mail.'

'Yes and Mum'll be sorry she missed you,' Joanna repeated. 'Before you go, how's the book doing?'

'I'm just rewriting one chapter and then it's finished.'

'Good for you,' she said and meant it.

*

Throughout the evening Joanna kept phoning her mother but she was always out. 'Typical Mother,' she said to Marcus. 'It's supposed to be the kids that are out while mothers stay at home.'

'I think you're thirty years out of date.'

Chapter 20

Later that evening Marcus opened the front door and looked out on the pall of rain. Sylvie saw his disappointed expression and made up her mind.

'Look, why don't you borrow my four-wheel drive and head for Port Douglas and the Daintry? Get out of the rain. There's no use waiting for the weather. It's set in for a few days and I can use my husband's car this week while he's away.'

Marcus looked at her. 'Are you sure?'

'Of course I am. You can book into a hotel in Port Douglas and from there you can take a day trip to the Daintry. It's a tropical rainforest and fascinating, well worth seeing. The trees are about fifty metres tall but their roots are only fifteen centimetres deep. It's amazing.'

'That's scary!' Joanna burst out.

Sylvie laughed. 'Apparently the trees are so tightly packed that they hold each other up. Then they're lashed together by vines, which creep over and round everything. It's beautiful in there. See it while you can. You may not get another opportunity.'

Joanna and Marcus exchanged glances.

'Then you could carry on up to Cooktown to see

Helen,' Sylvie suggested. 'The jungle up there is different again and you can dive on the reef on the way back. The weather may clear by then.'

They needed little persuasion to accept her offer. As they drove up to Port Douglas on Wednesday morning, they anticipated a happy relaxed break until they saw Helen in a few days. They didn't know she smelled danger on Thursday.

On Thursday evening after a long and fascinating day in the Daintry, Marcus was floating in the warm waters of their hotel pool, the night sky a safe dark canopy. Strategically placed flares and spotlights lit up palm trees and flowering bushes and the aquamarine water twinkled with a million stars. He felt he had been transported to some magical wonderland.

As he luxuriated in the tropical warmth he mulled over the day. They had been collected in a minibus as the birds started to sing and were able to watch the sun rising behind the mountains. The pinky orange ball lit up rows of exotic trees which lined the road, golden rain looking like splashes of sunshine yellow, huge red poinsettia trees and bushes of every colour from pink through red, through apricot. The tree palms were lumpy with coconut clusters, ancient maples trailed strangler figs and cosy brown cows dotted the fields.

The Daintry itself had been packed with palms of all kinds, tree ferns and eucalyptus and covered with lichens, mosses and grasses. He thought about the way the vines lashed everything together. Nature is clever, he mused.

All day the sky had been a highly polished blue and they had lunched by a crystal-clear stream, watching turtles swimming. He had been delighted to see the blue flash of a sacred kingfisher.

Marcus wondered what it would be like to merge with the consciousness of the rainforest. To become one with the trees and plants and animals. He tried to feel his way into the energy of the forest and was sinking slowly into a state of peace, when he heard urgent footsteps.

Opening his eyes he saw Joanna was running towards the pool. She looked panic-stricken.

She was holding the mobile. 'Marcus. I got through to Mum. We were chatting and then suddenly she cried out for help. I could hear sounds of a scuffle and the line went dead. Oh, Marcus. I should have listened to my premonition. Something terrible has happened to her. I know it has.'

Chapter 21

All day Thursday Helen had felt restless and anxious. She couldn't concentrate on a book and something warned her not to wander far from the hotel. She remembered Joanna's premonition and her own feeling that there would be danger on Thursday.

But when Jane phoned to say Ferdy had negotiated the creek and they could meet her that evening at the bowls club, she showered and changed, with a sense of relief that she had something to do. Then she sat on the verandah watching the furtive grey sunset until it was time to go out.

It was dark when she left the side door of the hotel. The safety light came on, startling a kangaroo, which was grazing by the wall. They stared at each other for an appraising moment. Then it turned and crashed away through the undergrowth. It startled and unsettled her. Outside the pool of light, the night seemed very dark. She walked nervously in the middle of the road until she reached the club.

About twenty people were playing bowls on the crisply shaved emerald lawn, which was generously floodlit. Men and women, mostly in whites, were eating and drinking outside. It was a comfortingly normal scene.

Jane and her husband were not among them, so Helen ventured into the large, icily air-conditioned club room. Nothing had been done and perhaps nothing could be done to alleviate the soulless feeling of the place. Helen shivered with cold and something else, a sort of tangible hostility.

There were groups of people sitting at small square tables, each covered in a dark green cloth with a vase of plastic flowers in the middle. No one looked up as Helen entered yet she had a distinct impression that everyone knew there was a stranger in the room.

She went to the bar where clusters of men were chatting and was totally ignored. She felt humiliated and knew she was covertly watched. A fierce determination formed inside her. She moved and stood in between two groups of men, directly in front of the barman. It was a challenging gesture and at last he had to serve her. He poured the drink she ordered without a smile, comment or eye contact. No one spoke. But bodies imperceptibly edged her out, pushing her from the bar. She picked up her drink and took it to an empty table, where she waited. Bubbling anger was an antidote to the apprehension of the day.

At last Jane and her husband Ferdy walked in with a strange tale to tell.

Ferdy was thin with side whiskers and a furrowed fox face. He looked rough and tough – the sort she would avoid in the street and he never stopped talking, a kind of compulsive verbal diarrhoea, which was nevertheless fascinating to Helen.

He told her that as a youth he had often gone into the

bush with his Aborigine friends and on one occasion lived with them for some months. He boasted that he had learned all about tracking and bush tucker and reckoned he could live easily off the land. Her inner jury was out on whether or not to believe him.

He sent Jane off to get drinks while he told Helen about contraception in the bush. 'After a bloke has had several children the elders would say "enough". Then he was whistle-cocked.'

Helen was intrigued. 'Whistle-cocked?'

'Have you got a strong stomach?'

She nodded and laughed. 'Go on.'

'They would cut the base of the penis with a knife. A straw or hollow twig was inserted into the urethra so he could pee. The tube through which the sperm runs was severed and then the wound packed with ash and clay to heal.'

'You're joking.'

'Naw. That's whistle-cocking. One hundred per cent effective it was. Sperm couldn't enter the woman.'

'What man would choose that?'

Ferdy uttered a throaty laugh. 'They didn't get a choice. The elders would order it when a man had enough children. They decided and you couldn't say no.'

Jane returned with the drinks. She had stopped and chatted to several people. Clearly everyone knew Ferdy, for several had waved or called out, 'Hi, Ferdy.'

Helen noticed with a kind of sarcastic detachment that they even included her now!

Ferdy talked on like an express train. Helen had the

oddest feeling he had something of importance to tell her. His small eyes kept flicking to her and sometimes to Jane and he would pause for a moment. But right now he was on another track.

'The old men initiated and slept with the young girls – nine or ten years. And the young men were given widows and older women past childbearing age. That kept them all out of mischief until they married.'

Helen asked him what he thought about the stolen generation. He downed his beer and sent Jane for another. 'Order the food while you're about it.'

He turned his attention to Helen's question. 'Lot of fuss if you ask me. They only took half-castes and fifty per cent of those would have died anyway because of the way the Blacks treated them.'

'They treated them badly?'

'They were tainted with white blood. No clan wanted them. Lots were abandoned at missions or starved.' Helen remembered what Philip had told her and wondered where the truth lay.

'If you ask me those that were taken were the lucky ones. They got educated.'

'Why were there so many half-castes?' asked Helen. 'Were the women raped?'

'Only a few. Mostly the Abo girls would hang around the white men and ask for it.' He leered and suddenly Helen did not want to know of his past.

Their meal arrived and Helen was determined to turn the subject to something positive. She asked about the Aborigines' legendary skills as stockmen.

Ferdy immediately launched into a story. 'I had a friend with a magnificent cattle station in the Northern Territories. It was all fenced and there was a beautiful house. Good stock and horses. Everything top notch. The Abos wanted it. Claimed it was sacred land. Probably was to them. Anyway they were given it and five years later they'd stripped it. None of the fences was repaired. The stock wasn't watered and the animals died horrible deaths. Then when the station was no use any more they abandoned it.'

Helen queried why the neighbours had not said anything.

He paused. 'They knew what was going on all right. They said they'd have been killed if they'd spoken.'

Oh God! So much for a positive subject, thought Helen.

When their plates had been cleared Ferdy glanced again at Jane, who nodded surreptitiously. Helen's quick eyes caught it.

'Had a strange experience today,' he said. 'Think it might interest you.' Again that sense of suppressed excitement.

Helen looked at him, her eyes alight with anticipation. 'Yes?'

'Well, I'm bowling along the dirt when I see a big dog, crossed with a dingo somewhere along the line, but this isn't wild.'

'Out there in the middle of nowhere?'

'Sure. Don't know where it could have come from. It walks into the road and stands there.'

'What did you do?' Surely he hadn't run it over.

'Well, I stopped. Didn't want to hurt it. I shouted at it but it gave me a look and walked slowly, keeping right in front of me. Then it headed off the road towards the Black Mountain.'

'The Black Mountain!' Helen had heard of the place. By the side of the road were piled thousands of huge black rocks. It was a sinister, desolate place. No Aborigine would go there. They said it was full of evil spirits and people had disappeared there.

'It kept turning to look at me as if to check I was following.'

'And did you?'

'Well, yes. I figured someone might be injured and the dog was taking me to him. Pretty soon he headed off the road and I had to get out and I followed him towards the piles of stones. It gave me the creeps I can tell you. It was eerie. Never felt like that before. I didn't like it.'

'You were brave,' said Helen.

Jane gave a slight snort. 'Or foolhardy. They say there are noxious gases in the caves and tunnels in the Black Mountain. That's why people die there.'

'Well, I was scared shitless. Oh, pardon me!'

Helen smiled. 'Go on.'

'I was glad the dog was in front in case there were snakes. Then it went behind a boulder and I followed it. When I clambered round the boulder the dog had disappeared. There were just rocks.'

'Disappeared?'

'Yeah. No sign of it. I was just going to turn and go when I heard a sound, like a clapping of sticks. And then a man appeared in front of me. Seemed to come from thin air.'

Helen blinked.

'He was old and black and naked. He was a karadji.'

'A karadji?'

Jane broke in. 'They're medicine men. Sometimes called a mekigar or a wirreenun, depending on the tribe. Karadjis come from central Australia.'

'So how come he was up here?'

Ferdy shrugged. 'They're powerful people. They can do magic and miracles. I've seen them do unbelievable things.'

'Like what?'

'Walking over fire, taking things out of people's bodies, healing illnesses. I've seen them make rain.'

'How do they become medicine men?'

'Oh, they have to go through terrible initiations. You don't want to know. And they become clairvoyant and psychic and healers and very powerful.'

'So they're shamans?'

'Yes, that's it.' Ferdy was becoming impatient. 'Anyway, the guy comes up to me without saying a word and puts his hand on my chest. I feel like, I can't describe it, strange heat going through me and the cough I've had for months just goes away.' He turned to Jane. 'Haven't I had a terrible cough?'

She nodded reluctantly.

'Well, I haven't coughed since or felt tight-chested,'

Ferdy declared. 'Then the old man takes a piece of rock or crystal from thin air.' He took a furtive glance at his wife who sat with tight lips, making it clear what she thought of superstition. 'At least it seemed like thin air. And gives it to me. He said, "For white woman from across oceans. You meet soon. Give her."

'And then, I kid you not, I took the bit of rock and looked up and he'd gone. Gave me the creeps. I legged it. When I got home and Jane told me about you, you could've knocked me down.'

Helen was longing to see the stone and Ferdy was rummaging about in his pocket for it. At last he brought it out, glowing red, with one smooth curved side, just like the others.

She could hardly contain her excitement as he passed it to her. 'The old man said, "Tell her it comes from Uluru." He clearly said this. "Remember to honour each other and learn from the differences." He rabbited on about all colours in a carpet being important. But there was something strange in his eyes when he said, "Remember to honour each other and learn from the differences." '

Helen nodded. As she took the crystal reverently, she murmured, 'Honour each other and learn from the differences.'

Ferdy and Jane dropped her off at her motel and she was so excited as she ran up the steps that she forgot her fear of danger. She was completely unaware of the two figures lurking in the bushes, watching her.

Chapter 22

Leaving the door wide open, Helen hurried across the room to pick up the phone, which inevitably seemed to be ringing whenever she came in.

'Hi Joanna. I'm so glad you called. Guess what! I've got another piece of the crystal ball!' Laughing with excitement, she placed the crystal on the table by the phone. 'Ferdy just gave it to me and you'll never guess what he told me!' By extending the phone cord and stretching out her leg, she was inching the door closed with her toe to stop the mosquitoes from flooding in when a large black hand appeared round the frame. She froze. No sound came from her mouth.

Joanna's voice was saying in her ear, 'Go on. What did he tell you?'

Dirk lurched into the room and grabbed the receiver from her hand. Too late Helen cried out but his hand was across her mouth and the cry was cut short. She struggled helplessly against his size and his brutality. Distantly she could hear Joanna calling, 'Mum! What is it? What's happening? Mum! Mum!'

In her head she was shouting, Help! Help! Oh, God, help! Then a thin black youth pushed into the room and plopped the receiver into its cradle. It felt as if her lifeline had been cut.

She couldn't move. Dirk had pinned her hands roughly behind her. A mingled smell of sweat and beer assaulted her. She felt nauseous with revulsion and panic, mostly panic. Her knees buckled and she stumbled.

With Dirk behind and the other one in front of her she was trapped. The thin youth peered into her face with small bloodshot eyes. It was a menacing gesture and she tried to shrink away but Dirk was an implacable wall behind her. The youth's breath was foul and hot. He staggered slightly. He was drunk but not drunk enough to make a noise or speak. They were both silent. Ominously silent as if they had planned this, like a commando raid.

With a sneer of triumph Dirk grabbed the crystal Ferdy had just given her and put it in his pocket. They half dragged, half pushed Helen from the room and along the verandah. She tried to knock over a chair. Anything to make a noise and alert help but Dirk anticipated her intention and pulled her back before her leg could connect with anything. They carried her between them, holding her so painfully tight that she could not struggle and could hardly breathe.

The lights were feeble. All doors were closed. There was no one around. No one to hear. No one to see.

As they emerged at the back of the motel, the floodlight came on and the kangaroo stood there once more, staring. Then he crashed away through the undergrowth. Surely someone must come. Helen prayed as she had never prayed before.

But her captors skirted the light, dragged her to a truck parked in the dark shadow of a tree and heaved her inside like a carcass. They got in, one on either side of her, squashing her. As soon as Dirk took his hand from her mouth she shouted, 'Help!' and it came out as the feeble wail of a small child. Faint and pathetic. Impossible to hear outside the truck.

The both laughed hysterically and unpleasantly, pleased with their conquest. Excited by her fear. Fighting down her dread, Helen tried to clear her mind. What could she do?

The youths took a moment to watch her maliciously as if she were a trapped animal at their mercy. 'We got her then, Billy, and Uncle George's stone – our stone!' said Dirk with satisfaction.

'Yeah, Uncle Philip said to get it back. Now we just got to get the money out of her.' They chuckled, a grating, horrible sound.

Nonchalantly Dirk opened a can of beer and chucked one to his mate. He wound down the window and threw the ring out. At that moment she knew they intended to kill her.

Billy? she thought. Billy? Where had she heard that name recently? Of course, he was Philip's nephew! Her stomach lurched. The youth who wanted to buy a car he could race round in and dump! She realised Dirk thought he'd taken the crystal Uncle George had given her but she sensed they did not know its true purpose or value. What was that about money? Did they want ransom money for her? Her thoughts were whirling in crazy loops.

There was no one out on the road. In any case no one would have remarked on a truck being driven erratically on a Thursday night.

Once she tried to throw her hand out to hit the horn. A futile gesture. Billy grabbed her arm and twisted it so violently she thought he had broken it. After that she became passive with hopelessness and pain.

They veered off to the left before they reached the shops. Where were they taking her? Some houses still had lights on but gradually these became fewer and then there was only blackness, barely alleviated by a miserable moon. Helen could smell her own fear.

I've got to talk to them. We must get to know each other. That's what hostages have to do, she thought. Her mouth was dry. 'Your Uncle George won't like this.' Her thin voice sounded plaintive. Evidently it was the wrong thing to say.

'Shut your gob, bitch. You got something we want and you better give it to us.'

'Anything. What is it?' Pathetic eagerness sounded in her voice. This was the first inkling of hope. 'What do you want?'

'The gold.'

'What gold?'

'Don't pretend, you stupid bitch.'

Helen was baffled. 'What gold?' she repeated. 'I haven't got any.'

Dirk took his hands off the wheel to hit her and the truck skidded on some mud and veered on to the soft grassy edge of the road. The full impact of the blow missed her as he put his hands on the wheel again, fighting to avoid a tree. But it still caught her across the head and sent her reeling.

No one had ever hit her before. The pain was excruciating. The possibility of more was unthinkable. How did people stand up against such violence? Holding her head in her hands she shrank back into the seat, shaking. Her mind was racing. Gold. What gold? What did they mean?

The mean-faced Billy pulled away her hands and grabbed her chin in a vice-like grip. He forced her head round. 'We know you got it and we intend to have it.' A hint of moonlight caught the whites of his eyes and they glinted, demonic. Releasing her chin he made a gesture to indicate he'd cut her throat. Her jaw throbbed in agony, her body was limp with dread, her mind a fog.

Now they were driving through dense tropical trees crowding in on either side of the road. Suddenly Dirk swung the truck off the road into a clearing and drove to the far corner, screeching to a stop in a large puddle.

Billy pulled her out of the truck so that she fell on her side into the foetid water. Her trousers were soaked and a swarm of mosquitoes rose around her. She could feel them biting at her face and ankles and in her hair. He laughed a slurred, drunken laugh.

Rage like she had never ever experienced spurted through her. I hate you, she thought. I'll get even with you.

A cool voice in her head said, 'Revenge is not the way.' But she could not subdue the voice of hatred and revenge which played round and round in her mind.

Dirk said with intended menace, 'She can walk in front as snake bait.'

Billy added, 'She'll knock the spiders from their webs too.' And they giggled drunkenly together, like two malevolent children.

'I'll kill you with my bare hands,' she wanted to scream. Her hands were sticky. Her eyes blazed and the anger cleared her mind. Already her remote mind was judging. It's better to be angry than afraid. It keeps the adrenaline flowing. But she wasn't going to risk bravado. In this state they could kill her easily, without even realising they were doing it.

Billy held a torch in one hand and a couple of six-packs in the other. The light arced as he lurched, illuminating dripping leaves, misty rain and impenetrable trees beyond. He staggered and almost fell into a large bush.

Dirk held a can in one hand. With the other he twisted Helen's arm and pushed her in front of him. Pain ran through her shoulder as she stumbled forward.

Every moment she expected to hear the hiss of death or feel the needle-like sting of a spider. Each step forward was a slipping, slithering, agonising nightmare. Thank God she still had shoes on. She could have been in thongs or bare feet. They wouldn't have cared. Fragmented thoughts passed through her mind but mostly the numb terror returned, which anaesthetised her.

When she could see nothing in front of her, Dirk pushed her through barbed leaves and clinging tentacles. She was helpless to resist his physical strength. And always there were the mosquitoes. Millions of mosquitoes. She could feel her face swelling up.

When she thought she could go on no further they reached a clearing. She could make out the shape of a hut. It was a wooden shack. A derelict, rotten, infested place. They pushed open the creaking door, which was half off its hinges, and Dirk flung her inside.

She tried to be courageous but as she was propelled into a corner, she cowered in the dark. She could feel something crawl across her hand and her heart stopped, but with an instinctive movement she flung it off and nothing bit her.

Dirk and Billy sat on the beaten earth and leaned against the side of the hut. 'What'll we do with her?' slurred Billy.

'Plenty of time. She'll tell us about the Gold of Power when we lock her in here with the snakes.' He appeared to like that thought and mumbled something to himself, laughing, his hair dripping down his face in the torchlight. They drank another beer each.

What would happen when they became very drunk? Helen tried to stop the numbness, which threatened to take over her mind. Now they had stopped moving she could feel the unbearable itching of the bites.

There is a moment beyond fear. Perhaps it comes when all hope is gone.

As the youths became steadily more and more inebriated, Helen focused on the wisdom contained in the Scroll. First she must still her mind. Hunched in the corner of the insect-infested shed, she forced herself to control her breathing. Her thoughts became quieter.

She breathed the colour gold around her. Now she knew that the angels and the powers-that-be could connect with her. Why didn't I do it before? she asked herself. But she knew that she had been too panic-stricken. She visualised daylight coming and being rescued. No sooner had she formulated the picture than something slithered across her foot and she let out a yelp of fear.

Instantly Dirk was aroused. He shone a torch on the sly shape disappearing through the door. 'A brown,' he muttered. But it seemed to shake him, for a brown is one of the deadliest snakes in Australia. He prodded Billy.

'Time to find out about the gold,' he muttered. Billy, however, was dead to the world.

Dirk clearly needed his mate's support. He settled back. 'One move from you and you're dead,' he shot at Helen. 'And if I don't get you, the jungle will.' He waved a hand towards the door where the faintest pearlescent shimmer alleviated the black of night. Then he took another swig of beer and his head fell sideways on to his shoulder. He breathed heavily.

Either asleep or feigning sleep, thought Helen. Her heart was hammering. I daren't move yet. He had left the torch on and it shone crookedly into the far corner. She could see insects crawling and flying in the beam of light. The thought of escaping into the dark jungle terrified her. More than terrified her. She was caught between the horror of staying where she was at the mercy of these violent drunks and the certain death of the jungle at night.

The dread that had been screaming in her stomach, spread over her whole body. She felt out of control and started to shake. I don't want to die. I don't want to die, she thought. Then she took herself in hand. I must not give in. I must stay calm.

Her visualisation of daylight coming and being rescued had been shattered into a million fragments. She must start again and take command. It was her only hope.

This time, as soon as she had calmed her mind, she put herself into a cocoon of protection. Then she pictured a web of golden rope being woven around Dirk and Billy, to keep them psychically bound. Such was her faith in the power of the inner world that she immediately felt safer. She dared to move an inch. Her whole body was stiff and aching with pain and bites. Now that she was calmer she knew her life depended on getting out of there.

The youths both seemed dead to the world. Carefully she moved her hands and legs. Neither of them stirred. There was a loose plank in the corner. For a fleeting second she thought she could hit them on the head. Knock them out. Kill them.

Where did that thought come from? She was horrified at herself, though another part argued that it was perfectly reasonable. It's never justifiable to kill, the voice in her head went on. Oh, shut up, Helen, she said to herself. Just concentrate on getting out of here.

The rain had stopped and the sky glinted with a silvery pink sheen. It was definitely lightening. Stiffly she rose to her feet. Cautiously, inch by inch, she crept across the floor. Watching the men. Dirk moved a fraction and she froze, holding her breath. But he settled back and she breathed again, heart thumping.

Dare she take the torch? She knew she must but Billy was still holding it. Suddenly determined, Helen picked up the loose plank. If he moves, I'll hit him, she decided. Lips tight, hands ice-cold now, she stepped over the inert form. Her body crossed the beam of torchlight and everything went dark. If anything woke them, that might. Holding her breath, she waited but they did not move.

Now the final test, she thought. She bent slowly and carefully and tried to ease the torch from Billy's flaccid fingers. Once he gripped, but it was a reflex motion and soon his fingers relaxed again and his hand fell from the torch handle. It clattered. The light moved.

Heart thumping, Helen snatched it up and crept slowly, ever so slowly out through the door into the jungle.

Chapter 23

Joanna was frantic. There were dark smudges under her eyes. 'What can we do?' she repeated. She was holding the phone out to Marcus in a gesture of supplication as he pulled himself from the pool. 'Mum's been attacked. I know she has.'

'Right. Tell me again exactly what happened.' Marcus's heart was thumping. He spoke slowly, trying to calm himself.

She told him again, quickly, desperately. There was a weight on her chest. She felt as if it would explode. 'Do something!' she wanted to scream. 'Help me!'

Marcus wrapped a towel round his waist. 'Come inside.' He put an arm more firmly than he felt round her shoulders and propelled her back to the room. In her shock she had left the door open. He shut it firmly. Then phoned a great many people.

The police were unhelpful. Through Sylvie he managed to get hold of Ferdy and Jane, who said they would drive to the motel immediately to check if she was there. They also gave him Uncle George's number and Marcus phoned him immediately. The elder listened intently. 'I'll find out what's happening and phone back,' was all he could say. Marcus sensed that he was shaken to the core.

There was nothing they could do but wait and time dragged.

'Come on, Joanna,' Marcus said to encourage her. 'You know what the Scroll said. We must use our thoughts to project safety to your mum and a positive outcome.'

Joanna nodded. 'Of course. Why didn't I do it straight away?' She sat down and together they stilled their breathing. Then they created a picture of Helen safe and well. They visualised gold surrounding this picture; gold, the colour of the angelic ray and the Christ ray. It was only later that they learned how much good this had done. It had helped to steady her and stay the worst possible atrocities.

It was an hour before the phone rang and they both leaped up. 'Quick!' urged Joanna unnecessarily.

It was Ferdy, Jane's husband. He sounded serious. 'I'm at Helen's motel. The manager's with us. Now stay calm but she's not here and there's no sign of her. It looks like there's been a bit of a struggle and the door of her room was open. The police are now involved and they say they'll start looking for her in the morning.'

'In the morning!' Marcus was horrified. 'Can't they do something now?'

He could sense Ferdy shuffling. 'They think it's too dark and wet out there but they'll make some enquiries.'

Joanna had heard. She was yelling, 'In the morning! They've got to look for her now!' He could hear her voice quiver under the anger.

Marcus took a deep breath. He must think clearly. 'Any idea who took her or why?'

'Not yet. Got to go. I'll phone you as soon as there's some news.' The line went dead.

There was a ball of anxiety in Marcus's stomach. Joanna was sitting on the bed looking at him, her face pale, her brown eyes tinged with grey. She felt sick.

'In the morning! They found her door open and some indications of struggle,' Joanna repeated. She was shaking her head in disbelief. Bewildered. Dejected. Angry and hopeless.

'The police are involved.'

'But they're not doing anything, are they?' she demanded, suddenly strident.

Marcus shook his head. 'Not yet.' He clenched his fists. 'It's insupportable.'

'I want to go now. At least we'd be there,' said Joanna. Marcus looked at his watch. 'It's after midnight. And Cooktown's beyond the bitumen, so it's dirt road for quite a way. It'd be madness to set off now.' He thought for a moment, aware of her eyes on his face. It was so unlike Joanna to wait for someone else to make a decision.

'I'll phone Ferdy back. See if the creek's passable. He must have got through today but it's rained some more. We'll see what he suggests.'

Another hour had gone by before they managed to get hold of Ferdy, who told them tersely, 'There's no news here. We think she was taken in a truck.'

'Who? Who'd want to take her?'

'We don't know.'

Fruitlessly they discussed the possibilities. Then Marcus asked if the road would be negotiable if they left now.

'Don't be a damn fool. Don't even think of doing it at night. Leave at first light if you must. The coast road isn't passable anyway, so you'll have to go inland.'

'How far is it?'

'Two hundred and eighty kilometres. About sixty kilometres of it's beyond the bitumen on dirt roads. If the creek's passable you'll be here by midday. But don't take any chances. If the water's too high, you'll just have to wait.'

'Would it be better to fly?'

'Quicker but you'll never get a seat. I'll phone you if I hear anything.'

Marcus relayed to Joanna what Ferdy had said. It made sense though it was not what they wanted to hear.

'Lie down and try to rest,' Marcus commanded. 'We'll leave first thing.'

It was like trying to nap on a bed of nails. Neither could sleep but maybe they slipped into a doze from time to time.

Uncle George phoned at 2 a.m. apologising about the lateness of the call. Both were instantly alert. The old man sounded weary. He had contacted a great many people since Marcus had spoken to him. Clearly he had not gone to bed. However he had nothing concrete to report.

Marcus had an uneasy feeling that the elder was holding something back. But why? He did not tell Joanna of his suspicion. She was looking ill enough as it was, her mood vacillating between anger and despair.

They left for Cooktown before 5 a.m. heading through occasional storms. Every time rain fell, Joanna tensed. Marcus knew she was thinking of the creek. Would it be passable?

As they drove through relentless mile after mile of scrubby desert punctuated with termite mounds, they had a strange feeling of isolation. All signs of human habitation vanished. It was somehow heartening when a car passed them and they were reminded that there was someone out there.

Ethereal mists writhed round the distant mountains. Everything seemed obscure. Once they clambered out to stretch their limbs. They stood on a high ridge at the side of the road, staring out over miles of flat land haunted with skeleton trees. Even when the sun emerged there was an eerie feeling and they were glad to get into the car and press on.

They talked over the possibilities again and again. Was her disappearance linked to the Codes of Power?

'Please, God, don't let it be the Elite who took her,' cried Joanna.

'They must know about the Codes of Power,' replied Marcus flatly.

'But how? And why Mum?' she asked bitterly. 'The

Scroll has only ever brought us danger and difficulty!'

'True!' agreed Marcus. 'But look what we've learned.'

'Oh, I know. And the good that's come about. All the same, is it worth it?'

'You know the answer to that,' Marcus reminded her. 'We've always been clear that this is more important than anything else in this life. It means we could be instrumental in changing the planet.'

'I know. But why Mum?'

'I can't answer that but I'm sure it's all linked to the Codes of Power. It must be mighty important. Look how the pieces of the crystal ball have started to come to us. It's all got to be connected.'

Joanna sighed and mused for a while before she spoke again, more calmly. 'I wonder if this area was the Garden of Abundance described in the Scroll. I'd like to live in a world where everything was abundant and people could merge their consciousness. And where everyone was transparent. No fear and no deception.'

He squeezed her arm. 'We will some time. That's why we're trying to bring the crystal ball together – to release again the original blueprint of the planet, so that the Oneness consciousness can come about again.'

The conversation continued on a happier note until Joanna felt a sharp kick in her stomach and immediately knew her mother was in danger. The hairs behind her neck prickled. A chill ran down her back. Marcus picked up her energy.

'I'm sure she'll be all right. Come on, let's keep sending her golden light. You know how powerful it is.'

'Perhaps we should phone Tony and ask him to send her light too?'

'As soon as we can get a signal again, we'll do that.'

Finally they agreed to concentrate their energy on picturing Helen in a cocoon of gold. That seemed the most positive thing they could do. It also helped to keep their spirits up as they raced along the endless road.

The only things that made Joanna smile were the road signs warning of bullocks. They depicted a bullock bigger than a car it was lifting up. 'Scary!' she giggled. Sometimes thin wandering cattle stood unmoving in the middle of the unfenced road, clearly determined to delay them. Joanna kept breathing away her tension and projecting the golden cocoon to her mother.

'I think we'll soon be at the creek,' Marcus told her.

Joanna was peering through the fly-spattered windscreen. 'Look, there are trees over there. They must be near the water.' Please! Please! Let us get through, she prayed.

The road dipped and a wide brown expanse of water lay ahead. In the very centre a wild current fought and bubbled and wrestled, carrying leaves and branches. They stared.

'Can we make it?' Joanna's voice trembled with despair edged with bravado.

Marcus's jaw clenched. 'I don't know.'

'We've got to get to her.'

They had both heard stories of cars being swept away in the floods but they did have the advantage of a four-wheel drive.

The dull ache at the back of Marcus's head became a sharp throb. 'We'll go in slowly. See if we can gauge it,' he offered, knowing it was madness. They inched forward. The water was too high but they had good purchase and they were halfway across and moving steadily. 'It'll be okay,' he thought.

Suddenly the wheels slithered and for a dreadful moment the current took them. Weightless, the vehicle lurched. A branch crashed into the side with a crack and they did not hear it.

Then they could feel contact with the river bed. The wheels gripped again. Marcus let out a breath. He dared to accelerate a fraction.

Joanna's shoulders dropped.

That was when they spotted the crocodile in the shallows, a huge scaly monster, swimming languidly towards them, only its eyes and tail visible above the water. It was watching them.

Fear sliced through Marcus's gut. They could not go back. They could not stop.

'Go faster!' screamed Joanna, eyes filled with horror.

'Can't.'

Joanna's armpits felt sticky. 'Can it flip us?'

Marcus did not reply. His hands were like a vice on the wheel.

He concentrated with all his power on getting the vehicle through, which left no room in his mind for anything else.

The crocodile was snaking beside them now, eyes and snout out of the water.

Joanna could not take her eyes off it. She forced herself to breathe as she pictured an impenetrable wall between them and the beast.

An eternity later the car crawled out of the water on to dry land. The crocodile submerged and vanished.

Chapter 24

The meeting with the crocodile unnerved them. 'What does it mean?' demanded Joanna. 'There must be some reason for it appearing then.'

'Have you got your Aborigine Dreaming book on you?'

'Sure.' Joanna delved into her bag and drew out a book decorated in Aboriginal drawings. She flipped over the pages. 'Here it is – crocodile dreaming.' She pulled a face. 'It says it's about respect and the reverse is cunning or heartlessness.'

'What's the story?'

Joanna scanned the page quickly and paraphrased. She was always too impatient to read anything out in full. 'Well, Pukawi the crocodile was a human in the Dreamtime – a man. He was very strong and bad-tempered so people were afraid of him. The clan decided to move to an island in the middle of a river where they'd be safe. They ferried everyone across one at a time and told the crocodile man to wait until last because they planned to leave him behind.'

'Surprise!'

'I know! However, he suspected their plot and decided to take revenge by swimming under the boat and turning it over.'

Joanna was enjoying the story and Marcus was glad to see the colour return to her cheeks. She laughed. 'But when he made himself a snout and swam to the boat they all turned into birds and flew away. The crocodile man decided it was better to be a crocodile and swore he'd kill any birds or people he met. And everyone respected him after that.'

'That's a fear-based respect!'

'True.'

'So the message is?'

'It says, if a crocodile comes into your life check whether you've been cunning, heartless, aggressive or resentful, which are croc qualities. Or you may need croc aggression to protect your young.'

'Maybe we need crocodile aggression to get your mum back?' Marcus suggested. Then he could have bitten off his tongue. He had been trying not to mention Helen. And now Joanna's face had that pinched look again.

She nodded. 'We'll do whatever we need to do. But it's the uncertainty that's so killing. If only we knew where she was.'

They had been over it a hundred times and Marcus knew it was pointless to reply, so he put out a hand and covered hers for a moment in a reassuring gesture. He noticed that the eczema to which she was prone when anxious had flared up and her hands were raw and scaly. Poor Joanna, he thought. He had never seen her skin in such a state and could not begin to imagine what she was going through.

Once more he visualised Helen in a golden bubble of

protection. Then he put one round Joanna too. She seemed to relax a little after that.

Five minutes later she commented, 'I had such a shock when that croc appeared. It was like a Ferrari which appears on your tail on the motorway.' And they both laughed.

They drove on through the endless dull red earth and scrubby bush, punctuated only occasionally with languid trees, termite mounds like old tombstones and rare signs of habitation. Skinny cows were more numerous than passing cars.

The sinister Black Mountain made up of huge granite balls loomed to one side of the road. A lone bird of prey wheeled over it and bizarrely an invisible animal howled.

Joanna shivered. 'Did you hear that? It sounded like a dog but there's no one around for miles!'

'I heard it too.' Marcus felt disquiet.

'It's spooky. I've got a horrible feeling about this place. Can we go a bit faster?'

Marcus was about to accelerate when an Aborigine, with a large dingo-dog, appeared in front of them. He stood in the middle of the track, peering at them. 'What the hell! Where did he come from?' Marcus exclaimed as he braked sharply.

Joanna was equally startled. 'I didn't see him. He was just there.'

The man was wizened, thin in the way of the very old and sporting a straggly beard and a battered hat. He leaned on a stick, immobile as a stork, watching them. The dog stared at them with bright eyes.

'I'd better go and see what he wants,' muttered Marcus uneasily. He glanced around but there was no other sign of life. The man did not move.

Joanna jumped down too and they approached the Aborigine. Marcus enquired in a solicitous tone, 'Can we help you?'

Joanna would have smiled if the conditions had not been so surreal. She thought he sounded very public school. An Aussie would have shouted, 'Hey, mate. Get out of the road.' But then that was why she loved Marcus.

The old man put out a claw-like hand and plucked Marcus's shirt. 'Come,' he said. He waved his arm vaguely in the direction of the Black Mountain. 'Come.'

'Just a minute,' butted in Joanna. 'What do you want? I don't want to go over there.'

The man fixed her with a glittering eye and for a shocked moment she thought, He's not old at all.

Then he cast his eyes down and repeated, 'Come.'

She frowned, thinking herself mistaken.

Marcus and Joanna looked at each other.

'I don't want to go anywhere near that place,' Joanna said vehemently, her nostrils flaring slightly, like a race-horse scenting danger.

'Nor do I.' Marcus was aware of the old Aborigine watching him as if appraising his response. 'How strange,' he reflected.

The old man made a pleading gesture and made a rocking movement with his arms.

'A child must be hurt,' said Joanna doubtfully. 'Oh, God. I suppose we ought to go with him.'

She inclined her head sideways as a question mark and cradled her arms to indicate baby. He nodded. She looked at the bare black rocks and shuddered.

'I'll go with him. You stay here,' Marcus said decisively.

Joanna did not want him to go on his own. Besides, she was not sure which was worse: to be left alone in the desert by the sinister hill of black rocks or to accompany Marcus and this stranger.

'I'll pull the car off the track,' she said and climbed into the driving seat. It took a minute or two to negotiate big stones by the side of the road and the frail old man had set off at a cracking pace with Marcus following him. As Joanna watched, she remembered that babies were women's business. Why would a male come for help?

She had heard that no Aborigine ever came here to the Black Mountain. They were superstitious and particularly terrified of this place. Something was terribly wrong. Quickly she jumped out and called after them but already Marcus, striding behind the old man, was some distance away. Panicky, not knowing quite what to do, oblivious of the scorching heat, Joanna ran after them, shouting, 'Marcus. Wait. Don't go any further.' But he did not appear to hear. She hurried blindly after them.

Chapter 25

As she ran after Marcus, Joanna's thoughts raced. Everyone had told her not to leave the road when in the outback and here they were following a strange old man, who did not seem old any more.

'We must be mad,' she panted and was surprised that the words had come out aloud. 'Marcus. Wait,' she shouted again.

She recalled that even the down-to-earth Sylvie had warned, 'Just drive as fast as you can past the Black Mountain. It feels evil.' It had astonished Joanna to hear Sylvie say it. Of course if it had been Helen that would have been different. At the thought of her mother, Joanna groaned, 'This is terrible. I want to get to Cooktown. We should never have got out of the vehicle.' She paused and cupped her hands round her mouth. 'Marcus! Stop!' she shrieked.

He had vanished behind a pile of boulders and she felt isolated and abandoned. Her heart thundered and she stopped to take a deep breath, then bellowed, 'Marcus!' Her voice echoed back from the devil's stones.

A snake darted in front of her. 'Oh, God,' she whispered. She was wearing shorts so her legs were unprotected. She glanced back. At least she could see the four-wheel drive, solid and reliable by the roadside. I'll go round that next boulder, she bargained with herself. If they're not there I'll go back to the car. Please, please be there.

Now that she had remembered the snakes and the vulnerability of her legs, she walked cautiously, watching every footstep. When she rounded the boulder, she could see a tunnel cut through the rocks. She could hear Marcus's voice coming from it, muffled so she could not distinguish what he said, but he was there. She was sure of it. With a deep breath, she took off her sunglasses and entered the gloomy tunnel, not tall enough for her to walk upright but neither did she have to crawl. It did not extend far but it seemed a thousand miles.

She emerged into a gloomy cavern, with a gassy smell, which looked as if it had been accidentally formed when the boulders piled up. Straggly rays of light crept through various cracks and holes, allowing strange black lichen to grow.

Marcus and the man were there, sitting side by side on a rock, under a stream of filtered light. Beyond them it was impenetrably dark. It felt scary and she shivered.

The Aborigine extended a hand and smiled. He looked neither emaciated nor old. Yet he was the same man. Joanna's thoughts whirled and a blaze of anger shot through her.

'Why the hell did you go without me?' she shouted at Marcus.

'Sorry,' he replied, looking dazed. 'I can't really explain it myself.'

The Aborigine held up his hand. 'Many things not understand. Me karadji from central Australia.'

Joanna had no idea who a karadji was and her tone was belligerent. 'So?' She paused for breath. 'What are you doing here and where's the sick child? Why have you brought us to this hellish place? We urgently have to get to Cooktown. Come on, Marcus. Let's go!'

The karadji held up his hand. He was totally composed and watching Joanna with the faintest hint of amusement in his dark eyes. Under his scrutiny her rage dispersed to irritation and, now that he did not appear to want to hurt them, a strange curiosity.

She turned to Marcus. 'Have you any idea what's going on?'

A suspicion had started to formulate in his consciousness that this person was an important link in their quest. He replied enigmatically, 'Except that there's no such thing as chance, none.'

She frowned at this response, then peered into the shadows. She still did not like the feeling in here.

'What's a karadji?' Marcus addressed the Aborigine slowly, enunciating his words carefully.

'Magic man.'

'You mean a shaman or medicine man?'

The old man grinned and nodded.

'Can you manifest things?' Joanna demanded curiously, though all she wanted to manifest right now was to get out of this spooky place.

He nodded, watching her closely with hooded eyes, waiting to see if she would ask for a demonstration. She did not and he was satisfied. 'No important,' he grunted.

She nodded, agreeing. Her fascination for such powers was waning. The only true power was spiritual growth.

She knew suddenly that he had read her mind, for he nodded. She was no longer afraid of him, only this eerie, evil-feeling mountain. Again he nodded.

'Codes of Power!' he said, concentrating on the pronunciation, like a child speaking his first words of a foreign language.

They stared.

He smiled. 'Yes, Codes of Power.'

They wanted to ask him a million questions. And he was watching them, reading their minds. Joanna bit her tongue. Would he know about her mother? Could he help Helen? As soon as these thoughts passed through her mind, he turned away and she knew she must not ask him – yet. The thought of her mother was still a sick weight in her stomach but she felt calmer. Perhaps this strange man could help her.

Marcus asked, 'What can you tell us about the Codes of Power? Do you have one of the crystals for us? Should we go to Uluru?' He had not meant to fire so many questions to someone who clearly did not speak much English. They just burst out.

The shaman pronounced with difficulty, 'You here learn. Big learn.'

He pointed to himself. 'Teacher.' Then he pointed upwards and opened his palms as if accessing information. Finally he closed his eyes.

For the first time they noticed terrible scars on his arms,

like gouge marks. They must be initiation scars, thought Marcus. He glanced at Joanna and knew she had seen them too. Then they focused on the karadji once more, watching in fascination. Evidently he was far away, for he almost seemed to glow.

When he opened his eyes he smiled.

'I bring you here for purpose,' he pronounced.

Marcus and Joanna looked at each other in profound surprise, for he was suddenly speaking fluent English, with only a slight accent.

He answered the unspoken question. 'When link into universal consciousness. We call Dreamtime, can communicate with everyone. Is beyond language.'

'Like telepathy?' asked Marcus.

'Similar. But here takes form of words.'

Joanna was thinking of the information revealed in the Codes of Power. 'So it's like merging your consciousness with a flower for instance and becoming that flower but in this case you're connecting to a person's mind?' she queried.

He nodded. 'Link into mental body of person you communicate.'

Wow! thought Joanna. That was something.

'Why the charade about the baby?' asked Marcus. 'Surely you could just have asked us to go with you?'

Joanna nodded. 'Yes, why?' she echoed.

'If I ask you, perhaps come, perhaps not.' He shrugged. 'This way check compassion. Simple test. When you think child in need you follow. Is good.'

Joanna noticed that his English was getting better.

Perhaps he was tuning in more clearly to the universal consciousness.

'Remember this.' He held one finger up. 'While you live on Earth in a physical body you are being tested. Spiritual guides and what you call angels set tests, which come to you as challenges in your daily life.'

'What do you mean by, what you call angels?'

He smiled. 'Every culture and religion has a slightly different concept and understanding of the mighty beings of light who serve the Universal Master of Creation, that which we call the Great Spirit. I was merely acknowledging this.'

'Okay.'

'Everyone has a purpose and all are led to their life path by guides and angels. They orchestrate the coincidences and synchronicities, which propel you forward. However as you know all humans have free will and can choose to resist the prompting of the light spirits. Very often humans listen to the voice of the dark angels and guides, for, as you know, here on Earth there are both. The task is to discern which is light and which is dark. The voice of glamour, greed, harm, selfishness or deceit is that of the shadow. Great Spirit radiates only love, hope, faith, peace and joy through his angels and guides of light.'

Joanna and Marcus were listening intently.

'Every human has a shadow side. It is part of the learning of Earth. You cannot deny your dark side. If you do your shadow will go underground and like a submerged bomb surface when least expected. You must shed light on your shadow and understand it. That is the way to integration and ascension.'

He paused for emphasis. 'All contain yin and yang, feminine and masculine. Because of duality the dark feminine and dark masculine have to be accepted and integrated or individuals and society cannot operate.

'We Aborigines act out our shadow in drama. Some of our ritual dances are violent, others sexual or they express need, greed and deceit. In this way we acknowledge and express the dark side of human nature, which is disruptive and unacceptable in a society.

'Westerners tend to condemn and suppress their shadow. So it emerges as drug addiction, war, murder or corruption. When individuals do not take responsibility for their shadows, they project the dark feelings out on to others and blame them. Society does the same thing.'

'How does society do that?'

'Oh, take one example. A rich nation builds its wealth on the labour of a poor nation. It hoards these riches and implements policies which keep the people of the other nation starving, uneducated and in debt. The people of the poor nation get more and more angry. Their outrage may eventually surface in acts of terrorism. Yes?'

'True,' agreed Marcus.

'The people of the rich nation will genuinely feel hurt and surprised that anyone should hate them so much that they want to attack them. Is that right?'

'It's true.'

'They don't understand because their collective shadow of greed and cruelty is denied.'

They nodded.

'However, in the example I give you, an opportunity for spiritual growth is offered. If the rich nation recognises its shadow as causing the terrorism, it will eschew revenge and instead put in place policies that begin to create balance.'

'Like using its resources to end starvation?'

'And setting an example by being ecologically responsible?'

'Making sure everyone in the world is educated?'

'Honouring spirit instead of the material?'

The old man just kept nodding. 'That would be a good start. I ask you who would commit acts of terror against such a wise nation?'

They sat in silence for some time. Considering.

'And the crocodile?' asked Marcus. 'Was that orchestrated by the Great Spirit?'

'Of course. It was a test.'

'A test!' Joanna shuddered.

'An initiate of the Codes of Power must be able to master the energy fields. You know this?'

They nodded.

'The physical, emotional, mental and spiritual bodies?'

'Indeed. The initiate must master the physical body, be moderate in food and drink and activities. The emotional body is more difficult. When you master fear and emotional attachment, then you control your environment. No creature will harm you.' He looked at Joanna. 'After the initial shock, you did well with the crocodile. Your fear levels were high and brought it closer but the wall you sent out with your mental body kept it at a distance.'

He turned to Marcus. 'Your emotional body was quite strong. It was natural to feel some fear. At your level that is to be expected. But you worked to master it and you too used your mind to keep the creature at bay. Good! Good!'

Joanna wanted to ask him about her mother but he read her mind immediately and once more waved the question away.

'The spiritual body is a much lighter and higher frequency. It is concerned with keeping your connection clear to the Great Spirit. Then you feel your spiritual guides and angels around you and they can help you. When you master your energy bodies, nothing can harm you. Nothing.

'Now, I must leave you for a time.' He stood up and glanced gravely at Joanna. 'Mother very big danger. I go.'

Joanna jumped up. 'Will she be all right?'

He ignored the question. 'Wait for me here. Do not try to leave. Remember what I told you. Master your bodies and you will be safe.'

Joanna opened her mouth to ask about Helen again but so stern was the expression in his jet-black eyes that she kept quiet. In her mind formed the word 'trust'.

'Remember, just as there are portals of light on the planet, there are also portals of dark. Only light can keep dark at bay.' He looked at each of them keenly. 'Use the time wisely,' he advised. 'You know that dark cannot penetrate light. And keep this.' They swore he smiled as he held up a piece of red crystal in a chink of sunlight, so that it glistened and glowed. Then he handed it to them. 'Remember all are equal,' he said and repeated in a sing-song voice, 'All are equal. Mother and father, male and female, sun and moon, compassion and courage: all same, all equal.'

Then he turned and walked swiftly to the tunnel between the rocks. No sooner had he disappeared from view than there was a strange rumble and crashing sound which reverberated through the Black Mountain. Some of the rocks had moved. A huge boulder fell with a terrible crash and completely sealed the entrance to the tunnel, followed by an avalanche of smaller stones, which filled the air with dust. When it subsided their worst fears were realised. They were trapped.

Chapter 26

The silence was eerie. Just the occasional rumble of rocks settling. A pebble dislodged, clanging as it landed, loud in the emptiness. Dust everywhere, which filled the air, then started to settle like fine grey snow.

Marcus and Joanna clutched each other, her face buried in his shoulder, partly for support and partly to filter the dust. Also she could not bear to look. She did not want to see.

At last she lifted her head. Marcus was staring, white-faced, at the huge boulder, which plugged the entrance to the tunnel. Together they got up and clambered over to it as fast as they could. It was no illusion. This was real rock. Desperately they tried to push but it would not budge. They fancied they heard manic laughter and looked at each other in terror.

'What shall we do?' Joanna's voice trembled though she tried to keep it in control.

Marcus thought deeply. 'This must be a test. We must stay centred.'

'I know, but do you think this is a dark portal?'

He nodded. 'Yes, I'm sure of it and we must keep our energy bodies strong and firm, no matter what happens.

And we must stay together. Come on. Let's check if there's a way out.'

She agreed. His masculine energy gave her strength and together they explored.

'There's nothing we can do,' he said at last after they had examined every chink and crack. 'We're totally trapped.'

'Try the mobile!'

He fumbled in his pocket but there was no signal. 'Too much to hope for a signal out here,' he said, his voice sounding like death.

Joanna found strength from somewhere. 'We can invoke the light and visualise help coming. Surely the karadji will get help?'

'Of course, he'll get help.'

'Marcus, do you think he was who he said he was?'

'I don't know.'

'He might have created this to test us?'

'Or he might have been hurt in the landslip! Oh, I'm sorry, don't let's give that thought any energy.' Doubts were starting to undermine them. They must hold hope. He must be strong for Joanna and they could not help Helen if they succumbed to fear. Suddenly he remembered the crystal the karadji had given them. He had put it into his pocket and now he pulled it out.

'He gave us the crystal, so he must think we can bring the pieces of the crystal ball together,' he said with more of a sense of reassurance than before.

'Oh yes! I'd forgotten. How weird.' She took the crystal from him and held it, immediately feeling better. 'Let's meditate.'

As they closed their eyes and started to focus on their breathing, they heard hissing. Simultaneously their eyes flew open. A snake, disturbed and terrified by the quake, was poised in strike position.

Joanna's heart stopped. She knew that she must not move, that she must master her fear. She felt strength flow to her from Marcus. He too was totally still. Giving each other courage they breathed together slowly, deeper and deeper. And gradually the snake relaxed and slithered away.

That was when weird noises started. Scratching. Then whispering, howling and wailing. Marcus's scalp itched. Joanna's cold hand found his. She grasped the crystal in her other hand.

'It's a test. Surround yourself with light,' he whispered.

Again they breathed deeply to calm themselves. In the gloom they saw a sinister shape slither. Marcus increased the pressure of his hand in hers and they focused on light.

Suddenly the sound of rocks moving made their hearts thud and thunder in their ears. They could feel the ground shaking. 'No!' screamed Joanna in her head. For a second she thought the rocks would fall and crush them. Then she shut out that thought as she struggled to maintain calm.

They smelled it at the same moment. An invasive smell of sulphur gas. Rotten. It seemed to suffocate them. This time it was Joanna who said, 'Light is stronger than dark.' Marcus nodded.

She could feel the smell flowing round her as if it were trying to strangle her. How can a smell do that? she wondered. Yet that was how it felt. I must stay centred in light. She invoked the Angels of Light. She invoked the Masters, Jesus Christ, Buddha, Krishna, Mohammed, Allah, Mother Mary, Quan Yin. Every great being she could think of.

In the gloom she could sense ghostly forms trying to get to them. They seemed to wail and call. It must be my imagination, she told herself. But she knew it was not. Something foul and horrible was happening here.

Holding hands, they continued to send out prayers and invocations. Marcus felt as if icy fingers were touching his face and shivered. He could not help it. Joanna felt his shiver and her hair prickled. Then the spooky figures around them seemed to be touching them. As one they started to chanted 'ohm'. The shapes fell back. They lost all sense of time.

They were thirsty, hungry and trapped but as the nightmare threatened to enfold them, those bodily sensations faded into insignificance. Together they 'ohmed' aloud and focused with all their concentration on the light. They knew these creatures of the darkness could not harm them while they were surrounded in light. They knew it must be a nightmare, some ghastly illusion from which they would wake up. But they had to use all the power of their minds so that they were not overcome.

A long time later they heard voices. Real human voices, or so it seemed. They opened their eyes and looked at one another for reassurance. Was this too an illusion?

The voices called out again in unmistakable Queensland accents. 'Anyone there?'

'Hi there.'

'Cooee.'

The nightmare diminished. The wailing and moaning, the slithering shapes and even the foul smells went. Only the ghastly sensations of having been touched by cold slimy fingers remained and the goose-pimples on their arms.

Marcus and Joanna shouted and yelled. Marcus picked up two stones and banged them against a rock. Soon they knew there were men out there coming to rescue them. Three big, solid, real men.

It took time. The men had to go back to the station to get more help. Joanna begged one of them to remain and, seeming to understand, they agreed. Two stayed and talked to them through a gap in the rocks, while the third went to fetch support and to get hold of a digger from the road works five miles away. With human contact the horror of the dark world disappeared and so did their goose-pimples.

At last an arm appeared through a hole and handed them a plastic bottle of water.

'Better than champagne!' Joanna grinned. Her voice was hoarse from shouting and the dust.

'Bliss,' agreed Marcus.

The men kept up a constant stream of encouragement through the enlarging hole. The man with the big voice, called Zed, shouted, 'An old Aborigine feller, driving a four-wheel drive, told us about you. He came to the station and said he'd seen you go into the mountain. Then he said he heard the rocks move and couldn't find you again. So he drove your vehicle to get help!'

Joanna and Marcus stared at each other.

'We were pretty doubtful I can tell you,' the voice went on. 'What was an Abo doing here in the first place? I asked myself. But he was driving a spanking new four-wheel drive.'

'Yes, that was ours!'

'Thieving bastard! But there was something about the bloke. Not like an ordinary Abo at all. So we came over to check. Just as well. You owe him one, I reckon.'

'You're right!' shouted Marcus through the growing gap. How could anyone explain what had really happened? He did not even know himself. 'We were lucky, I guess!'

'Well, he's gone off with your vehicle,' Zed went on. 'We went inside to get some clobber together. When we got out he'd gone. No sign of him and the four-wheel drive with him. He must have driven like a bat out of hell. Guess that's the last you'll see of it.'

Marcus and Joanna looked at each other in concern. It was Sylvie's vehicle. 'It'll be all right,' he whispered. 'There's some reason for all this.'

Joanna nodded. 'He's gone to help Mum! I'm sure of it.'

'I hope so!'

For some reason the heavy feeling in Joanna's stomach had lifted and she realised she had not thought about her mother for some time. 'Please let her be all right!' she breathed and rubbed the red crystal.

It was another tedious hour before the hole was large enough for them to crawl through. 'By the devil. You're a lucky pair,' the great burly Queenslander greeted them, when they had both emerged, covered in dust and grime. 'Odds of coming out of there alive must be one in a billion.'

Chapter 27

Helen thought she had faced her worst nightmare but now, alone in the dark jungle, with no idea where she was, the terror intensified. She was torn between treading heavily to warn snakes and insects of her approach and creeping quietly so that Dirk and Billy would not find her. Somehow she could not persuade herself that they were not already after her.

'I must get a grip,' she told herself sternly. With every ounce of her willpower she stilled her mind again and built a protection around herself.

From the Scroll she had learned how important it was to keep your thoughts pure and harmless. That is the ultimate protection. No darkness can penetrate when there is pure light around you. Of course, she knew that being human this was all but impossible. However, she was also aware that when she had been sending out thoughts of hate and killing to Dirk and Billy, it had opened up a chink in her aura, rendering her vulnerable.

All the cells in her body revolted against the idea of radiating love or forgiveness to those animals. Her jaw ached where Billy had hurt her. Her head throbbed where Dirk had hit her. Every inch of her body felt bruised and bitten. Bitter gall rose in her throat. She could not feel anything other than hatred for them and her thoughts turned to violence and torture. What she'd like to do to them was nobody's business. They deserved it. But she stopped herself again, knowing she must not let her thoughts go down that route. The thoughts we choose create our own heaven or hell and that was the way to hell. Also she knew the violent energy would only come back to her. For her own sake she must let it go.

The path twisted ahead, muddy, murky, overhung with trees and bushes, which seemed intent on tripping her and tearing at her clothes. Tendrils tried to fasten themselves to her. Thorns ripped at her trousers and scratched her hands.

The torchlight stabbed the darkness and revealed low-hanging webs across the path, large spiders lurking in the middle of each one. Poisonous spiders. She shuddered. 'Keep calm. Keep calm,' she repeated. 'Whatever happens, Helen, keep calm.'

She started murmuring the mantra, 'Keep calm.' And it helped until something large moved in the bushes beside her and nearly gave her a heart attack. She stood immobile with terror while her pulse thundered in her ears.

Eventually she crept on through the darkness, shining the torch towards every rustle or movement. From time to time she stood stock still listening. She could not hear any sound of pursuit.

Then the awful thought struck her: They're Aborigines. They're trackers. Wherever I go they'll be able to find me. For all she knew she was going deeper into the jungle. Yet again she formed a picture in her mind and focused on it.

She pictured herself coming out into the open and people being there to rescue her. She pictured Joanna, Marcus and Tony smiling at her. She could not get any further, for sudden tears choked her. She felt her shoulders heaving. 'Don't give way, Helen. Keep focused,' she warned herself. 'Stay centred.'

She kept moving on and on through that long night. Birds started to cough and whistle and call. At last she could see without the torch. Black scary leaves turned green. Threatening shapes became branches. She could make out that a pair of black eyes watching her from the shelter of a bush was a bird. At last as the sun was beginning to break through the pink-grey clouds, she felt safer.

All at once the trees thinned and she found herself at a sandy beach. Her first thought was safety. Her second, that Dirk and Billy could easily find her here. Her third, crocs. Maybe this is where the large croc was seen.

Skirting through the trees, watching for any sign of movement, she hid behind a large rock. One foot was in a puddle and she no longer cared. She felt too exhausted to move. I'll wait here until people come. Surely someone will come here today. Then the thought came unbidden. What if Billy or Dirk find me first? She closed her eyes and swayed in panic. Then, fiercely back in command, with her last ounce of energy she crept to a cluster of rocks, which afforded shelter, and started to amass a pile of stones. If they found her, she'd throw these. Whether that was sensible or not, she felt better. So much for my pledge to harmlessness, she thought bitterly. She just was not strong enough to live up to her ideal.

The sun strengthened and she looked at the red, raw, bleeding eruptions that itched and burned on her skin. Crouching, waiting in the open she wanted to scream at the relentless unbearable irritation.

Yet she forced herself once more to centre and calm herself. Again she called on the powers-that-be for help. She tried again to surround herself in a cocoon of harmlessness. She felt much more aligned and peaceful but she could not overcome her fear.

The sun was high when Dirk woke from his drunken stupor. His head ached. His stomach heaved and he was in an evil temper. Almost immediately he realised what had happened.

He kicked Billy in the side. 'Gerrup, idiot. She's gone!'

'What? Leave me alone,' Billy muttered.

'She's gone. Escaped. The white bitch. Gone. The gold's gone.'

Billy opened his eyes. The word 'gold' had reached him.

'Gone?' he repeated dully.

'Get up. We'll soon find her.' Dirk's face looked thunderous in his rage. He dragged his friend up roughly by the arm. Together they set off down the jungle path. Neither was at his best but they could still do rudimentary tracking.

'She bin down here,' Billy shouted. It jarred Dirk's thick head.

'Don't you shout, you fleabite.'

They exchanged unpleasantries while they followed Helen's track. She had gone round in a circle. When they realised they laughed and jeered. They felt superior, invincible, now that they knew her weakness and her folly. They were hunters at the end of a chase.

Helen had walked for several hours before she reached the bay. It took Dirk and Billy just forty minutes. They knew where she was immediately. 'You go that way. I'll go this,' Dirk commanded his friend. 'We'll catch her in the middle.' He was grinning.

What they did not know was that Helen had called in the powers of light.

When she saw Dirk approaching from the trees, she felt icy calm. She picked up a good-sized chunk of stone in each hand. 'I don't want to use these,' she whispered to the powers-that-be. 'Please stop them from coming any closer but if I must I will defend myself.' Then she pictured the stones stopping the youth. Aim had never been her strong point but now her life depended on it. She wondered where Billy was and something made her turn her head. Her stomach screamed when she saw him coming up behind her.

For a second she glanced at the sea. No escape that way. Crocs and stingers were a major disincentive. Better to face the men. Never had she felt so alone, caught as she was between the jungle, the sea and two dangerous men.

She ducked down and crept to one side of the rock. When Billy was within range she threw the rocks one after the other. Then whirled round and, picking up more, chucked them at Dirk.

One rock had hit Billy on the head and he fell but she missed Dirk. 'Hey,' he shouted. Helen picked up more and more rocks and threw them. One hit him on the shoulder and another on the leg. He was hopping, blazing mad and ready to kill her. Never in all her life had she seen such a look in anyone's eyes.

Then an amazing thing happened. A big blue four-wheel drive appeared and scrunched to a stop. A very wrinkled old Aborigine clambered out and hollered in a surprisingly strong voice across the bay. Dirk turned and saw him. He went pale under his black skin. Then he turned and ran.

It seemed to be at the very same instant that a fishing boat appeared and chugged towards the bay.

The old Aborigine shuffled through the sand towards Helen. He gazed at her in silence. He saw her bruised and bitten face, her scratched and torn clothing. Her fear. Then he reached out and placed his palm a few inches in front of her solar plexus. Immediately she felt a warmth and comfort shooting into her. She knew he had sealed her aura. Who is this man? she wondered.

'You okay.' It was a statement not a question.

She wanted to shout, 'No, I'm not okay. I'm a victim. I've been kidnapped and dragged through the jungle, and hit and terrorised. I thought I was going to be killed. Help.'

But as she looked into his faded black velvet eyes, she could not speak. She felt drained and utterly exhausted but not afraid.

Billy groaned and sat up. He took one look at the old man and scrambled to his feet. Helen wanted to scream, 'Stop him.' But the Aborigine just watched as Billy staggered away looking over his shoulder, his face stricken with terror.

The ancient one was silent as he observed him. Then he turned to Helen. 'They know they can't get away.'

She nodded.

The boat was coming closer. She could see Bob and Sally from the wharf café and a blonde woman she recognised as a frequent customer. They were peering anxiously over the side, calling and waving. Bob steered in as close as he could and then waded to the beach. They were all shouting, 'Are you all right?'

Even Sally, who was nervous of stingers, though Bob had scanned the clear water carefully, waded ashore. 'We heard about you being kidnapped on the local news. Everyone's out searching for you. Seems like your daughter alerted the police, who took no notice. Then she contacted old George and he got things moving.'

'I'll kill 'em if I catch them,' Bob said ominously. 'Just look what they've done to you.'

Helen's face and arms were covered in red blotches and giant mosquito bites, which itched infernally. One eye was swollen and part closed and she appeared to be a mess of bruises, scratches and dirt. Her hair, grasped and torn as it had been by briars, was a tangled mess. Under her tan, white rings ran round her mouth and eyes and touched the corner of her nostrils, giving her the air of one who is severely traumatised.

'They've not raped you then?' the blonde woman asked bluntly.

Helen had never thought of rape. Thank God. The thought made her shake.

'That's enough,' Sally rebuked her friend sharply and added gently, 'That was our greatest fear.'

'They said they'd kill me,' said Helen almost matter-of-fact, whether in shock or relief they did not know.

Their eyes flickered with revenge. 'I'm going after them,' shouted Bob but Sally held him back.

'The Abos will punish them far worse than ever we can. Anyway the police'll get them.'

'I'd like to get them first,' he growled and Helen felt a sense of satisfaction that someone was fighting her corner.

The old man had disappeared. No one saw him leave but he and the four-wheel drive had gone. Helen wanted to thank him but she couldn't even do that and the world seemed unreal. She felt as if she were walking an inch above the ground and everything seemed very slightly out of focus.

They were bombarding her with questions, offering her water and calling the police to say they had found her. And all the time she was operating on automatic pilot, smiling, calm and not really with it.

She felt like she had at her sister's funeral. Then everyone had said how well she had taken her death. But she knew that she had disassociated from the pain and was merely acting the part of the charming, gracious hostess. In fact most of her was in some kind of limbo.

All she wanted to do now was to sleep.

Chapter 28

Two burly officers had hot-tailed it to the beach and asked Helen numerous questions. They insisted on taking her to the hospital, accompanied by Bob, Sally and her friend, before zooming off to seek the thugs.

It caused quite a stir when Helen was helped out of the police car at the hospital. She limped in accompanied by a retinue of interested folk summoned by Bob's many phone calls. They were milling around her, importuning her, helping her where it was not needed or desired. All she really wanted was to rest. Hospital was the last place she wanted to be.

It was strange. She had felt really worried about Marcus and Joanna, convinced something was wrong. Even while she was in danger she had flashes of Joanna calling to her for help. Now she told herself it was her imagination heightened by her ordeal. The sense of them being in trouble had disappeared but she would feel happier when she saw them again.

Everyone seemed to be asking her questions. They were solicitous, angry and sometimes downright impertinent. She wished that she could shout at them to go away and leave her alone but she demonstrated the stiff control of an English lady in extremis. This was her salvation and, in many ways, her problem.

Sally's friend whispered to her in the irritating tone a certain kind of woman reserves for animals and children, 'Don't you worry about anything, dear.'

Helen felt like hissing at her.

She caught sight of Uncle George standing apart from the rest. He looked deeply grave as if the cares of the world were on his shoulders. Suddenly she wanted to hurt him. Dirk was his nephew. Why hadn't he disciplined him better, taught him about humanity, controlled him better? Anger bubbled inside her and she felt she might explode if she spoke to him. So she gave him a cold stare.

Minutes later she remembered his words of wisdom and forgiveness and felt instantly ashamed. She glanced in his direction again but he was looking down, his face drawn and haunted.

Damn! she thought. I want to raise my consciousness, yet I fail every test. Tears pricked the back of her eyes. She was exhausted. Just go away, everyone. I can't cope much longer.

As so often happens it was a nurse who shooed them away and conducted her to a cubicle. She ooh'd and aah'd over Helen's cuts and bruises as she cleaned her up and even made her laugh.

While she waited for the doctor to see her, she drifted into sleep, a menacing world of spiders and snakes, dark tunnels and staring bloodshot eyes, waking an hour later, sweating and moaning. The nurse came hurrying in.

'A nightmare, love? Not surprising after what you've gone through. Oh, you're shaking. Poor thing, I'll get you a nice cup of tea.'

It was mid afternoon before Jane collected her and drove her in merciful silence back to the motel.

As they passed reception the manager's wife called out in her friendly way, 'Just you let us know if you need anything, Helen. Anything at all. Your daughter's phoned and I've told her you're safe. They're on their way.'

Helen's lips trembled with relief and she clamped them tight. She waved her gratitude.

By now bruises were emerging, like spilled ink over her body. Volcano-size bites were erupting on her face and ankles and the shock was wearing off, leaving her nerves feeling grated. Every limb ached. She was so stiff that Jane had to support her up the steps. 'I'm like a creaky door. I need oiling,' she joked as Jane helped her into bed.

But the latter was not amused. She remained tight-lipped and Helen was not sure whether Jane was angry with her or if she blamed herself in some insane way. She only knew that Jane was kindness itself and yet underlying it was an unspoken hostility.

Once Jane spat out, 'Wait till the Abos get those two. I wouldn't be in their shoes for anything right now.' She spoke with a kind of glee, as if she were picturing a vice tightening over their testicles. Perhaps she was.

Helen felt uncomfortable about this. I've had terrible angry thoughts myself. Yet I don't like the idea of her wanting vengeance, she thought, so I'm guilty of double standards. She soon rationalised. But then surely rage is a healthy part of my healing process. And right now I could flay Billy and Dirk alive. But that doesn't mean I want other people to torture them. No!

Jane broke into her thoughts. 'You sleep now. You're quite safe here.'

Helen thanked her and wondered how someone so seemingly judgemental could be so kind and giving. It was a conundrum, which she did not have the energy to pursue.

As she lay on the bed her body felt as if it were rising and falling in nauseous waves. She had declined pain relief. Now she wished she had not been so single-minded. Joanna would have persuaded her to take a middle road. Oh, she wished someone would give her healing, physical, mental, emotional and spiritual healing. That would take all pain away.

I do hope Joanna and Marcus get here soon, she thought. She kept seeing Dirk and Billy in front of her, their bloodshot eyes peering at her with evil intent, their voices leering. 'You're snake bait. Infested with browns. Gold. Gold of Power.'

Muddled with pain and tiredness it all swirled round and round in her head and so did her sense of outrage. Her mind drifted through anguish and torment into free-fall. Coming, going, floating. In and out of slumber. She did not realise she was whimpering and moaning as she tossed and twisted under the sheet, sometimes curling into a foetal ball, at others stretched out and rigid.

She sensed figures in the room and came back for a

moment. It was too much effort to open her eyes but it felt safe. She drifted again. Voices whispered. It was all right. She did not need to wake. Again she disappeared far away. A cocoon surrounded her. A warm, secure, golden cocoon. She drifted deeper in safe, healing sleep.

Much later she opened her eyes. The bedside light was on, throwing a soft pink shadow over the room. By her bed sat Joanna and Marcus. She knew they had been giving her healing.

'Thank God you're here,' she whispered in delight.

Joanna held her hand. 'You have been in the wars,' she said.

It was such a ridiculous statement, the sort of thing a mother said to a child with a cut knee, that Helen found herself smiling.

'We phoned Tony and he called back twice to see how you are. He was very concerned and sent his love. He said he'd phone again.'

Helen felt a small buzz of pleasure. 'Thanks. That's nice of him,' she said in a non-committal, offhand sort of voice, which fooled them not one bit. Why can't I express my delight that he phoned? she asked herself, but she soon remembered how her mother had laughed at her and put her down as a teenager if ever she looked at a boy. She felt a spurt of annoyance at the memory and thought wearily, Yet another thing I need to heal.

Joanna broke in. 'Tell us all about last night, Mum. What really happened?'

So while Marcus put the kettle on for tea, Helen went over the entire events of the night. She told them every painful, horrific detail, and by the time she had finished she felt considerably better. Joanna, however, was looking numb and sick.

Jane brought them dinner. The grapevine had ensured she knew of Marcus and Joanna's arrival and with typical Australian generosity she had brought enough food for them all.

'Well, this is a real mess!' she said by way of greeting as they introduced themselves. 'I haven't heard anything about those fiends. But Philip, you know, the elder I took you to see' – she glanced at Helen – 'he's Billy's uncle. He left Cooktown this afternoon. He's on their trail. And George has been meeting up with everyone. They're talking, talking. They'll get them soon.' This latter was meant as encouragement to bolster Helen. In some ways it did but Helen was beginning to have strange, complex and confused thoughts. She no longer lusted after undiluted vengeance.

Jane did not stay long. 'I'll see you tomorrow,' she said. 'I called Sylvie and she said, if you want to you can stay with her in Cairns as long as you like. Good place to recuperate. Oh, and not to worry about the four-wheel drive the Abo took. It's insured. She can borrow a vehicle to come and fetch you if you like.'

Helen marvelled once more at the Australians, not just their capacity for giving but the way they would happily drive for a day to collect someone and then drive back.

'What four-wheel drive? Who took it?' asked Helen.

Joanna replied, 'Sylvie lent us her four-wheel drive to come to Cooktown and it was taken, but . . .'

Her mother eyed her, sensing there was much more. 'What do you mean taken?'

Marcus broke in. 'The Aborigine didn't steal it. He saved our lives and when we got back here it was parked in front of the motel. Nothing was taken. And the keys were handed in at reception!'

Jane stared at him open-mouthed. 'That's a turn-up,' she grunted. 'They're light-fingered as hell. Wouldn't trust one as far as I could see him.'

Helen wished Jane would go. Then she could find out what had happened to Joanna and Marcus. The Australian picked the thought up nicely.

'Well I've got to dash. Enjoy the meal. I'll pop in tomorrow. Let me know if you need anything.' Several mosquitoes zoomed in as she opened the door. 'Nice to meet you two. See you!'

When the door shut Joanna explained to her mother, 'He was a karadji. You know, an Aborigine shaman.'

'A karadji! Who was? What's been going on?' Helen felt so much better that she pulled herself up in bed. Curiosity is a wonderful antidote to pain.

Joanna brought her up to date from the moment they realised her mother had been kidnapped. It encompassed their journey, the crocodile crossing, the karadji and what he had told them, the horror of the entrapment and rescue, and the way their rescuers had taken them back to the station, fed them, insisted on phoning the motel for news and had finally driven them to Cooktown, where they had found Sylvie's four-wheel drive waiting.

Helen was appalled, horrified, concerned and spellbound in such measure that they felt justifiably proud of the odds they had overcome to be at her side.

'Why didn't you tell me this before?' Helen demanded. 'I feel dreadful. I've done all the talking.'

'We felt your ordeal was greater, I guess,' Marcus responded, with a shrug and wry smile.

'Besides which we had each other. We talked and talked and that helped to work some of it through.'

Helen nodded, as ever surprised at their maturity.

'And Zed and the others were great guys. They were so down to earth. It took the spookiness out of it,' added Joanna.

'Also there was the energy of the karadji. He was quite something. I think he helped to hold us steady. It was horrific enough but somehow he'd warned us we were going through a test and must stay centred. I guess we knew it was a challenge of faith.'

'Yes, it felt more like a nightmare than something real, especially when we smelled that ghastly smell and heard those wails.' She shuddered and goose-pimples rose on her arms. 'Even now I think I must have imagined it.'

'Many a person has ended up in a mental hospital after a lesser experience,' said Helen soberly.

'True,' agreed her daughter. 'But we did know we had to focus unceasingly on the light. Once that stuff all started up I forgot about being trapped. In a weird way . . . Oh, I can't explain.'

'I agree,' said Marcus. 'It was undoubtedly the most horrific experience I ever want to go through. At the same time it was unreal. All of it. Even the crocodile. And the karadji.'

'But we do have something to show you.' With a beaming smile, Joanna pulled the crystal from her bag. It glowed red in the soft lamplight.

As her mother gasped, she said triumphantly, 'The karadji gave it to us. It's from the crystal ball. Part of the blueprint is "All are equal."'

Chapter 29

Next morning the sight of puffy, bruise-coloured clouds made Helen wince. She was glad to see the jewel-blue background peeping through.

Marcus informed her that there was still no news of Dirk and Billy. They had vanished and no one could believe it. The thought that they might get away scot-free made all Helen's thoughts of forgiveness and mercy disappear in an instant.

'Those thugs could be anywhere.' Her voice was harsh with anger and a trace of foreboding. 'Someone must be hiding them. They've got to be caught and punished, preferably castrated.'

Joanna was taken aback. She had never known her mother's moods to swing like this or for her to be vindictive. She needs time to get over it, she thought, glancing at Marcus, who responded with a concerned look. This was not a Helen he knew.

'Would you like some healing, Mum? It'd do you good,' suggested Joanna.

'I'd love some,' agreed Helen with relief, for she was well aware that she was reacting from the distorted perspective of victim consciousness. At that moment she could not see it in any other way.

When Joanna and Marcus gave her healing she accepted the extraordinary energy with a sense of profound gratitude. It felt like a gentle electric current flowing through her.

An hour later she felt a great deal better. Her body ached less but the biggest difference was in her spirits. The healing had the effect of pulling out the fear and anger she had been feeling. It realigned and centred her. Then it closed and sealed her aura so that she was no longer vulnerable to the negativity of the world. She felt cocooned in safety. By the time she opened her eyes she was in touch with her accustomed wisdom and higher nature.

'Helen, you look so much better,' Marcus exclaimed. 'That was a powerful healing coming through.' He held up red and tingling hands and looked at them as if surprised. Ever since he had learned that he could be a channel for healing, he had practised under Helen's guidance, and never ceased to be awed at the energy flowing through him and the effect it had on people and animals.

Joanna laughed. She too was a good healer and loved giving and receiving it. She knew it kept her healthy too. 'You're looking a bit spaced, Mum!'

'I feel wonderful. Thanks, you two.'

'A pleasure,' replied Marcus and meant it. 'We'd better have breakfast. Uncle George said he'd be over this morning to see you.' He was eyeing Helen closely, for she had been bitter towards the old man the previous evening, blaming him for Dirk's actions.

Helen felt guilty. 'He's such a good man,' she said. 'And I was so angry with him. Poor thing. He probably feels terrible about it all. After all, Dirk is his nephew.'

'Dirk's a thoroughly nasty, vicious, unpleasant youth and deserves all he gets,' exclaimed Joanna hotly. 'Besides, he was after the Codes of Power because he thought you meant gold which would give him power. Just imagine how he would have abused it!'

Part of Helen agreed but as soon as Joanna had uttered the words of condemnation, another more detached and compassionate part of her remembered that Dirk was a very damaged and confused youth, from a fragmented culture.

'What they did was inhumane and dreadful but they must have been horribly hurt themselves to do that,' she conjectured. 'Vengeance won't help the situation and I'm sure there's a higher purpose behind it all.'

This made Joanna burst out into sarcastic laughter. 'Mum, you're priceless. It's okay for you to judge him but not for anyone else and now you've disassociated and gone into being all pure and holy.'

Marcus ventured bravely, 'Perhaps being disassociated, wise, pure and holy is a good place to be, especially after what you've gone through, Helen.'

Helen felt all the warmth of being supported. 'Thank you.'

Joanna turned turkey red with mortification.

Her mother smiled at her sympathetically. 'And don't forget what you've gone through in the last couple of days. I'm not sure how I'd have coped with being trapped in a rock fall like that and as for being haunted, ugh!' She shuddered. 'It must have been horrendous for both of you.'

Joanna felt mollified.

'You know, Joanna, I'm sure the anger I feel towards Dirk and Billy will come up again and again before it's resolved. Forgiveness and transmutation isn't that easy. It's just that you gave me that marvellous healing and that's helped me view it all for the moment from a higher dimension.'

'I know, Mum.' She gave her mother a hug and they both felt better.

They had scarcely finished breakfast when the phone rang. Uncle George was at reception. Marcus walked along the verandah to meet him.

When the elder entered the room, he looked shorter, more stooped and greyer than he had done when Helen had first met him. Lines seemed more deeply etched on his face and his brown eyes were faded.

He looked at Helen with an anxious expression, full of concern for her, tinged with personal dread about her response to him. His hands open in a gesture of appeasement, he walked towards her hesitantly as if he expected to be reviled. 'How are you? I'm so terribly sorry.' His voice blurred slightly as if he was very tired.

When Helen looked at the old man, she saw his pain and conflict. Saw his concern for her and his revulsion at his nephew's actions. He blamed himself and she knew he had punished himself more severely than anything she could inflict. He had suffered enough. Her heart melted. She disassociated from the nightmares and the pain and gave him a smile both gracious and welcoming.

'I'm all right. Getting better. Thanks for coming.'

Relief flooded his face and she felt as if she had given him a reprieve. Instantly she apprehended that if she judged him, it would lock him into his own personal prison for a long time. She had once been told that humans can condemn each other to hell for eternity by refusing forgiveness. She felt compassion for this man who had been so damaged by the Whites and had the mercy and understanding to forgive them, yet now was being vilified for the actions of his family.

She had no doubt that in the town there were many fingers pointing at him. In that instant she aligned herself with him. If he could forgive far worse things perpetrated on his people, she too would strive for the clemency that leads to permanent forgiveness. Together they would stand for justice with mercy. For an instant she felt noble and strong.

She did not speak but he read her mind and felt it in her energy fields. He nodded humbly. 'Thank you.' But he still had the heavy look of someone with a burden in his heart.

Joanna had been watching the exchange. 'Mum, you've always claimed that the darkness serves the light, so how do you think Billy and Dirk served you?'

'Truth to tell I've been thinking about that. I even thought about it while I was being held in that ghastly hut but then I was too involved in the danger of it all.'

'Helen, trust you to try to find a higher reason even when you're in danger!' Marcus chuckled. Then he continued more soberly, 'They certainly made you face your worst fears.'

'But it must have been more than that!' exclaimed Joanna. She turned to Uncle George. 'The Scroll tells us that in this plane of existence everything acts as a mirror or offers us challenges to promote our growth. So what Marcus and I went through at the Black Mountain and what Mum was subjected to, happened so that we would grow.'

'And though our personalities might hate it, our Higher Self has agreed that we undergo the ordeal.'

Uncle George was listening intently and nodding. 'I can understand that. We believe that the Great Spirit sends us what we need to experience.'

'But why did we go through it? Why the crocodile? Why was it Mum who was captured?'

Uncle George smiled benignly. 'We do not ask why.'

'Of course not! "Why" is left-brain activity!' exclaimed Helen with a blush, for she loved to probe and analyse.

'It does seem you're going through some sort of initiation,' added Uncle George.

'Initiation?' Joanna and Marcus looked at each other. 'The Scroll says that the Codes of Power is an initiation, which certain people have agreed to undertake.'

Uncle George nodded imperceptibly.

'Why are initiations so difficult?' asked Marcus.

'Initiations are entry into a higher level of consciousness,' Uncle George told him. 'That means being tested to see if you are ready. The initiation into the Codes of Power is an advanced one with appropriate challenges.'

Marcus grimaced. 'Your traditional ones for boys into adulthood sound bad enough!'

'Did your nephew go through initiation?' asked Helen. She knew most young Aborigines in towns no longer experienced this part of growing up.

Uncle George shook his head sadly. 'No, he didn't. I know some consider our initiation rites barbaric but they do serve a purpose. They really bring discipline and true manhood. Very few go through them now, so they wander round in gangs, confused, aimless and dangerous because they have nowhere to channel their aggression.'

'They say that children wrapped in cotton wool become disillusioned, dependent, undisciplined and remain immature,' said Helen.

'My father always maintained that military service was a good initiation for teenagers in England,' said Marcus with a laugh. 'He said it made a man of him! But I'm glad I didn't have to do it.'

'Perhaps university is the modern soft initiation option,' surmised Joanna.

'The Scroll said that when enough people have been initiated into the Codes of Power, the blueprint of the planet will come to fruition,' Marcus commented.

'I think the world's led by grey men, who aren't initiates. They're in their heads only and not in their hearts and they don't have the wisdom and courage to take the world forward into the Golden Age,' observed Joanna.

'I think you're right,' agreed her mother.

'Well, lots of people are undertaking initiations so that everyone can grow,' Marcus reminded them. 'Perhaps it will throw up new, stronger, wiser leaders.'

'I hope so,' said Uncle George.

Marcus's mobile rang. It was Philip, Billy's uncle. He said he was phoning from Sydney. 'The boys were sighted here so I flew down. Don't you worry, I'll bring them back.' He sounded jovial, expansive even.

Marcus's expression was blank. Joanna knew it well. It meant he was suspicious. He asked a few questions and listened intently but his face betrayed nothing. Then he thanked Philip and clicked off.

'That was Philip. He said he was in Sydney but . . .' He read the caller's number from the handset. 'That's not a Sydney number, is it?'

'No!' said Uncle George. 'I think it's somewhere in the centre.'

'Did he have the money to fly there?'

'And where would Dirk and Billy have got the money from?'

'They don't have that sort of money,' answered Uncle George. 'And he's never flown before nor have the boys.' He was clearly uncomfortable.

The question in their minds was not whether Philip was lying but why. Joanna voiced it. 'Why does he want us to think they're all in Sydney when they aren't?'

Uncle George had gone white under his dark skin. He had a terrible look on his face and his voice was like thunder. 'He's shielding them. He's lying to protect them.' His eyes were like stones. 'I think I know why.'

They waited and he continued, in a tortured voice, 'After you visited me, Helen, a man came to see me, a man so repugnant I didn't even want to remember.' He passed a hand over his forehead as if to wipe away the memory. 'He offered me money for information about the crystals.' The old man almost gagged on the word 'money'. 'I said, "No." Then he said I could have whatever I wanted if I helped to find the remaining pieces of the crystal ball. He offered me power. He said the ball conferred power and I could have whatever I wanted, women, political power, fame, anything. How dare he! I didn't mention it before because I was ashamed, ashamed someone could feel he could bribe me.'

They all felt the weight of the insult to his very soul.

'How dare he,' agreed Helen.

Uncle George continued, 'But Philip's different!'

'You think he approached Philip?' gasped Marcus.

'I know he did. Philip's not proof against offers of money or power. I fear he'd sell himself for a fast car and revenge.'

'How do you know he contacted Philip?'

'The evening after you visited him, Philip phoned me. He was boasting that he was coming into money and I wouldn't be the only one people looked up to. I dismissed it as one of his money-making schemes. He's always trying to get compensation money. I didn't connect it to the man's visit until just now, when I suddenly realised that the man must have contacted him too and given him the money for the flights.'

'What did he know about your crystal?'

'He knew it was part of a bigger one.'

'And of course Dirk took the one Ferdy gave me, presumably thinking it was yours,' said Helen.

'Yes,' agreed Uncle George. 'That's understandable. They were very similar. But Philip didn't know about the Codes of Power or the true purpose of the crystal ball.'

'So he thinks it's financially valuable but no more?' mused Joanna.

'I suspect the man promised him some sort of power – perhaps only the power money brings. I don't know. When I think back to our conversation that night, it feels it could have been more. He was kind of gloating.'

'Who was the man? How did he know you had one of the crystal pieces anyway?' Marcus demanded.

Uncle George shook his head. 'I don't know. He gave me this.' He handed Marcus a business card.

In one corner were the initials St V. Marcus shivered and his mouth went dry, though in his heart he knew already. 'One of Sturov's men,' he said and they looked at each other with frightened eyes. 'I guess they know about the Codes of Power and they must assume we're looking for the pieces of the crystal ball, so they're contacting everyone we speak to.'

'Do they know you gave the piece of crystal to Mum?' asked Joanna.

Uncle George shook his head. 'No, but Philip does. The day after the man came to see me, my house was broken into and ransacked. Philip happened to come by and said that the only thing I had of any value was the crystal. I thought it was a strange thing to say but assumed he was being sarcastic. I mentioned I had passed it on to you, Helen. How stupid of me! I never thought to keep a secret from one of my own.'

'No, of course you didn't.' Helen's heart ached for the proud old man.

'Did Dirk know you'd given it to Helen?' asked Marcus.

'Not from me, he didn't. I expect Philip told Billy, who would have told him. Why else did Dirk take the crystal when they kidnapped you, Helen? He just assumed that the one he saw in your room was the one I gave you. But I doubt if he knew of its meaning or importance. Philip probably said he wanted it back for the honour of the race.'

'What can they do with one of the crystals on its own? I thought they all had to come together to be active?'

'I'm not sure but without it we can't complete the crystal ball, which holds the Codes of Power. It was given to me for safe-keeping and it might be thousands of years before it comes back again.' The old man put his face in his hands and rocked in a gesture of helpless despair. He frowned and murmured as if to himself, 'I don't trust Philip. We'll have to watch him.' Then he looked at Helen. 'I'm sorry, my dear, we've got to get it back. We've got to find Dirk!'

If he thought she'd let fear show, he'd underestimated Helen. Now that there was a reason greater than her personal safety her eyes glittered. 'We will find them. And in the meantime we must keep the other pieces of crystal safe,' she replied.

'At least Sturov's henchmen won't harm us while we're looking for the remaining pieces,' commented Marcus soberly. 'They'll hope we'll find them. That's when they'll try to get the ball off us.'

Mother and daughter looked remarkably similar as their jaws clenched in defiant determination. 'Over my dead body!' they announced as one.

Chapter 30

Helen's mood continued to fluctuate. By the following day she had developed an intense desire to know all about Dirk, as if understanding would assuage the nightmares.

She persuaded Joanna to drive her round to see Uncle George, who winced when he saw her hobble to the door. 'How are you feeling, my dear?' he asked, taking her arm and gently drawing her in, like an old-fashioned English gentleman.

Joanna followed, wrinkling her nose at the same smell of sweat and coffee, which her mother had noticed on her first visit.

Helen did not beat about the bush, though she was nervous of his response. 'Uncle George. Please, will you tell me about Dirk. I want to know how he came to be . . . well, like he is. How he could do such a thing?' She sat down abruptly on a hard chair. Joanna drew a second one up close as if to support her mother by being as near as possible.

The elder was regarding them both, a look of concern and sadness on his face. 'What do you want me to tell you?' His voice was gentle.

A sense of relief flowed through Helen. He understood.

He was neither defensive nor blaming, just sad and wanting to help. It comforted her and made her feel safe.

'Oh, about his childhood. What made him like that? I don't know why I want to know but I do. It's strange,' she added, 'I don't feel the same way about Billy. It's as if he were a weak and vicious kid, who followed his friend. But Dirk!' She shook her head. 'He was so angry and brutal. I thought he was going to kill me.' She shivered and Joanna put a hand on her arm. 'To be honest there's also his connection to you,' she added, looking the old man full in the eyes. For a moment she struggled as if wanting to express the flood of conflicting emotions that welled up in her, the sense of betrayal as well as the anger, but no words came.

Uncle George watched her, trying to comprehend her feelings. His eyes softened. Helen could see that, though he was still upset by his nephew's actions, there was now no trace of guilt. Something had changed within him. Dirk was his blood but not his conscience. And for no reason that she could define, her anger towards him diminished.

'What was he like as a small boy?' she repeated.

'When he was little he was a cheeky scamp of a lad, so bright and alert – full of life and mischief. He had the most wonderful smile.' She thought a tear glistened in the old man's eyes.

'Whatever did happen?'

Uncle George sighed and scratched his head without

realising what he was doing. 'His father, Sammy, couldn't find work. He wanted to. And he tried. He was a proud man.' The old man shrugged, a gesture of despair. 'Have you any idea how demoralising it is for a young man to have no work, especially when he has children to feed? They lived in appalling conditions, surviving on handouts. Sammy had the black cloud inside him sometimes. Then he used to get very angry. Yet whatever he did, Dirk adored his father. Followed him everywhere.'

Helen was silent for a moment. 'And then?'

'Sammy got more and more frustrated. He'd always been a drinker but now he was drinking far too much. When Dirk was nine, Sammy got into a drunken brawl. Pulled a knife and killed someone.'

Helen gasped.

'He went to prison for life.'

Helen said slowly, 'And Aborigines can't cope with prison. Their spirit just dies.'

Uncle George's voice dropped, full of pain. 'Young Dirk lost interest in everything. Two years later, when he was eleven, his father hanged himself in prison. Dirk never came to terms with it.'

Shock hung like an icicle. Helen let out a little sigh.

'It was terrible for the whole family. My sister, you know, his grandmother, was devastated. But Dirk took it hardest. He hated everyone. He never forgave his father for leaving him and he never forgave the white judge who sent his dad down. After that he had a real chip on his shoulder. He was always stealing and getting into fights.'

'What about his mother?'

Uncle George's voice sounded flat. 'She was a sick woman – diabetes. I'm sure you know it's a terrible scourge in our communities.'

They nodded.

'Anyway, Dirk's mother succumbed to alcohol too and became prone to violence. I believe she hit the kids, and no mother in our culture ever does that. We love and honour children. They are our life and our future.' He paused to realign his thoughts and emotions.

'She did visit Sammy a few times when he first went to prison but she found another man within six months. He was an alcoholic too.' The old man spread out his hands as if to push away the feelings.

'That's tough on the kids,' said Helen.

'Very. She died two years ago. Dirk was very angry with her too. He bummed around and no one could do anything with him.'

'No wonder he was twisted up,' commented Joanna.

'It doesn't excuse his behaviour or his cruelty,' pointed out Uncle George sternly.

'No,' agreed Helen. 'But it does go some way to explaining the pressures inside him. He was in a living hell.' She had a way of connecting deep into the heart of a person's pain, which enabled her to understand and empathise but made it hard for her to be objective sometimes.

The elder concentrated on making little circles with his thumb. 'You're right. He was in hell.'

Joanna said, 'Mum, you're always saying that only a deeply hurt person can hurt another.'

'Yes, I know.' Helen sighed. She so much wanted to forgive but within her the forces of compassion were still battling the forces of anger.

Chapter 31

'Hey, there's an e-mail from Tony, headed Lemuria!'
announced Marcus the following day. He was sitting on
the verandah outside his and Joanna's room, which was
next to Helen's, his laptop on the tiny table, totally
absorbed in the screen.

He was oblivious of the glorious orange butterfly which
sunned itself in a patch of filtered sunshine on the deck;
unaware of the sea, shimmering like soft grey mother-of-
pearl in front of him, nor did he hear the quarrelling
lorikeets or smell the sweetness of the tropical blooms.

'Joanna! Come and see this. Helen!'

In an instant they were by his side, peering over his
shoulder in the cramped space.

'Go on! What does he have to say! Scroll down a bit,'
urged Joanna.

Marcus quipped to Helen, 'Is her middle name
Impatient?'

Helen laughed. 'It would have been the pot calling the
kettle black. I'm just as bad. Come on, read it aloud. I
haven't got my glasses. What does Tony say?'

Marcus read aloud: ' "We know from the Scroll and
other published material I have been studying about
Atlantis that—" '

'He's been reading about Atlantis!' exclaimed Helen.

'Good old Tony,' said Marcus, thinking fondly of his mentor, who had been of such a scientific, sceptical inclination before he came across the Scroll.

'Go on, Marcus. What does he say?'

Marcus continued, ' "That the consciousness of later Atlanteans was separate from nature – just as ours is now. For example if we study a rock or a petal, we can touch, smell and taste it and examine its texture, colour and shape. It is an external comprehension. Because we explore it but don't identify with it we feel separate from it, so it seems all right to alter its components. In Atlantis scientists often examined and explored matter in order to change it and make it into something else.

' "Because there was no reverence for nature in later Atlantis they experimented with changing the properties of plants, cloning and expanding technology." '

'It's true,' agreed Joanna. 'We discussed that when he phoned us in Cairns. And what's it got to do with the Scroll?'

'I think those are Tony's comments,' replied Helen.

Marcus continued, 'Yes, he goes on: "We talked about this last time I spoke to you but it has been amplified a little in the latest translation. I have the sense that a different priest was talking and the scribes were writing it down verbatim." '

'That makes sense. There can be more than one perspective,' said Helen.

Marcus carried on. 'Then he quotes from the Lemurian section of the Scroll.' Marcus's voice changed subtly as he read: ' "If we wish to understand a lizard, we lovingly touch the lizard and immediately our consciousness merges with the consciousness of the reptile. We become it. The lizard is connected to the network of nature, so there is instant communication with that lizard and with every lizard throughout the world. Connection is complete. It is part of the Oneness and part of us.

' "Everything is divine so how could we desire to change it? How could we harm it?

' "The way we grow and evolve is by merging our consciousness with different aspects of nature and fully understanding it. Then we individuate again but retain the knowing of the essence of the other. Thus everything expands and evolves.

' "A lump of rock or an animal is of equal value in the eyes of the Great Spirit, just as your finger or leg are of equal value to you. They are part of you.

' "We value the essence of every living thing. We have no fear of another creature or of lack. We know all our needs will be provided. Therefore we do not need to own anything. All belongs to One and is shared." '

'That's something the Aboriginal culture brought forward.'

'And the honouring of all nature too.'

'Yes, that too. It's amazing really how they carried the consciousness of Lemuria throughout aeons.'

'Go on, Marcus.' Joanna nudged him gently, still impatient.

He continued to read the e-mail: ' "We have control over our consciousness so we can merge it with anything and can lighten our frequency so that we leave our bodies and travel anywhere.

' "When we meet together to share our knowledge, we travel in our light bodies and share by merging our consciousness. It is very beautiful because there is always goodwill." '

'That's beautiful.'

'Yes, isn't it.' He continued: ' "We live a sacred life. We honour beauty and are surrounded by it. Beauty nourishes us and therefore there is no illness. Light flows constantly through us." '

'That's interesting,' mused Helen. 'I suppose all our illness and disease is caused by lack of light.'

'Do you think if we each brought more light through us, we could eradicate all illness?' queried Joanna.

'I'm sure of it,' replied her mother. 'If physical sickness is the final manifestation of mental, emotional and spiritual dis-ease, then light would surely dissolve the physical problems.'

Marcus nodded. 'It seems we keep hearing the same message. They knew it in early Atlantean times too.'

'This part of the Scroll was written at the end of Lemuria and the beginning of Atlantis, wasn't it?'

'That's what it said. But presumably the priests entrusted to take this information across the ocean to Atlantis were high-frequency beings. Perhaps they didn't lower themselves like the rest.'

'They must have been the purest of the pure to be allowed entry to the Cathedral of Atlantis on the Sacred Heights.'

'Yes. And quite remarkable to have maintained their integrity in the darkness of late Lemuria!'

'It must have been almost impossible.'

'It's what light-workers are being called on to do right now though and no one said it was easy,' reminded Helen.

'Shall I continue?' said Marcus patiently and the women nodded. He scanned down the page. 'This next bit seems to be about dwellings and temples.'

'Well, go on,' cried Joanna eagerly. Marcus smiled and ruffled her hair.

' "We do not need dwellings but we create crystalline light structures for housing or temples. Houses are not a protection from the elements but a space where we can be still and centred, away from the consciousness of the rest of the world. Here we integrate and purify our frequency.

' "In the beautiful crystal temples we gather to exchange energy and learn. All communication is telepathic and the Great Masters beam whatever the student is ready to assimilate. The information imparted is always in alignment with the soul's evolution and openness.

' "Our leaders are highly evolved souls from each community, who relinquish their freedom to serve the people. There are no laws. All is decided in accordance with the highest consciousness. Our aim is to preserve the sacred life of Lemuria.

' "One person becomes the Supreme Being, who is the God-like ruler of all, and who reigns until departure from this dimension. All the people everywhere send streams of pure, beautiful and holy thoughts to the Supreme Being every day in order to maintain the highest consciousness of this God-King. Therefore everything flows from the highest to him and then from him." '

'That's remarkable,' Joanna could not help interrupting. 'Just imagine if our leaders and politicians were chosen because of their integrity and high consciousness.'

'And then the people beamed the highest energy to them to maintain it,' added her mother. 'Wouldn't that make a difference.'

Marcus had been reading ahead. 'This is the last bit of the e-mail. It's fascinating,' he murmured.

'What?' said Helen and Joanna simultaneously.

'It's about death or leaving the planet. Listen! "When a tree or animal or person wishes to transit to another plane, they telepathically impart this information into the ethers. Then flowers are brought to surround whoever it is. Flowers have such a high and pure energy that they assist all transitions.

' "The souls transiting raise themselves and evaporate into light." '

'Wow! A bit like ascension used to be!' exclaimed Joanna.

'We still use flowers at times of transition,' said Marcus. 'Think of weddings and funerals.'

'When someone dies in an accident people put flowers there, which helps the spirit, who's probably in shock, to move to the light.'

'And if someone's in hospital we send flowers to raise their light to help them recover.'

'And births. They must help the incoming soul to enter,' said Joanna thoughtfully.

'That's true. I wonder if they had sex in Lemuria?' mused Helen.

'Trust you to think of that, Mum,' said Joanna, laughing.

'That's not fair,' retorted Helen. Then she realised she was being teased and laughed.

'Let's hope the next instalment comes soon. There's lots more I want to know.'

'Tony says that there will be more information in the next few days, especially about the initiation and he sends his love. He adds best wishes for your recovery, Helen. He says he'll phone again soon.'

Chapter 32

Within a couple of days Helen was feeling much better. Yes, she ached and she had been woken once in the night by another nightmare but she accepted this was her unconscious mind still processing what had happened. Knowing that this would diminish with time and the intercession of spiritual healing, she was optimistic that the worst was over. Now she wanted to find the missing piece of the crystal, even though that would probably mean seeing Dirk again. A very determined part of her wanted to face him, for then he would have no power to distress her ever again. Her intuitive antennae were telling her to follow them to the centre. If that meant crossing the creek by the Black Mountain and returning to Cairns before flying to the red centre, so be it.

She had a sudden sense of urgency to follow this intuition. It was time to leave Cooktown and she must say goodbye to Sally and Bob at the café.

As she dressed quickly she reflected that in the overall scheme of things she had been well supported. She had survived a challenging ordeal and been rescued at the moment of greatest danger by the lone Aborigine, who she suspected was the karadji. The pieces of the crystal ball had come to them with divine synchronicity. Perhaps she should just trust that this would continue to happen with the missing segments and that the stone taken by Dirk would also be returned to them.

She sensed the closeness of the angelic presences and murmured aloud, 'Please help us to find all the pieces of the crystal ball.' Then she remembered with a start that the verbalisation of the desire was left brain. She must balance it with right brain. So she pictured the ball complete and the three of them holding it triumphantly in their hands. It felt good.

She emerged from the cool of her room into furnace-like heat, where steam rising from puddles and grass added a mystic feel to the morning. She strolled down to the café to eat breakfast and say goodbye to Sally and Bob. They clucked over her delightedly, like enthusiastic birds on return of a battered chick.

A couple of beefy blokes at the next table flexed their muscles. Obviously they, like everyone else in the place, knew what had happened. One growled he'd like to hang the bastards who'd kidnapped her. Helen realised it was his way of supporting her but refused to be drawn into a victim's trap of recrimination and revenge. Now she wanted justice with integrity.

Also a steely resolve was starting to form within her. 'Whatever it takes, I will find Dirk and retrieve the crystal. And I will pass the initiation of the Codes of Power.' She held her head high. 'No matter what.'

She was sure that if she held that intention the pieces of the crystal ball would come back to them. She just knew it. What she did not know was what the full initiation entailed.

Nevertheless the vision lit a flame in her heart, which reflected in her eyes. The two muscle-bound men observed this and translated it as the fire of revenge. They could not conceive of any loftier emotion.

'Don't you worry. We'll get them,' the bigger of the two reassured her. 'They'll wonder what hit them.'

Helen smiled and thanked them. It would have been pointless to respond differently.

Just as she finished her coffee and scrambled eggs, Joanna and Marcus walked in. 'Ah, thought we'd find you here. You look tons better this morning, Mum.' Joanna gave her a hug.

'I feel it,' she replied.

Marcus searched her eyes before he hugged her. 'Yes, something's definitely lifted.'

She laughed. 'I can't hide anything from you, can I?' She told them of her decision.

'Okay,' responded Marcus. 'We'll all go.' He felt buoyed by her optimism.

'I don't want to drag you away,' she protested half-heartedly. In reality, she was delighted to have their company and could not imagine chasing after Dirk and his cronies on her own.

'Don't be daft, Mum. Of course you can't go on your own.' Joanna was almost sharp in her response. 'Have another cup of coffee and let's decide exactly what to do.'

'First we must get the four-wheel drive back to Sylvie,' said Marcus.

'We'll have to pass the Black Mountain and go through that creek again.' Joanna shivered violently and Marcus put a hand on her shoulder. She half smiled in acknowledgement. 'But you're right. We'll take it back and then fly to Alice or wherever.' She got up to order coffee, her mind on the long, hazardous drive ahead.

Helen drove to Uncle George's house to say goodbye. She suspected the old man had tears in his eyes as she hugged him. 'I'll see you soon,' she said and meant it but as she gazed into the ancient black eyes she was overcome with a sad feeling that they would never meet again.

Later that day they passed the Black Mountain, sensing the evil emanations even more powerfully than before. Their experience had made all the legends and stories about it more real.

'It's more horrific than I dreamed,' murmured Helen. Her arms went goose-pimply. 'What a nightmare you went through.'

'It's over now,' said Marcus firmly and once again his masculine energy helped to steady them.

They negotiated the swirling waters of the creek with a shudder but without mishap. There was no sign of a crocodile.

'Thank God.' Joanna let out a sigh of relief as they reached the bitumen. 'I didn't like seeing the Black

Mountain again, but I have to say the thought of meeting another crocodile was much more terrifying.'

Marcus nodded. 'Well, we came through it all. I reckon we must have passed that test or something else would have happened.'

'Don't even think it!' exclaimed Joanna, punching him affectionately. She had perked up considerably now that the danger was past. 'Hey, Mum, it wasn't your challenge to meet a croc face to face, then?'

Helen shivered and laughed at the same time and even managed to feel guilty that she had not had to encounter that horror. 'I don't think I'd have coped with that.'

'You coped with some pretty terrible things,' Marcus reminded her. 'All of us have.'

'I don't have that weird sense of isolation driving back on this road though the trees and mountains are still misty and ghostlike,' commented Joanna. 'I suppose on the way we were so worried about you, Mum, that we hardly saw anything. And that was before we reached the creek.'

'And now we're safe and well. All we've got to do is get the crystal piece from Dirk, trust the other pieces come to us and face any challenges we are set with equanimity and courage.' Helen tried to sound upbeat and cheerful. 'Nothing to it.'

They laughed, though it seemed a superhuman task.

Cairns was still grey and dripping. 'Like a warm England,' Joanna commented gloomily next morning, staring through the window of Sylvie's house at rain-drenched palm trees. A bedraggled bird sat on the fence, looking as if it wished it had flown to sunnier climes for the rainy season. 'At least it'll be hot in Alice Springs,' she commented to anyone who was listening.

At that moment the phone rang and she snatched it up. It was a sombre Uncle George to tell them that Philip had just phoned again. 'He lied again,' the old man told her, his voice heavy with sadness, shame and a hint of indignation. 'He said that he was in Sydney but that the boys had slipped away. Just as he did before. He said he was sure he'd catch them soon. I don't know.' He sighed deeply and added formally, 'It's most unacceptable.'

'Did the number he phoned from come up on your handset?'

'Yes. He phoned on a land line and he was nowhere near Sydney but I talked reasonably to him. He didn't suspect I knew he was lying.' His voice sounded as if he had indigestion.

Poor Uncle George, thought Joanna. What a lot for a man of integrity and honour to swallow.

'Where did he phone from?'

'A place called Mount Isa. Tiny little place. We have relatives near there. They must be staying with them, unless . . .'

'Unless what?' Joanna felt alarmed.

'Well, if they are after the Codes of Power they may have discovered something.'

'Oh no!' Joanna felt horrified. 'I thought they believed it represented gold and that's what they wanted. Do you really think they might be looking for the pieces of the crystal ball? I thought they'd be waiting for us to find the other pieces?'

'Possibly. They may not know how many pieces there are or what they represent. They don't understand it's an initiation to help the planet. I'm pretty certain they just think it is something that will give them power.'

'And of course it will, won't it? If they get hold of the pieces of the crystal ball?'

'Yes, of course it will. They can use that power in any way they want. But they can't help humanity unless they pass the initiation into the Codes of Power.'

'Oh no!' she repeated.

'This is all conjecture, my dear.' Uncle George's voice hardened suddenly. 'Let's concentrate on getting that piece back.' By now Marcus, Helen and Sylvie were standing round the phone. Sylvie had got out a large map and they were all looking at it.

'Here's Mount Isa. God, it's in the middle of nowhere. Halfway to Alice. Surely they can't be driving to Alice!'

'Show me!' said Marcus.

Sylvie pointed with her finger to a dot on the map, a few hundred miles south-west of Cairns. 'You could fly there,' she suggested. 'You're welcome to take my four-wheel drive again but it'll take you a coupla days to get there.'

Helen said unexpectedly, 'Thanks, Sylvie. I think we have to drive. It won't be too bad if we take it in turns but we're on a sacred journey. It's much more than facing Dirk and retrieving the piece of crystal. I feel we may miss something if we fly.'

'I've got the same feeling,' agreed Joanna. 'Two days sounds a fearful distance to us Brits, especially through the middle of nowhere. But it feels right. Sorry, Uncle George, are you still there?' She spoke into the phone again.

'Of course,' replied the elder courteously, his voice gentle again. ' And I think you are right about driving. You are on what you would call a shamanic journey. You will be given the help and the tests you need. Call me when you are near Mount Isa and I'll talk to Philip again but be careful. Remember he may be a tool now for evil men!' He sounded immeasurably sad.

Joanna shivered at the mention of the evil ones of the Elite who were trying to control the financial markets of the world through drugs and banking and corrupting many huge companies. They were formidable in their desire for power. However she replied as brightly as she could, 'Thanks, Uncle George. We'll need some help in tackling Dirk, Billy and Philip. They're all strong men!'

'Don't think in terms of tackling them,' advised the old man wisely. 'Find a way of getting them to hand the crystal over harmoniously, if you can.'

'Sorry! You're absolutely right!' Joanna flushed at her own aggressive statement. 'I'm sure we'll be helped.'

'I'm sure you will. May the Great Spirit go with you,' he replied.

She felt a lurch of fear as well as excitement as she clicked off the phone.

*

On Sylvie's recommendation they headed inland through the Atherton Tablelands. 'It's a bit further but different from the coast road. You might as well make it a bit of a holiday,' she advised.

'Let's do it,' they agreed simultaneously.

And now they were twisting up the snakelike road to the higher ground, through wet tropical forest. Below they could see the flooded plains, for all the world like some vast brown inland lake, unbroken except for the occasional tree top holding its head up above the waters.

'I expect it's still eternally raining in Cairns,' remarked Joanna, delighted to be out of it. 'Trust us to be here in the rainy season.'

'This feels more like an adventure,' agreed her mother, sitting back to enjoy the sight of the rolling hills and pastureland, mountain streams and true bridal-veil waterfalls, glistening in the sunshine.

She had a guidebook on her knee. 'The Atherton Table Mountains used to be totally covered in forest and used for training for jungle fighting,' she read. 'According to the book this area sustained huge cedar trees. It was rich volcanic soil, but then with typical disregard for nature, the trees were butchered and the area turned into Chinese market gardens. Lots of Chinese settled in Eastern Australia apparently. They grew peanuts, avocados, mangos and all sorts of fruit and vegetables. It must have been wonderful.'

She gazed out at the rich and verdant land for a moment. 'Anyway, after the war land grants were given to soldiers to settle here and they cultivated the area.'

'It's beautiful,' agreed Marcus.

'I feel as if I'm on holiday,' said Joanna.

'Well, we are meant to be,' pointed out Marcus. 'It's just that our holidays turn into something else.'

'Yes, they do have a tendency to do that.'

'Having a quest makes it more fun,' pointed out Helen from the back, with blatant disregard for truth or the danger they had experienced.

'Oh, Mum, you are funny,' Joanna shouted with laughter.

Chapter 33

They decided to let their intuition lead them, stopping where it felt right or where something in the guidebook caught their attention. And so they found themselves on a walkway in the middle of the rainforest, surrounded by camera-laden Japanese tourists, gazing at a monstrous curtain fig tree, which the information board told them was five hundred years old.

'Pretty impressive,' said Joanna, gazing at the thirty-nine-foot diameter of aerial tree roots cascading down from the host tree. 'It's like a tree waterfall.'

'It's true Australian size,' agreed Marcus, intending a compliment in a land where everything was at least twice as large as in Europe.

They enjoyed the detour but all the time they were wondering if it was relevant to their quest for the Codes of Power and whether they really ought to be racing after Philip, Dirk and Billy.

Nevertheless, feeling like real tourists, they stopped for coffee and cake in a gorgeous rural village called Malanda, set in verdant pastureland rich with cows. Here Helen was totally entranced by a squat, square building on the village green, charmingly painted with rustic scenes. It turned out to be the public loo but she insisted on photographing it from every angle.

'Why can't we paint our buildings like this?' she demanded. 'Just think of our stations and subways. They're ghastly. Murals like this would change the energy of the place completely. And school children could do it really well and generate a sense of pride in their locality.'

'You're right, Helen. You'll have to do something about it,' Marcus told her with a smile.

She grimaced. 'Can you imagine the red tape involved in getting our public places painted beautifully? It would tangle up an army of council officials for years.'

Minutes later as she wandered round the village, Helen was even more enchanted by the life-size statue of a farmer with his horse, pulling a sledge on which sat a dog and two milk churns.

Several of the friendly locals took time to chat to her as she gazed at it. One old man touched her on the shoulder and told her, 'My dad was a dairy farmer and when I was a child I used to sit on a sledge just like that and be pulled along with the milk – and the dog too!'

'Ooh!' she exclaimed, surprised. 'Wasn't it bumpy?'

'No! On the grass it was surprisingly smooth. Oh, those were the days.' The criss-cross wrinkles on his face smoothed out as he smiled at the memory.

'What fun!' Helen could imagine it. And just to live surrounded by the beauty of the lush valleys and quiet glens must have been something. Oh yes, she thought, this place is beautiful but is beauty relevant to the Codes of Power?

She sensed that everything on their journey might be a key to something important.

And so they drove on and on towards the desert, overnighting at Charters Towers, which used to be a big gold-mining town and still sported streets of attractive old houses. The gold rush had left its mark and a local proudly told them it was the home of Australia's first stock market. Nevertheless it had the air of a proud old matron, clinging to the illusion of her past glory.

As they strolled round examining the elegant façades in the faded streets a flock of common galahs, red-bellied and grey-topped, screeched like warring children from a drooping tree while their feathers were scattered like confetti on the ground.

They ensconced themselves in a spit-and-sawdust pub drinking beer, which seemed the thing to do. 'From tomorrow we'll be well and truly in the outback,' remarked Marcus.

'Desert seems a misnomer when everywhere is flooded. We're lucky, I suppose. It could be breathlessly hot.'

'It will be,' commented a local, overhearing their conversation. 'Wait till you hit Mount Isa, there's just desert, desert and more desert. And hot. You'll know all about heat in the centre.'

'We're only going as far as Mount Isa,' replied Joanna.

'Yeah, most people give up there and get a plane or a bus. It's just too much desert,' he said lugubriously. 'No wonder the dinosaurs died off.'

'Dinosaurs!' exclaimed Helen.

'Yep, dinosaurs. You're on the Flinders Highway now.

We call it the Dinosaur Highway because lots of dinosaur remains were found here. Oh yes! Six-foot-long goannas, sabre-toothed tigers, giant kangaroos. The ones we get now are mere babies.' He sucked his teeth as he contemplated it.

'And there were ichthyosaurs and ammonites, like giant squid. They were all here. Oh and kronosaurus or something like that. They were forty feet long. Just think of that.'

'But why here?' asked Joanna. 'This is desert.'

'Now it is. It was a huge inland sea right here.'

The local drank up his beer, wiped his mouth with his brawny arm and said as he stood up, 'All a long time ago. They say it was a Garden of Eden once but it's desert now. Take plenty water with you when you go. G'day to you.' And he shuffled off to whatever life had in store for him.

'The Garden of Eden! That means we're right in the centre of old Lemuria!' exclaimed Helen in awe when he was out of earshot.

'I don't think we're here by chance, do you?' asked Joanna excitedly, her cheeks pink with more than suntan. 'We must be specially vigilant tomorrow for signs from the universe!'

Despite the prospect of a long, dreary drive ahead they set off in the morning with heightened anticipation. There must be something here for them. Something more than the prospect of facing Dirk, Billy and Uncle Philip. 'Not that he deserves that title of respect,' muttered Joanna.

'Maybe not,' replied Helen. 'But we have to treat him

with respect if we want him to respond to us with respect.'

'I hate it when you're right.'

Marcus laughed and put in, 'That's how I often feel about both of you.'

Joanna grinned. 'Ooh! I'll take it as a compliment.' And they drove off laughing with spirits lightened.

In spite of their positive expectations the most exciting things they saw all morning were an anteater crossing the road and a kangaroo standing behind a squat bush so still that he looked like an extension of it. They also passed a few enormous road trains, approaching in great clouds of dust, which were bigger and more dangerous than any dinosaurs.

The endless ribbon of patched tarmac with its red sand edging became tedious, the mile upon mile of spiky grey-green spinifex giving the illusion of lush countryside palled. The sky, interminable blue, was only broken by the white-hot sun and the air-conditioning in the car could no longer do its duty. Sweat dripped down Helen's back as she drove. Just as she was beginning to feel drowsily hypnotised by eternal sameness, she noticed a black object on the road ahead. It looked like a rock but she realised it was moving towards them.

'Hey,' she said, alerting the others. 'It's a bull.' Indeed a big black bull was trotting in the middle of the road straight at them. She slowed down. The bull did not deviate. It headed like an arrow in their direction.

'Stop, Helen!' shouted Marcus. She braked. The bull lowered its horns and moved faster.

'By God, it's charging us!'

'Hold on!'

'Make your aura huge!' shrieked Joanna. Holding on for their lives, their hearts pumping wildly, they tried to do this.

Helen's hands were like vices gripping the steering wheel. It could kill us! What about Sylvie's car! It'll write us off! The fragmented thoughts raced through her head in the seconds before inevitable impact. Everything went into slow motion. And then at the last instant the great black beast swerved and ran past them. Automatically they swivelled and watched it trotting away into nowhere.

'Whew!' Marcus said. 'That was too close!'

'Wherever did it come from?'

Joanna shivered. 'It was a bad omen!'

'Don't say that,' said Marcus quickly.

'Of course it was,' she flared. 'Everything has a meaning. You know that. Here we are in the middle of nowhere and we're charged by a black bull, for goodness sake.'

'Okay, okay,' Marcus placated. 'We were all shaken up.'

'It's a good job you reminded us to make our auras bigger,' put in Helen. 'I guess that made a difference. The animal sensed our sheer size and didn't want to take us on if we were that big.'

'You taught me to do that, Mum! Animals do respond to how big your aura is.' Joanna reached out and touched Marcus's hand. 'Sorry I snapped. I guess I'm tensed up.'

'Join the clan!' He gave her a squeeze. ' And you're right. Of course it has a meaning. But not necessarily a bad omen. What does a bull mean metaphysically, Helen?'

'Not sure. Look in the Dreamtime book.'

'It won't be in there, Mum. It's not indigenous to Australia.'

'Of course it isn't. How silly of me.'

'Tamsin told us that all indigenous Australian animals hop or bounce and don't disturb the infrastructure of the soil, which is apparently very fragile. We introduced the animals with cloven hooves like cattle, sheep and horses, which trample the ground and do incredible damage. It's one of the Aborigines' great griefs.'

'Oh dear! I thought rabbits were the worst we did!'

'No, there's a long list of creatures we've foisted on Australia.'

'And so,' interrupted Marcus, 'A black bull is a big, powerful, destructive, alien beast.'

'And it tried to attack us but left us alone because of our size.'

'It was more scared of us than we were of it.'

'So perhaps that represents the energy of Philip and the others. They want to take us on but they're scared.'

'They're not exactly aliens.'

'Maybe their energy is foreign to what the Codes of Power represents.'

'Maybe. At least it is a warning that there's danger around and we must face it carefully.'

'And non-threateningly.'

'That's true. You never hooted your horn or flashed your lights or did anything that could have been termed aggressive, did you, Helen?'

'To be honest I never thought of it,' she replied. 'But I agree it is a warning to be careful.'

Chapter 34

Most of the towns they passed boasted a petrol station, a general store and a couple of dejected-looking houses at most.

Joanna said she was gasping for a cold drink. 'Anything other than water!'

'Okay. We'll stop at the next place,' agreed Marcus, who was driving. And an hour later he pulled up with a flourish outside a clump of square, flat buildings, a super-market, a pub and unlikely as it seemed, a real-estate agent. 'Here you are! Utopia!'

As they tumbled out into the heat Helen gasped, 'I feel I'm being desiccated like a prune.'

'Me too.' Joanna wafted the eternal flies from her face. 'But it's surprisingly green. The rain seems to have pene-trated even here.'

A cluster of Aborigines sat in the shade. As always they were slightly slumped. So many of them have the head bowed posture of the emotionally defeated, thought Helen. Yet they have big shoulders and hips. They have such strength.

She watched them covertly as they walked into the pub. The men had big bellies. Each of the women had an untidy haystack of hair, frizzed round their faces into a halo, and they wore torn dresses. She hurried past them into the cool interior and, while Marcus bought drinks, took a seat by the window where she could watch them. After ten minutes or so, without seeming to speak or communicate in any way, they got up in one movement and wandered off. 'It's like birds acting with one consciousness,' she said to Joanna.

'Yes, it's extraordinary, isn't it. They must be very telepathic together.'

'I suppose people who live close to nature are tuned in to it and each other.'

'I guess so.'

Marcus and Joanna, with the intrepidity of youth, strode into the blistering heat to look at an emu, which was kept in a wire-netting enclosure. Helen intended to follow them but the temperature proved too formidable and she lingered in the shade.

An old Aborigine, thin and feeble, with grey stubble, battered hat and bare feet, hobbled towards her. A hungry-looking dingo-dog slunk behind him. 'Spare change missus?' he muttered. Helen was taken aback. That's what the beggars in London said. She didn't think Aborigines begged.

She looked at him and he grimaced, exposing uneven teeth. A front one was missing. She knew that a tooth was often knocked out during initiation and wondered if that's what happened to him. He looked very old. The life expectancy for a white Australian is almost eighty, while for Aborigines it is fifty-five. He must be pushing the statistics up, this one, she thought. However does he live out here? The thoughts were pulsing through her mind. She had a policy of not giving to beggars. Too often she had read that they spent it on drugs and drink. Clearly he's not a drug addict, she thought.

He smiled as if catching her thought – perhaps it was her imagination – and rubbed a hand over his stomach.

'You're hungry?'

He nodded, eyes downcast yet strangely all-seeing.

Something propelled her. 'Wait here.'

She went into the bar and bought a meat pie, bread rolls and a can of Coke. It was all they sold. The old man was waiting for her and took the offering without a word. He broke the pie in half and gave one portion to the ravenous dog. Then he turned away and shuffled off round the side of the building, his feet scuffing up puffs of dust.

Helen could hear Joanna's voice floating through the heat from the direction of the emu compound. 'I'm fried alive.'

'Just think, emus are out in this all the time.'

'They're adapted to the heat,' Joanna replied with her magical laugh, which always made her mother want to laugh too.

They came into sight and Helen could see that under her cap Joanna's face was tomato red. 'Hey, you need to cool down,' she called, concerned.

'You're right.' Joanna was fanning herself with a magazine. 'I'll just get another drink, then we'd better be on our way. It's my turn to drive.' She took off her cap and ran her hands through her damp hair. 'Anyone else want anything?'

Helen and Marcus shook their heads.

'I'll be with you in a moment then.'

Marcus and Helen crossed the dusty, stony area to their vehicle, which they had left under the only tree.

'Your turn in front, Helen.' Marcus opened the passenger door for her and they both saw that on the seat lay something wrapped in a rag.

'Whatever's this?'

'Don't know.'

Helen picked it up gingerly. Through the rag she could feel something small and hard. A suspicion entered her mind. She looked at Marcus and an electric excitement ran between them.

Quickly she tore the wrapping off and revealed a piece of crystal. A red crystal with a curved edge.

'It's a piece of the crystal ball!' she gasped. 'It must be, mustn't it?'

Marcus held it up. 'It's got to be. But where did it come from? Hey, Joanna! Quick!' he called to her as she emerged from the pub into the sunshine. 'Look, it's another piece of the crystal ball. Look!'

She was with them in an instant, ecstatic, laughing, jumping with delight. 'Who put it there? There wasn't anyone around,' she said, puzzled.

Helen replied slowly, 'Except the old man. The Aborigine I talked to. Do you think it could have been him?' She told them of her meeting with the old man. 'But he didn't say anything. He didn't meet my eyes. He just asked for spare change and indicated he was hungry.'

'What was the dog like?'

'Sort of dingo-like.'

Joanna and Marcus exchanged glances. 'I bet it was the karadji.'

'I didn't recognise him from when he saved me from Dirk on the beach but I don't suppose I looked at him properly then. I was in much too much of a state.'

'He was probably testing you to see if you'd be generous. Good job you were, Helen. Which way did he go?'

'Down the side of the building. Why?'

Marcus sprinted off and the women got into the four-wheel drive, wound up the windows and put the air-conditioning on full. He returned within moments, lobster red and dripping with sweat.

'No sign of him,' he panted as he opened the door.

'Get in quick. You're letting the heat in.'

'I thought he might be there and would give us a message or something.' Marcus looked disappointed.

Helen held the crystal in her hand. 'Now what Code does this one represent, I wonder?'

'The karadji was teaching us about caring and sharing,' said Joanna. 'It's obvious to me. He was testing you.'

'And then he shared with his dog, to show you.'

'Yes, that's true. Do you think we'd have been given the crystal if I hadn't bought him that food?' said Helen, feeling strangely humble.

'Presumably not. Though I think we'd probably have been offered another opportunity, don't you?'

'Why me? Am I the one who needs to be tested on caring and sharing?' Helen hoped her feeling of upset did not show but, of course, they sensed it immediately.

'Helen, you're a very generous person. I think we're all in this together.' Marcus leaned forward and put a hand on her shoulder.

'What do you mean?'

'I just have a feeling that we're undertaking this initiation together. As if the tests are being shared out.'

'Is that possible? I thought initiation was a very individual thing?'

'It is usually. But this feels very strange. I'm sure the three of us are in it as one.'

'I wonder,' said Joanna. 'You're right that it's peculiar. But don't worry, Mum. You're a very giving person. I think Marcus has got it right, though. You did it for all of us.'

Helen sat back, gazing at the strip of dusty road reaching to the horizon and beyond, lost in thought as they drove on.

'Hey, what are they?'

Joanna had slowed down. A group of large, grey birds were walking gracefully on the red earth, bobbing and gyrating.

'They're dancing!' exclaimed Marcus.

'I know what they are. They're brolgas,' exclaimed Joanna. 'How exciting.' She stopped the car. The Australian cranes continued to move in stately fashion, ignoring them completely.

'So they are,' agreed Helen. 'I'm so glad we've seen them. There's a Dreaming story about them, isn't there?'

'Yes, there is. Look in the Dreamtime book, Mum.'

Helen searched in Joanna's bag and pulled out the book. She found the page and scanned it. 'Oh yes, I remember the story. In the Dreaming there was a tall girl called Brolga, who loved to dance. She spent all her time out on the red sand dancing and making up new steps. The tribe was very proud of her and she was excused her share of food gathering because she entertained them all. Many men wanted to marry her but she preferred to concentrate on her dancing.

'One day she was caught by the evil cannibals of another clan and managed to escape by turning herself into a bird. When the tribe came to look for her all they could see was an elegant grey bird, dancing. They knew it was Brolga.'

'What a lovely story!' exclaimed Joanna.

'What does seeing the brolgas represent?'

'It represents discipline, commitment and creativity. It's interesting too because the Dreaming stories are often about aspects of the personality that are not allowed in Aboriginal society. They are teaching stories.'

'What do you mean?'

'Well, in traditional society everyone is equal and is discouraged from standing out except in ceremonial dance. Brolga seeks fame and glory at the expense of marriage and her womanly duties. To the Aborigine individual aggrandisement is considered to steal power from everyone else.'

'Is it! In the West everyone seems to want to be individual and successful and stand out.'

'It doesn't work that way,' said Helen. 'For everyone who is a star or a leader, there are lots of people keeping them in that elevated position.'

'That's true,' agreed Marcus. 'I'd never thought of it like that.'

'I suppose,' added Helen, 'that the traditional Aboriginal society functioned harmoniously without a hierarchy. Instead they were in tune with the spiritual world.'

'And to think this bird reminds us of all that,' said Joanna, moving into gear and gliding away gently so that the brolgas were not disturbed.

Chapter 35

Several very long hours later, hot, cramped, stiff and weary, they were glad to see the mining town of Mount Isa ahead. The dust and dirt had been newly washed by rain.

'I never want to sit in a car again,' groaned Helen.

'Nor me! My head's splitting,' agreed Joanna. 'What a nightmare journey. We must have been mad to say we'd drive.'

'We've got to drive back yet,' Marcus reminded them.

'Don't even mention it,' grumbled Joanna. 'When we've got that crystal from Dirk I want to lie in a cool swimming pool for days.'

Though it had never been far from her mind, when Joanna spoke Dirk's name aloud Helen's stomach lurched. Soon she would have to face him and retrieve the crystal. She felt it was her task and her responsibility. She hoped he was alone, for she could not cope with seeing Billy as well. Suddenly the fears she had been keeping at bay with sheer willpower flooded in. What if they hurt her? What if Dirk and Billy tried to capture her again? Even worse, were they working in collusion with the Elite? As the old memories returned her palms were sweating and hairs stood up on her arms. She stopped her train of thought abruptly. She must face it with courage and this time she had Marcus and Joanna to back her up. Also Uncle George was respected by the elders here. If necessary they would help them.

She must not let doubt in. She cancelled the fear thoughts she had been having and visualised them dissolving in the silver-violet flame of transmutation. Then for the hundredth time she visualised herself facing Dirk fearlessly and saw him handing the crystal to her. All her resolution returned and she was no longer afraid of any of them. She was geared for the meeting next evening.

But when they had settled into a hotel they spoke on the phone to Uncle George. What he told them gave them a horrid shock.

'What do you mean they've left Mount Isa?' Marcus realised his voice was curt almost to the point of rudeness. 'We've driven for three days to get here.' He could see Helen and Joanna looking at him, their faces haggard with exhaustion.

Uncle George was softly apologetic, which did nothing to assuage Marcus's annoyance. 'I have spoken with relations. Philip knows now that I have deduced his true whereabouts.'

'Did he know we were on our way to Mount Isa?'

'He probably guessed. He and the boys left today for Tennant Creek where there is more clan. They know no one will follow them there. It is too far.'

'Where is this Tennant Creek?'

'Another day's drive across desert. An old mining town,' replied Uncle George wearily. 'And when they get

there they can take the Stuart Highway north to Darwin
or south to Alice Springs. They've escaped, I'm afraid.'

Marcus felt pole-axed. His head thumped with the heat
and the eternal movement of driving. 'I'll phone you back
later,' he said abruptly and cut off the line.

'You heard that?' he said to the others, opening his
palms in a gesture of despair. 'They've already left.'

Marcus and Joanna looked at Helen, wondering how
she would react. They knew this was her personal battle
with Dirk, as well as their joint quest to retrieve the
crystal.

'Let's look at a map,' she said wearily. 'Then I want a
shower and a drink before I think of anything. I can still
see endless road and scrub when I close my eyes and my
legs won't walk straight.'

The map showed that Tennant Creek was another long
day's haul across desert. It was the opposite direction
from Alice Springs, heading towards Darwin.

'Oh hell!' exclaimed Joanna. 'You're right, Mum. We
can't take a decision tonight. It's miles and we're all done
in.'

Yet each one was thinking, Just another day. One more
day. We can't give up. We vowed we'd never give up.
We've got to get the crystal to fulfil the blueprint of the
planet.

When she had showered Helen fetched the four crystals
Marcus and Joanna were carrying between them and laid
them out on her bed, with the two she was looking after.
We've really found seven with the one we will get back

from Dirk, she thought determinedly and her eyes sparkled again at the sight of them. They're more precious than diamonds.

She was trying to fit them together into a ball when Marcus and Joanna knocked on the door to collect her for dinner.

'Come in! Look, several of the pieces fit each other.'

Marcus touched one of the pieces reverently. 'To think these contain the energy for the blueprint of Earth. Can you remember what each piece represents, Helen?'

'I hope so!' Helen picked up one of the crystals and cradled it in the palm of her hand. 'This is the first one that was given to me by Uncle George and it represents the fact that humans are caretakers of Mother Earth.' She replaced the first and picked up the second. 'This one was left by the old Aborigine at the motel and is about everything being brought into balance. Right and left brain, yin and yang, east and west, male and female.'

She passed it to Joanna, who held it carefully.

'The third one is interesting.'

'Ah, I recognise it. It's the one Stephen gave to me,' said Marcus, lifting it gently. 'Life is meant to be a celebration – or corroboree. And celebration offers gratitude and raises our energy to the divine.'

Helen picked up the fourth crystal. 'This is the one Martha gave to you, Joanna. The blueprint of the planet is to maintain harmony between humans and the natural world. It's our responsibility as humans to do this.'

Marcus indicated the empty space in the line. 'The one

Ferdy gave you should be here – about honouring each other and learning from the differences.'

'It's a pretty clear message,' agreed Joanna.

'Yes!' said Helen. 'And we will get it back. It's the one the karadji gave him at the Black Mountain. To ram the point home he talked about all the colours in a carpet being important.'

She had told them this a hundred times but Marcus laughed and replied, 'It's interesting he should have been given that one by the karadji!'

'Yes, isn't it?'

'And the fact that he held up one finger. Presumably that indicates oneness. We are all one.'

'I wonder if it has changed Ferdy or Jane!'

'I bet it has,' pronounced Joanna. 'You can't hold one without being touched by it. Anyway next there's the one the karadji gave us at the Black Mountain.' She managed to say it without a shudder. 'All are equal.'

Marcus continued for her. 'And the sing-song way he said, "All are equal. Mother and father, male and female, sun and moon, compassion and courage: all same, all equal."'

He replaced it on the bed and picked up the last one.

'And here's the one we got today, which we think means that everyone is to care for each other and share what they have.'

'Meaning there's enough for all if we share it.'

'Well, we know there is.'

'I hope we get the other ones,' said Helen.

'Oh ye of little faith. Of course we will.' Joanna at least had no doubts.

Mount Isa was a dreary, noxious mining town with nothing to recommend it. 'You mean people live here from choice?' commented Joanna, appalled, when they walked down the street for food.

'Apparently so!'

'Luckily we're all different,' said Helen. 'Otherwise we'd all live in the same place and do the same thing.'

Joanna laughed. 'That puts it in some sort of strange perspective I suppose. After all we all represent different coloured dots on the canvas of life.'

As with everywhere in Australia people seemed to have the time and tendency to talk. The waiter who served their meal told them the creeks all the way to Tennant Creek were flooded. 'I doubt you'll get through,' he said dubiously. 'Hey, Kev. Are vehicles getting through Tennant Creek?'

The older man he addressed came over. 'Some lorries got through today. What are you driving?'

'A four-wheel drive.'

He puckered his face in thought. 'Mebbe. Mebbe not. It depends. If it rains again, forget it. But if it stays hot, you might make it. Where are you headed? Darwin? It's a hell of a journey.'

'Probably Alice.'

'Naw. You take the other road to Alice. You can get through that way.'

'Thanks.' They could see no point in explaining that

they were searching for a man and a crystal in the middle of red Australia.

'Enjoy your food,' he said and wandered off.

'If we can't get through, then neither can they.' Joanna voiced all their thoughts.

'Maybe we'll catch up with them at one of the earlier creeks if they're stuck.'

'They can't get off the road, can they?'

They looked at one another. Helen said, 'Being Aborigine I'm sure they can. But they're urbanised. They probably won't want to tackle the bush in this wet. It'll be more dangerous too. The snakes will be much more active and venomous.'

'Anyway we have to take the chance. Let's go first thing in the morning,' urged Marcus.

Helen and Joanna looked at each other and groaned. 'Okay!' they agreed in unison.

Chapter 36

Helen felt very stiff in the morning when she woke. Her back felt tight and in spasm. When Joanna came into her mother's room to see if she was awake, she groaned, 'My back's terrible. I think I was sweating in the car because the air conditioning couldn't cope but at the same time it was cold enough to keep my clothes damp.'

'Oh, Mum. You poor old thing.' Joanna was concerned. ' Are you going to be able to travel today?'

'I've got to be.' Helen was not going to let the excruciating pain stop her.

'Your back represents your support system,' Joanna reminded her. 'Don't you feel we're supporting you? Or don't you think the universe is looking after you?'

'I don't know. I'm sure there's some of that,' admitted Helen. 'The back also tenses up when we don't face our fears and feelings and shove them behind us. Perhaps I've been too accepting without dealing with the real feeling.'

'Well, that would be your pattern, wouldn't it, Mum? I guess it's a bit of a family trait. Anyway, I'm going to give your back a good massage and some healing. Then we'll see how you are for travelling.'

'Oh, thank you. Bless you. You're an angel.' Yet again Helen thanked the universe for her daughter, who she sometimes felt annoyed with but usually admired and adored.

They left rather later than intended but Helen's back felt much better as a result of being nurtured, supported and massaged.

When Helen thanked Joanna, she quipped back, 'I'm just demonstrating caring and I'm sharing my gifts in accordance with the blueprint for the planet.'

'Good on you.'

The sky was part overcast and part brilliant blue. It felt appallingly hot, though sporadic rain kept the dust down. The journey ahead seemed interminable. Up to now they had been buoyed by a complete faith that they would reach Mount Isa, find Philip, Dirk and Billy and persuade them to hand over the crystal. They were certain they could manage this, possibly with an agreement not to press charges. But the news that Philip and the boys were running from them made the possibility of success less certain.

'At least they aren't stalking us for the crystals we've got already!' remarked Joanna.

'No!' agreed Marcus and was suddenly struck by the appalling thought that the men might be enticing them into a trap. He did not voice this fear but resolved to be doubly vigilant. He had a sense that Philip was dangerously crafty.

Everyone had warned them of flooded creeks ahead and they were soon aware of tracts of desert underwater around them.

So they were in tense and uncertain mood as they drove towards Tennant Creek, half hoping to catch up with the men at some flooded creek, half dreading what might happen in the middle of nowhere, yet committed to go on.

'Look, there are a couple of trucks coming towards us. They must have come through the creeks,' pointed out Joanna.

'That's good. So they're passable.'

'Unless they turned back. There has been a lot of traffic on this road.'

But the next piece of flooded road was passable and the one after that, just! 'I wouldn't like to risk it if it's any deeper,' said Marcus, a worried frown creasing his forehead.

The next flood was different. Two cars had pulled off the road and the drivers were evidently examining the possibilities. It was clearly impassable and their hearts sank.

'We'd better get out and hear what the others say,' said Marcus, turning off the engine. They piled out into the breathless heat and walked over to the cluster of drivers who were waiting patiently by the roadside. Dirk, Philip and Billy were not among them, so they must have got through earlier.

Damn! Damn! thought Marcus.

There was not an ounce of shade anywhere and the sun bounced and shimmered off the red desert and khaki waters alike.

'What are the chances?' he asked a couple with a child, who were debating whether or not to wait.

'We're hoping for a big truck to come by so we can follow in its wake.'

'How long have you been waiting?'

'Only about twenty minutes. Four cars in front of us got through behind a truck. We should make it in the next lot. So should you if you're quick.'

'You're obviously used to doing this?'

'Done it a few times,' the young husband admitted. 'You have to if you live out here.'

'We're going to family in Darwin for Christmas,' the wife told them. 'Everyone's trying to get home. That's why there's so much traffic.'

Helen realised with a shock that she had forgotten all about Christmas in the anxiety about retrieving the crystal. She looked at her watch. It was the 21st already. Where would they be for Christmas? she wondered.

'Hey! There's a bus coming,' shouted a blonde woman and suddenly everyone was scrabbling into their cars, ready to follow it.

Marcus was behind the wheel in a flash with the engine on, waiting, alert and expectant. Helen and Joanna leaped in with alacrity. The bus slowed down and for a moment they thought it was going to stop but it took the creek at a steady pace, sending out a huge bow wave. The cars tucked in close behind it. Their four-wheel drive was third in line and another car coming up quickly just made it behind them.

'Wow! That was exciting,' yelled Joanna, her eyes shining. 'I hope the next one's as good.'

*

But the next flood was vast. The red-brown waters from the creek covered acres of desert and the road was impassable. Dozens of cars, lorries and buses were lined up along the roadside waiting for the water to subside. They pulled up at the end of the queue and then all three of them got out and walked past the waiting vehicles to look at the water. They were also watching for Dirk, Billy and Philip.

'We've been waiting for two days already,' one strained-looking woman told them. 'They reckon it's going down an inch an hour as long as it doesn't rain again.'

'When will it be passable at that rate?'

'Tomorrow maybe. I hope so. We managed to get beds in the hotel but we'll turn back if we don't get through tomorrow.'

'Good luck.'

The three of them took off their sandals and paddled in the thick red-brown water. Ahead crowds of people were wading up to their waists and several children and dogs were swimming.

Someone shouted, 'Watch out for crocs.'

The English trio hurried back to the dry road but most people just laughed. 'In Katherine there were crocs swimming in the main street when the creek flooded,' a deeply tanned, white-haired man informed them.

'Is that meant to make us feel better?' muttered Joanna but Helen expressed enough horror to satisfy him and he laughed a deep belly laugh.

A cry went up. 'A lorry's crossing.' People scrambled

out of the way as a huge road train made it across. Everyone cheered.

A black rain-cloud crossed the sun and gave them temporary relief from its intensity. Apparently the fear now was of flash floods, as rain was falling higher up the river. Rumour and counter-rumour raced from mouth to mouth.

'A truck'll take cars across for $100.'

'Crocs have been seen down the creek.'

'Heavy rain's coming.'

'No chance of getting across for Christmas.'

'Lorries are going to start moving across any minute now.'

An old guy with a dog came by and said he was really anxious to get his truck across as he'd got seventy head of deer to get over. Really lovely animals with antlers. 'I've got to get over or the children won't get any presents,' he added and walked off chuckling.

In the excitement Helen forgot all about Philip, Dirk and Billy. She went off to the ladies' at the back of the general store and café, which was having a bonanza time and opening extra hours. The thermometer said 45 degrees. No wonder she felt sick and light-headed with dehydration.

She came out of the ladies', bought herself a cold drink and was just stepping out of the café to go back to the car when she saw Dirk. After all the anticipation it was un-expected. Her legs wobbled. Adrenaline rushed through her. She felt suddenly terrified.

A second later he saw her too. His eyes became huge,

his face grey. Then he turned and raced away on his long legs.

Helen forgot her genteel English upbringing. She screamed, 'Catch him! Get him!'

The sound coming from her mouth shocked her. It was loud, so loud. Everyone stared.

Half a dozen men, who not unnaturally assumed she had been mugged, closed in on him from every direction. Dirk swerved and doubled back but he didn't stand a chance. For a horrified moment Helen was reminded of a fox being chased by hounds. The youth crashed to the ground and two men held him down. Macho men, bored, weary and delighted to be heroes, they relished this.

'Give it back to her,' threatened the biggest man. He pulled Dirk up by the hair and made as if to bang his head on to the stony road.

Suddenly Helen felt huge, strong, powerful. 'Yes. Give it back to me,' she said, standing with her hands on her hips.

'Arm bin paining.' Dirk had lapsed into pidgin and set up a howl. The man made a chopping movement towards his arm and he went quiet.

But Helen stood her ground. 'Where is it?'

The whites of Dirk's eyes showed. 'Billy 'ave 'im.'

Helen was suddenly angry. 'I don't believe you. Give it to me.'

Someone shouted, 'The police are here.' With that Dirk thrust his hand in his pocket and pulled out the crystal. He threw it to the ground. ''Im come back. I go.'

Helen could see the shock on the faces around her that

all this fuss was for a bit of stone. She did not care. She scrabbled to pick it up, her face filled with relief and delight as she cupped it in her hand. The men loosened their grips and, slippery as an eel, Dirk slithered from them in a flash and ran for his life.

Marcus and Joanna, hurrying towards the scene, saw him jump into a battered truck driven by Philip and they raced away, the boys shouting obscenities and making rude gestures, while the older man was hunched over the wheel looking grim.

'I've got it! I've got it!' Helen called to them. They ran up to her and hugged her, all jumping up and down with excitement. She thanked the heroes who were very macho and matter-of-fact.

The police car stopped with a crunch amid clouds of dust and half the crowd melted away while the other half moved in, craning to hear what was going on. The crowd was well satisfied when the police made calls on their radios and, turning their vehicle, sped off in pursuit of the fugitives. They looked at each other eagerly, clearly asking, 'What was that all about?' The finger of excitement touched their tedious day.

Helen's perspective had changed so much over the last few days that she really did not care whether they were caught or not. It was a thought she was to regret. They were yet to cause a great deal more trouble, for weak men can become cunning and vicious when influenced by those of evil intent.

Marcus's conjecture that Sturov's henchmen had allowed Dirk to keep the crystal chip in order to entice the English trio who held the other crystals was accurate. As long as the Evil Ones knew where the crystals were, they were content to let the three of them be. He surmised they planned action when the remaining crystals were found. Then they would try to take them so that the dark forces of the planet would hold the power. They would control the finances and health of the world and keep people in subjugation. Marcus went tense all over at the thought.

In the meantime Philip, inflamed with thoughts of wealth and power, resolved to retrieve the crystals for himself. Now Marcus, Joanna and Helen had two sets of enemies, not one.

Chapter 37

Most people waited patiently for the flood to recede but Marcus, Helen and Joanna drove back to Mount Isa, once again waiting for a truck to tail at the next creek. It rained intermittently on the way and they guessed the people hoping to pass through the Tennant Creek flood might not reach Darwin for Christmas.

'What shall we do about Dirk and the others?' asked Helen.

'Nothing.' Marcus shrugged. 'Leave them to the police or the elders. But how do you feel about it, Helen?'

'I feel strangely indifferent. I have to admit when I saw him, my knees shook and I was scared.'

'He was more scared than you,' pointed out Joanna.

'Yes, but I wanted to meet him with courage and compassion, fearlessly.' Helen sighed.

'Oh, Mum, stop beating yourself up. You're human. Almost anyone else would have been lusting for revenge.'

'Courage is not about being fearless,' pointed out Marcus. 'It's about facing something even though you are afraid.'

'True, but if you are completely without fear, the situation dissolves.'

'Ah well, we haven't reached that level yet but we are

still questing for the Codes of Power, so we must be doing something right.'

'Look, there's a dingo,' yelled Joanna, pointing out of the window, and to their delight they saw the wild desert dog trotting through the scrub. Possibly because they were travelling at a more leisurely pace they saw several kangaroos and two emus, which helped to pass the very long journey.

They did not want to spend more time than they had to in Mount Isa. No way. That was one thing they were in agreement on. Marcus wanted to drive on to Alice Springs. 'We've got to get there as we're so close,' he tried to persuade them, but Joanna and Helen went on strike totally and utterly at this suggestion.

'Yes, but not immediately,' declared Helen. 'Tomorrow I shall lie by the pool all day.'

'Me too. What else is there to do? If there's anything to see that doesn't involve sitting in a vehicle, I'm game.'

'Okay. I get the message.' Marcus laughed. 'I know when I'm beaten. Let's contact Uncle George. He may have some suggestions.'

'Shouldn't we book a hotel in Alice Springs?' asked Helen. 'It might be difficult to find accommodation at this late stage.'

'Something'll turn up. You'll see,' replied Joanna and Helen remembered how, even as a child, she expected good fortune and it was usually bestowed on her.

And so a couple of nights later they were ensconced in a luxury hotel in Alice Springs, excited to be in the red heart of Australia for Christmas.

'You know, luxury comes from the Latin *lux* for light,' commented Marcus. 'It just shows that the spiritual world wants people to have the best.'

'Yes and I could get used to it,' replied Joanna, with a toss of her head and a huge grin as she plumped herself down on a comfy chair.

Marcus indulged Helen with a large gin and tonic, which he informed her would keep malaria at bay. 'There isn't malaria here, surely?' She was startled.

He chuckled. 'Plenty of mosquitoes and billions of flies but you're okay, no malaria.'

'Thank goodness for that. Malaria's not nice. I keep pinching myself, you know. I can hardly believe we're really here in the middle of Australia! It's so beautiful!' Helen sipped her gin as she looked out of the window at a glorious red sunset. 'I think it's the most fabulous sunset I have ever seen.'

Joanna smiled warmly. 'You've always wanted to come to Alice Springs, haven't you Mum?'

'Yes.' She laughed. 'Neville Shute has a lot to answer for. *A Town Like Alice* was one of my favourite books for years. Not that it's anything like I expected.'

'How's Alice different?' Marcus asked.

'Bigger, more concrete, more sprawling. I didn't expect huge malls and masses of tourist shops and cafés. I thought it would be a bigger version of some of the tired little towns we've passed through but it's a concrete jungle with all the usual chain stores. It could be anywhere.'

'Are you disappointed?'

'A little, but I may change my mind when I've seen the Royal Flying Doctor Service building and the Telegraph Station and School of the Air!'

'Oh, you've turned into a real tourist,' he teased.

She smiled but added more seriously, 'I suppose I didn't expect there to be so many Aborigines wandering around, looking out of place in the middle of a jazzy town.'

'It must be strange for them. Their land is covered with a modern metropolis and they lurk on the fringes.'

'It must be like owning a beautiful home and suddenly it's gatecrashed and full of party-goers who make you feel like an outsider,' commented Joanna. 'But they're a bit scary round town because there's such a palpable anger around them.'

'You're right,' agreed Marcus. 'All dispossessed people are angry but it's still scary to be around. Anyway I'm going to see if there are any e-mails.' He was busily pulling his laptop from its bag and setting it up as he spoke and within seconds exclaimed, 'Great. There's an e-mail from Tony about the Codes of Power.'

Instantly Joanna and Helen were at his side. 'What does he say?'

Marcus laughed. 'Hang on. Basically he wants to know where we are.

'We ought to ring him,' suggested Joanna.

'We could ring tomorrow and have a chat with him,' agreed her mother. 'That would be lovely.'

'He'd like that.' Joanna laughed. 'And it would be great to talk to him again. I like Tony,' she added, looking sideways at her mother.

'I still think he finds you hard to understand,' replied Helen, remembering their earlier conversations. She giggled. How much of it was gin and how much genuine amusement no one was certain.

'Right. The Scroll. This is what Tony's e-mail says,' said Marcus, ignoring them. 'Here is some more information about Lemuria, which is revealed in the Scroll. Professor Smith has also discovered a section which summarises the qualifications for passing the initiation to the Codes of Power. He'll send them in a few days.'

'Fantastic! Go on!'

Marcus read aloud: ' "As always happens when the veils of illusion are thin, the spirits of parents and child consciously communicate before birth. The child prepares for entry into the experience of Earth and is made welcome by all." '

'That's so lovely,' commented Joanna. 'I wish we could still do that.'

'I guess lots of parents do talk to the incoming soul even now, though often it's not conscious,' said her mother.

'Didn't the Scroll say they did that in the early days of Atlantis too?' queried Marcus.

'I think you're right.'

'It meant every baby felt welcome and special.'

Marcus continued. ' "Every soul to be born is chosen

and welcome. Then the sexual connection takes place."'

'That's amazing,' said Helen. 'Sex is such a powerful urge at the third dimension.'

'The Scroll says something about that,' continued Marcus. 'Wait a moment. "We early Lemurians are operating at a fifth dimensional frequency, beyond sexuality. In fact many are androgenous or very little separates the sexes."'

'How did they reproduce then?' asked Joanna, curious.

'Yes, I'm agog to know,' agreed Helen.

'Apparently it was done by a conscious will and energy transference. It says: "There are two parents, who dedicate themselves to providing the caring and wisdom for each child who enters. To become a parent is considered to be a very important spiritual responsibility."'

'A bit different from nowadays, when too often it's "an accident" and many parents think the child is bottom of their pile of responsibilities,' Helen said gloomily. 'I hate to see the way we devalue children these days.'

Marcus continued. ' "The veils of forgetting are thin and the incoming soul is in touch with the spirit world and receives spiritual sustenance from angels and ancestors at all times."'

He paused. 'Hang on. Let me scroll down a bit further. Ah. It talks about their homes. "Our homes are made of crystal, so we are sheltered by light."'

'That must have been in early Lemuria?'

'Presumably.'

'The crystal dwellings must have carried quite an energy.'

'Yes. It says here: "Our dwellings, whether they are places to nurture a child or a teaching centre or celebration cathedral, are made of pure crystal, which is programmed according to the purpose. The great leaders, those who we nourish with our thoughts, in turn use their power to programme the crystal. So a baby might enter a cave of rose quartz crystal, which is programmed with an energy of loving harmony."'

'Oh, that's beautiful,' murmured Helen softly.

' "And a child who is learning will enter a building which is programmed according to the level of knowledge he or she is at. For instance a being who is learning about the higher dimensions might enter an amethyst crystal dome where the higher teachings, telepathically imparted to him, vibrate in the very structure of his surroundings. A soul wishing to learn about the spiritual nourishment of plants and foods might enter an amber world."'

'How fascinating!' Joanna nodded. Helen too was nodding in agreement. 'I wonder if they used music to help with learning?'

Marcus scrolled down. 'Oh yes. Listen to this. "Because all is vibration and certain notes help information to be absorbed into the cellular structure of a being, teachers and the angelic forces as well as the learned ancestors play the notes which are absorbed first by the crystals and then amplified, so that the student can better learn."'

'Mmm!'

'Amazing!'

'It's all quite different from Atlantis and yet similar.

It's obviously more ethereal than the Aboriginal way of living.'

'Yes, I think the Aborigines earthed and grounded the Lemurian energies.'

'Did they eat in Lemuria, I wonder, or did they live on prana or light?'

'A bit of both. According to the Scroll, they breathed in prana for much of their spiritual sustenance and then lived on fruit and vegetables, honouring the plant for supplying them. The act of gratitude conferred much nutrition.'

'So it's like blessing food. It raises its energy and it automatically feeds the body better.'

'Well, blessed food becomes alive, doesn't it? So it must be more harmoniously absorbed.'

'True. But it's more than that. It seems they linked with the cosmic vitality needed to make a plant grow. Through absorbing the consciousness of the food they became healthy and full of extraordinary life force.'

'Good heavens!' responded Joanna. 'What else does it say?'

'Not much. It repeats what it said before: "All is transparent. Everyone is so connected to the divine that there are no secrets. No one has anything to hide. Therefore it is impossible to lie or cheat. Truth and transparency are the currency of our age." '

'I suppose if you can read everyone's mind and their aura, there is no point in hiding anything!'

'So no one had a shadow. They were transparent and ethereal.'

'So where do Aborigines come in as carriers of this Lemurian energy? No one could call them ethereal.'

'They grounded it and brought it fully into Earth. Yet they kept their connection to the spirit ancestors and the Great Spirit. Before the white invasion their auras were totally clear. They communicated with animals and nature and were the custodians of the natural world. They did this with integrity.'

'Yes, they kept the harmony between animals, the nature kingdom and the spirit world. And—'

'And they dedicated their lives to doing this,' interrupted Joanna. 'And they celebrated life in a way we would find extraordinary now. I guess they really did live the qualities of Lemuria.'

'What was it about the white invasion that stopped their connection to the ancestral world?'

'Their roots with the Earth were smashed. Their beliefs derided. All that they held important was taken from them but it was even more than that.'

'Surely the food and drink made a difference.'

'Right. There's nothing like drugs and alcohol to close the portals to the higher realms,' said Helen, finishing her gin and tonic with a wry grin.

'No, Mum, there isn't!' agreed Joanna, laughing. 'But I guess once in a while it's okay.'

'Is there anything else?' demanded Helen, speaking in an ever so slightly slurred voice.

'No. That's it.' Marcus smiled. 'Would you like another gin and tonic, Helen?'

'I'd love one.'

Chapter 38

In a seedy part of Alice Springs, outside a dingy concrete and corrugated-iron house, surrounded by bare earth, crashed cars and much rubbish, some dark and angry conspirators had gathered. Among them were Dirk, Uncle Philip and Billy, full of hatred and thwarted pride.

'We want them dead!' muttered Dirk, slurping from a beer can.

'Yeah. All of them!' gloated Billy, a weak youth, now emboldened by alcohol and his friends. 'Them Whites!'

'Shut your gob! It's my decision and I say George too!' shouted Philip, who felt betrayed by George. George his old school friend, who talked about reconciliation and was respected by all, while he, Philip the great stockman, was mistrusted and often derided by the clan. Now George had given his heritage to those Whites. That was his crystal too – in trust to the Aborigine race. Yes, after several beers he greatly felt George's insult and his atavistic rage was beyond reason.

Then he remembered that he was going to get money and power – the sort of power George did not have. He'd be able to pull the birds, those men had said. He gloated, his anger mollified. He'd get that crystal ball on his own.

He was not given to keeping secrets, yet he hugged this one close. He'd show George. He'd show them all.

That afternoon he had phoned George, who had spoken to him reasonably, calmly and wisely but spelled several things out extremely clearly. He was appalled at Philip's actions. He could not condone, support or excuse him or the boys.

'You're a white arse-licker!' shouted Philip.

George refused to react. He repeated his statement even more slowly and patiently. 'Come back and face justice.'

'Huh. White justice. After the way they've treated us. You think I'm going to let them boys go to prison?'

'Just imagine if our people tried you,' George reminded him.

'You wouldn't!' Philip was shocked at this betrayal.

'Oh yes I would,' replied George softly but very wearily. All his life he had tried to promote understanding, reasonable action and tolerance. And now his own family was behaving in this totally unacceptable way. He ran his arm over his face to wipe away the sweat.

His heart raced uncomfortably and he sat down abruptly on a chair, leaning his head on his hands.

Helen wanted to see a snake show, which was advertised at a hotel down the road. Joanna shuddered. 'No, thank you. You must be mad, Mum. It's the last thing I want to see.'

'Well, I'm going anyway,' announced Helen. 'We can eat there if you like and then I'll stay on for the show.'

And so it was decided, though in the end Marcus said

he'd stay with Helen too. 'I've always wanted to hold a snake,' he admitted to Helen, out of Joanna's earshot.

'Me too! They're fascinating creatures, but I don't want to face one out there in the bush.'

So Joanna wandered back to their hotel and Marcus and Helen stayed to learn about snakes.

A lean, bald man of average height, wearing heavy boots and gaiters on his legs, walked in nonchalantly, carrying a writhing sack in each hand. Then he went out to fetch more.

'Are the snakes in there?' whispered Helen.

'I guess so.' As Marcus leaned forward Helen was aware how tanned he had become. The sun had bleached his hair, making it fairer and his grey eyes were alight as ever when he was excited. Helen felt happy for her daughter. Marcus is a good man, she thought. It's important to be with someone who's interested in life.

When several sacks lay casually on the floor, the man introduced himself as Sid. 'I'm known as Hissing Sid, the Snake Man,' he jested. 'I've been bitten many times and developed some kind of immunity to snakes.' He held his hand up. The middle finger was a stump and Helen shivered involuntarily. 'This time I was not so lucky.'

After telling them how lethal the snakes were and that they must keep quiet and still so that they did not frighten them, he untied the drawstring of one of the sacks and tipped a long, sleek, brown serpent out on to the floor. It reared up instantly. Sid stood immobile. Yet every inch of him was alert as the snake watched him intently, ready to strike. Helen found her heart beating loudly. Sid moved a foot and instantly the snake swivelled towards it. Sid became still and so did the snake. They remained in tableau for perhaps a minute. Sid moved a hand. The snake slithered until its head was two feet away from the hand. As his hand moved, so did the snake's head. It watched the hand intently, moving in synchronicity with it. Sid became motionless and so did the snake.

Sid demonstrated effectively that the snake would be still as long as you were. 'They're scared of you. They don't want trouble. If you give them warning that you're coming, they'll get out of the way. If you startle them and they feel threatened, they'll bite. Never underestimate them. One bite from this beauty and you've got less than an hour to get help.'

Carefully he replaced the gracefully curving snake in the sack with a pronged stick and unfastened the second sack. A second snake, even more venomous, according to Sid, slithered out, ready to attack.

'If you are bitten,' Hissing Sid continued, 'don't panic. Keep the part that's infected immobile. Bind it if you can to prevent the spread of venom and walk slowly and steadily to a place where you can get medical attention. Remember most bites can be treated effectively.'

'Shouldn't the poison be sucked out?' someone called out.

'No. It's an old wives' tale. Don't do it and don't cut it. Stay as still as possible so that the poison doesn't move to your heart – and get help.'

Helen and Marcus looked at each other. 'Let's hope we never have to put that to the test,' he murmured.

She nodded. 'Let's hope so.'

For light relief at the end, Sid brought forward a huge python. He asked for volunteers to hold it and Helen and Marcus both went forward. So did several other tourists. They all stood in a line and the python, bizarrely named Polly, was placed over their shoulders. Polly's skin felt smooth and delightful, and she moved fluidly around them. Marcus stroked her.

'Relax there,' Hissing Sid said with a smile to Helen and she tried to ease her neck. Polly snaked from her to the next person down the line as if she was the branch of a tree and Helen had to confess to a sense of relief when Hissing Sid took python Polly back and placed her round his own shoulders.

When they returned to the hotel they told Joanna all about their evening, and it proved as well that they did.

More and more Aborigines had gathered outside the dingy house. All had been drinking steadily. Dirk, Philip and Billy were very drunk. Another was a karadji, a witch doctor, who was not drinking. At one time he had been a healer. Now he exchanged his powers for money. His energy could be used for good or bad and he did what he was paid for. The people knew of his power to use the energy of the invisible worlds and they were wary of him. He sat in a dark corner and watched, for he had a nose for trouble brewing.

The magic man gave the dishevelled impression of one who is in disharmony. He had a straggly beard, tangled hair and a cigarette hanging from the corner of his mouth. His filthy trousers and scruffy shirt, exposing thin bare arms, gave him a scarecrow look.

By midnight Dirk was telling everyone loudly about the evils of the white people, especially certain ones he knew, and also of Uncle George, who had thwarted him. He wanted to get even with him. Philip, in a slurred voice, agreed. Someone suggested darkly that they get someone to 'sing' their enemies and when the older man agreed, he pointed to the famous sorcerer, sitting almost invisible in the corner.

'He'll do it. My sister-in-law got terrible boils the day after he "sang" her.' The man cackled a strange high-pitched laugh at the memory.

Unsteadily Philip held up a kerosene lamp and the old witch doctor raised a hand to shield his eyes. One was opaque, covered with a cataract. The other squinted slightly. The elder smiled craftily. With George, his troublesome voice of conscience, and those Whites out of the way, he'd get the crystals and the money. Why not! he thought.

'You want me to point the bone?' the witch doctor demanded in his own language.

Philip acquiesced. 'Four people. Three white.'

The witch doctor grunted. 'Too many. One.'

'You do four.'

'Two most!' And from that he would not budge.

'How much?'

The scarecrow named a sum.

Philip growled. 'It was never done like this when I was growing up.' He turned to Dirk and Billy.

'Just do the old white woman,' sneered Dirk.

'Naw. Do the long-legged juicy girl,' disagreed Billy, the corners of his mouth turning up in a disagreeable smile. The ugly-hearted hate those who are unattainable especially those who are beautiful in body and spirit.

At that all three of the men smiled unpleasantly. The discussion, sometimes heated, went on for two hours or more. Interested people sat on the ground, ignoring the mosquitoes, and listened.

Dirk and Billy, several cans of beer later, shouted in triumph and chortled. It was agreed. 'You pointing the bone to white woman, juicy-legs Joanna and George, the treacherous traitor.'

The old sorcerer set about the incantations connected to the curse. He intended to use his power and all the arts of black magic to sing his victims to death.

Healing is a mighty power, channelled by those of high intention, who can call in the divine energy and transmit it to those in need. Miracles can result, when the sick person receives the blessing. And in this plane of duality, for everything in the light, there is its counterpart in the darkness.

Curses too have a huge power, brought through from the powers of darkness, those Evil Ones, who balance the beings of light in the inner planes. Their venom can penetrate the aura of the victim and cause death or misfortune.

It is not necessary for a victim to know consciously that they have been cursed. Their unconscious mind will pick up the intention and open them up to receive the effects, especially if they are sensitive or superstitious.

The old man spat on his palm and rubbed the spittle on two stones. He wrapped dead grass around them until they became effigies of Uncle George and Joanna. Then he started dancing, beating the red earth with bare branches, shouting promises to the totems, calling maledictions on the intended victims. He increased the rate until he was dancing and yelling at fever pitch. This continued for an hour or more.

At last, exhausted, he stuck bones from a dead chicken into the heart of each effigy and sank to the earth with a wailing cry. 'They are cursed. They will die.'

Far, far away in Cooktown, Uncle George woke next morning with a raging fever. His family was very disturbed.

Joanna too woke early next morning with a weird sense of foreboding. Marcus was fast asleep and there was a faint sound from the other side of the interconnecting door where Helen was having disturbed dreams.

Joanna rose quietly, donned her shorts and T-shirt and crept out into the relative cool of the early morning. It was a clear bright day and she had no idea why she should have this queer feeling of oppression. It was as if her heart felt heavy. She shook her head, irritated with herself.

The sky was misty pink and mauve and it promised to be a scorching day. This was a good opportunity to be by herself. She decided an early morning walk on her own would soon restore her humour and set off out of the hotel along a dusty track towards the rising sun.

Gnarled and sparse bush veiled the red baked soil and, vitalised by the unexpected rains, there were greenish spinifex hummocks as far as the eye could see. From the car these had offered a false impression of fertility but now she could see that the ground was baked hard and cracked between each hummock. The rain had caused a temporary carpet of extravagant wildflowers to spring up. Clusters of poached-egg daisies with pale yellow centres and white petals worshipped the sun. Brightly coloured desert peas ran riot.

A gaggle of desert finches fluttered and twittered at the base of an emaciated tree. She could see the tracks of tiny desert mice and lizards who had been abroad in the early morning. An eagle floated above the track waiting.

It was not yet too hot. She should have been in heaven with nature laid bare before her but this dread feeling lurked somewhere in her and over her, like a big black shadow. It felt like death, worse even than her premonition about her mother. She shivered as if an ice-cold finger had touched her.

There was not a soul or a vehicle to be seen.

And then a goanna plodded through the vegetation. She had to get a closer look. Forgetting all warnings, she moved off the track, picking her way among the spinifex hummocks and crept towards it. As she approached, it froze. So she stood still and watched for a long time. Then something moved suddenly beside her. Startled, she stepped back and slipped, falling awkwardly. The venomous snake sheltering under the hummock was disturbed as she landed by it. Her arm, thrown out to break her fall, threatened it. It attacked, fastening its jaw round her wrist. Its fangs poured out venom. She clutched her bleeding arm and screamed and screamed into the empty desert. The snake released its grip and vanished.

Chapter 39

Sometimes fortune favours us. Maybe it's fate or karma. Maybe the angels were looking after Joanna. At that moment a truck passed. Because it was early morning and not yet too hot, the vehicle's windows were open. The driver heard her screams and stopped.

Joanna trembled, feeling faint with pain and panic as she tried to control her breathing. 'I'm not ready to die! Oh no! No!'

She remembered what Marcus and Helen had told her the night before and kept her arm immobile as she hurried back to the road. Her knees were wobbling like jelly as if they would not hold her weight. 'Bites can be treated,' she kept repeating to herself. 'Stay calm. It will be all right. Oh, help! Help!'

The driver, a sturdy woman with blonde hair tied back and a capable mien, had jumped out and was hurrying towards her. 'You got bitten by a snake.' This was a statement. 'What was it like?' She had her arm round Joanna and was helping her into the truck.

Joanna was feeling faint but the woman was firm. 'Describe it. Don't faint on me.'

'It was brown and thin – about four feet long. Just brown, ' Joanna gasped.

'Right! I'll get you to Sid.' She was talking into a mobile as she drove. 'Stay conscious and keep still for heaven's sake.'

'Who's Sid?' Joanna murmured in a dozy voice and the woman cast her a sharp glance, looking concerned.

'Sid's a friend. He works with snakes and has all the serum. Quicker to go there than the hospital.' Joanna's eyes kept closing and the woman forced her to talk.

Fifteen minutes later they crunched into the driveway of a small bungalow, fronted with straggly weeds. The door was open and a man rushed out. Hissing Sid had evidently been waiting.

He opened the door of the truck and half lifted Joanna out. 'Hi, Freya! You made good time. Serum's ready. Thank God she could describe the bastard.'

'The bite was partly deflected by her watch-strap. That must have helped.'

'Sure thing.'

'She looks bad. Will she be all right?'

'I don't know,' he replied gravely.

They laid Joanna on a couch and Sid asked her some questions before he gave her the anti-venom serum. She was very sleepy, which worried him. He said quietly to Freya, Joanna's rescuer, 'There's something strange about this. Because of the watch-strap I don't believe she absorbed that much poison. It's as if there's something more, an aspect that we don't know about.'

'Yes, I know what you mean. There's a heaviness about her which I don't understand.'

'I don't like it at all,' he muttered, frowning.

*

By mid morning Helen and Marcus had been out looking for Joanna and were becoming increasingly concerned. 'Yes, of course, she might get up and go for an early morning walk,' argued Helen. 'But not for so long. It's really hot now. Something must have happened to her.'

'Oh, you know Joanna. She's met someone and gone off somewhere. She likes to be a free agent,' replied Marcus with a careless joviality he did not feel. 'Maybe she got a whiff of something to do with the Codes of Power. Nothing would have stopped her,' he added.

'No.' Helen stopped him firmly. 'She's more thoughtful than that. She would have come back and told us if she wanted to go off somewhere. Something's happened to her. I can feel it in my bones.'

'I thought you might say that.' Marcus sighed uncomfortably. 'I'm beginning to get really worried.'

Five minutes later the phone rang and Marcus grabbed it.

'What? Oh no! I'm so sorry!' he said in shock. 'Thank you for letting me know.' He clicked off, looking white and shaken.

'That was Jane from Cooktown. Uncle George died suddenly this morning.'

They stared at each other in disbelief.

Visionaries of old would use snake venom to produce altered states of consciousness in which they could enter higher dimensions. This was done in a controlled way yet often led to death.

Unaware of this and in a totally uncontrolled way, as she lay on the couch in a strange house Joanna slipped into a peculiar trance-like state. She experienced a vision of great clarity. The colours were vivid and extraordinary, like nothing she had ever seen on Earth.

She saw a basket being held by herself, Marcus and her mother. They were handed seven beautiful glowing apples. Each time one of them was given an apple they put it into the basket. They needed another four apples before the basket was full. A beautiful voice told them that they must search for and find three of these by themselves. They were about to set off on the search when a black cloud came down and surrounded Joanna. She could not hear or speak but she knew that one apple was on a shelf in the room where she lay. A second apple was in a cave by a multi-headed mountain surrounded by red sand. Then she looked through water in a pool and she could see the third apple. She tried to reach it but could not. She fell in and thought she was drowning. She gasped and kicked as she struggled to surface.

She must tell Marcus and her mother where the apples were. It was so important. But fight as she did, she could not wake from her weird state. Gradually she lapsed into sleep or unconsciousness.

Hissing Sid eyed her with growing concern. Then he nodded in response to the query in Freya's eyes. 'We'd better get her to hospital.'

Dirk and Billy continued drinking after the pointing the bone ceremony. They started a brawl and Dirk got kicked over. He fell into a crate of bottles, slumping over in a drunken stupor, not knowing his head was badly cut.

When Uncle Philip roused him it was already midday. Congealed blood all round the wound and smeared over his face made him look really badly injured.

'Better get you to hospital,' Philip muttered through his pounding headache, glaring round at the hung-over, drunken forms. 'None of these could help you.'

He pulled Dirk to his feet and half dragged him to the truck. On the way he gave Billy a kick. 'You come too.' He grabbed the slumbering youth by the scruff of the neck with his spare hand and hauled him up.

Billy started to protest loudly. Then the sight of Dirk's bloody head shook him and he almost retched. As Uncle Philip started the engine he muttered, 'Anyone'd think they'd pointed the bone at him.' The look he got from the elder silenced him. Among superstitious people that is not a joking matter.

Freya looked carefully though Joanna's bum bag for a telephone number they could contact. But Joanna had set out for a short walk with a little money and nothing else. 'Look, all I can find is this slip of paper with a mobile number on it,' she said to Sid.

'Better phone it then. Maybe they can throw light on who she is.'

'All right.' Freya dialled the number and plunged into a garbled explanation to the stranger who answered. The woman sounded quite taken aback.

'I don't know anyone like that in Alice Springs,' she

said. 'As a matter of fact I'm on my way there now. I'm in the airport in Sydney waiting for my flight.'

At least she might be able to identify her when she arrives, thought Freya in relief. 'Could you give me your name?'

'Tamsin. She's been bitten by a snake. That's crook. Will she be all right?'

'Hope so. She got the serum pretty quickly but she has been unconscious and—'

'Oh, my God!' Tamsin interrupted. 'I know who it might be. Joanna! Oh no! Not Joanna! Describe her again.'

Freya did so.

'Could be her. Look, I've got her partner's mobile number. Try that. They're calling my flight.' She gave Freya Marcus's mobile number. 'I'll be in touch as soon as I arrive in Alice. I do hope she's all right.'

By late morning Marcus and Helen were getting seriously worried. 'I think we should phone the police,' said Marcus.

'It seems daft. She's a grown woman who's travelled round the world for years. But I've got this awful feeling.' It was probably the twentieth time she had said that.

And then the phone rang. It was Freya, who could only tell them that someone had been bitten by a snake and was unconscious. She directed them to the hospital.

'Bitten by a snake! Joanna!' Helen gasped, her face white-yellow. 'Is she going to be all right?' All she could think of was Hissing Sid with his finger missing and weirdly puckered cheek. For a while she did not even grasp the graver possibilities. Would not allow herself to think of anything else. Marcus did not disillusion her.

They ran to the car and drove to the hospital as fast as they dared, clenched and silent.

Joanna had regained consciousness when they arrived and was sitting propped up in bed, face matching the whiteness of the pillows. Her eyelids were half closed but she managed a ghostly smile when she saw them.

'She's going to be all right,' the nurse reassured them. Marcus and Helen nodded, with eyes only for Joanna. They sat by her bedside, taking it in turn to hold her hand, the one that was not bandaged.

'You were lucky that Freya passed and stopped for you.'

'I know. She and Sid were wonderful.'

Conversation was strained and spasmodic as it often is in hospital. Eventually Helen decided it was time to leave Marcus alone with Joanna. 'I'm going to find a cup of tea. I'll be back soon.' She went in search of a cafeteria and felt much better after refreshment and a time of quiet reflection.

On her way back to see Joanna, as she walked through the waiting room she came face to face with Philip, Billy and Dirk. Her stomach screamed in horror. But here there was no danger. She had even lost all desire for vengeance.

To her eternal credit her first thought was of Uncle George. She stopped as she walked past them. 'I'm so sorry,' she said, her voice sounding slightly wobbly, 'to hear about Uncle George.'

'What about him?' They eyed her suspiciously.

'Oh, I'm sorry. Didn't you know?'

They shook their heads dumbly.

'He died suddenly this morning.'

They looked at one another in blank horror. If they expected to feel elated at this news after they had paid for him to be 'sung', they were wrong.

'Aaah-weeee,' wailed Billy. He stood up and beat his head with his fist.

Philip pulled him down. He was staring transfixed at something or someone behind Helen. She turned but no one was there.

'He was a good man. I'm sorry,' she repeated and walked on. She still could not believe it. So sudden and he was doing such good work.

Behind her she could hear them talking volubly among themselves in their own tongue.

Helen just missed Tamsin, which was probably fortuitous, for the latter stood for some time waiting to enquire where she would find Joanna. As Tamsin waited she became aware of three Aborigines talking urgently in a tongue she understood fairly well. It was not her first language, nor her second, but like so many Aborigines she was an excellent linguist. As she found herself listening she frowned.

Billy had stopped wailing and was now laughing and babbling in excitement. They were boasting about the death of Uncle George whom they had had 'sung' the night before. They talked about a young white woman, Joanna juicy one, who had also been 'sung'. 'I wonder if she'll die too,' smirked the tall thin youth with the nasty gash on his head. They appeared awed at the possibilities they had unleashed. Yet it was tinged with guilt and horror.

The older man was very quiet. 'I was at school with George,' he said at last. 'He was my mate.'

Oh, my God, thought Tamsin. They've had Joanna 'sung'.

She, part black, part white, well understood the depths of the Aboriginal darkness as well as the wonder of their light.

She swivelled and stared fully at them – a sad, patched and dirty, messy trio, who looked at her with eyes bold and frightened at the same time. They knew she had overheard and understood. Somehow they also divined that she was in some inconceivable way connected to what had happened.

With one accord they got up and ran out of the hospital, Dirk's head still untended and congealed with blood.

Chapter 40

As soon as Tamsin discovered where Joanna was she hurried through the doors of the hospital to her ward. Helen and Marcus stood up to greet her as she walked in.

'How is she?' asked Tamsin immediately, taking in Joanna's pallor, yet pleased to see that there was some spark of life in her eyes, which were now open.

'A lot better,' replied Marcus thankfully. 'She's going to be all right. Thank goodness you were able to give Freya the mobile number. We were going crazy with worry, weren't we?' He glanced at Helen who nodded.

Tamsin sensed that they were going to tell her the whole story so she spoke quickly, with that touch of dramatic urgency, which she knew would cause them to hear her out. 'Listen, Marcus and Helen. I've got something urgent to talk to you about. Can you come outside with me for a moment?'

They stared at her in surprise.

In normal circumstances Joanna would have been agog to know what Tamsin wanted to say that was evidently not for her ears, but now she just smiled vaguely and closed her eyes. Not a good sign, thought Tamsin, adding, 'Now!' with a slightly peremptory edge to her voice, which reminded Helen of Joanna on occasion.

They looked at each other. 'Of course,' said Marcus and led the way.

Tamsin's face was set in grim, hard lines, which made her look much older than her years. She described the Aborigines she had seen in the waiting room and told them succinctly about the conversation she had overheard, including the mention of the name, Joanna.

'You mean black magic?' asked Marcus, when she had finished. A year ago, before he understood the information divulged in the Scroll about energy transference, he would have dismissed this as superstitious nonsense. Now he did not. But while he grasped the concept intellectually, he still thought it affected only superstitious people.

Helen's face was set in a mask. She fully understood Tamsin. 'We must put her in extra strong psychic protection immediately,' she said.

Tamsin nodded. 'Yes, that we must do. I think we also need to counter the curse. I will find a karadji who can do this.'

'She did say she felt dreadful this morning as if there was a weight on her heart and she couldn't understand it,' said Marcus. 'I wonder if that was it. Oh, my God. It's inconceivable.'

'No, it's not,' replied Tamsin. 'It's happened.'

'I've just thought of something,' exclaimed Helen. 'Do you think they put the voodoo on Uncle George?' She turned to Tamsin. 'He's a very wise and wonderful elder we knew in Cooktown. Uncle to one of the men you've described. He died unexpectedly this morning.'

Tamsin thought back on the conversation she had overheard. Uncle George had been mentioned. 'Oh yes! They cursed him too.'

Helen had turned grey. She had admired Uncle George so much. He was so wise and generous, so forgiving and understanding. 'How could they do such a thing?' She could not, would not believe it.

But Tamsin was speaking again. 'They could easily have had you "sung" too. I will find a local magic man to clear this curse.' She turned away. 'They deserve to have it turned back on them.'

Marcus stopped her. 'No. There's been too much of that in the past. Let it stop now. By all means get any curses lifted but that's all.' Deep inside him he really could not believe that Uncle George's death and Joanna's snake bite could be a result of an Aboriginal curse. Despite what he had learned from the Scroll his scientific mind rendered it beyond his comprehension.

'Nevertheless,' announced Helen firmly, 'we'll place a universal mirror around each of us, facing them, so that anything they send towards us will be returned to them. That just speeds up the return of karma.'

'Okay,' Marcus responded. 'That feels right.'

Tamsin left urgently on her quest to find a magician who could rescind the curse with a more powerful ceremony, while Helen sat quietly by Joanna's bedside, surrounding her in a universal mirror of protection.

Within a couple of hours the colour had returned to her cheeks and she was laughing.

Joanna told Helen and Marcus that she had had a

vision after the snake bite. 'It's strange. It's the most vivid picture I've ever had. It was so real and I know it's important. I think it's about the crystal ball.'

'Go on. Tell us!' said her mother eagerly.

'Well, the three of us were holding a basket. And we were handed seven beautiful shiny green apples one at a time, which we put in the basket.'

'Right. You think that represents the seven pieces of crystal we've been given?'

Joanna nodded. 'I can't think of any other explanation. I knew we needed four more to fill the basket. This voice said, "You must search for the next three by yourselves." Then just as we were leaving to search for the apples a black cloud came round me.'

'I wonder if that represents you being stopped by the snake bite.' Helen nearly said, 'Stopped by the curse,' but they had not told Joanna yet. She was vulnerable and possibly susceptible.

'I'm sure it does,' agreed Joanna. 'That's what I thought too. Oh and there was something else. The black cloud seemed to clear and I knew that one apple was on a shelf in that room where I was.'

'So one of the pieces of crystal is in the room in Sid's house? Is that what you're saying?' questioned Marcus.

'No. I'm just telling you the dream.'

'All the same,' said Helen. 'We must talk to Sid. Maybe it is there.'

'I think it is,' replied Joanna carefully.

'I'll phone Sid and talk to him.' Marcus was already pulling out his mobile.

'No! Wait until Joanna's better. Then we can ask him,' suggested Helen. 'There's no rush. All is being divinely directed.'

'Even the snake bite?' asked Marcus.

'Quite possibly. The universe works in mysterious ways.'

'I haven't finished telling you two about the vision,' interrupted Joanna and they immediately turned their attention to her.

'Go on!'

'There was a second apple in a cave by a multi-headed mountain surrounded by red sand. Then I looked through water in a pool and I could see the third apple. I tried to stretch my hand into the water to pick it up but I couldn't reach it. I fell in and thought I was drowning. I think that must have been when I went unconscious.'

'A multi-headed mountain surrounded by red sand,' repeated Marcus. 'I wonder where that could be.'

A jovial nurse bustled in to tell them Joanna needed to rest now. 'I suspect she'll be discharged in the morning.' They could hear the nurse chatting with careless insensitivity. 'You were a lucky young woman from what I hear. You got the right serum quickly enough. Those snakes are killers.'

When Joanna was discharged she wanted to thank Sid personally for helping her and to talk to him. They arranged to visit him in the afternoon. 'My snakes are drowsy then,' he joked.

'You don't have them loose in the house, do you?' Joanna was shocked.

But he reassured her, laughing. 'Do you think I'm a madman?'

And so Marcus drove her and Helen over to Sid's house.

'You're a lucky young lady,' he said, when they met.

She laughed, her usual easy good humour restored now that she felt better. 'Now where have I heard that before! I wanted to thank you for all you did, Sid.'

'My pleasure.' He eyed her long bronzed legs clad in scanty shorts with a predatory expression. They followed him into the cool of the bungalow, a bachelor pad judging from the untidy piles of papers and junk everywhere.

'You were lucky Freya passed at that moment. She's got a cool head and she knew where to bring you.'

'I know. I want to say thank you to her too.'

'She'll be around soon. She wanted to see for herself that you were okay.'

Responding to their fascination, he told them enthusiastically about his lifelong interest in snakes. 'Got it from my father. He was just the same. My mom hated them. Wouldn't even go into the garage where the cages were!' He laughed. 'I always said she'd die of a snake bite and my dad would die of old age but it didn't work out that way.'

'Oh?'

'No, a King Brown got him. Can't do much about that.'

'And your mom?'

'She's still going strong.'

They heard a car door slam. 'That's Freya,' Sid said easily, and sure enough Joanna's rescuer walked in, very pleased to see her looking recovered.

'I sure was worried about you.' She laughed. 'You look great.' She helped herself to a Coke from the fridge without asking and when they were all sitting Joanna broached the subject of the crystal chip.

She told them briefly that they were looking for a crystal piece from Uluru with a curved edge. 'It's part of a crystal ball,' she added.

Sid and Freya glanced quickly at one another.

How odd, thought Marcus as he saw a mask descend over Sid's face.

Sid shrugged and said casually, 'There must be millions of bits of crystal like that. What's so special about it?' It felt as if they were all holding their breaths.

Through the mask Sid was observing Joanna with the same one hundred per cent attention with which he watched his snakes. His eyes were very clear, psychic eyes and she knew she must not lie to him. She turned to Helen and Marcus, raising her eyebrows as a question mark. 'I think we should tell them about the Scroll and the Codes of Power.'

They in turn were scrutinising Freya and Sid as if checking their souls. Suddenly Marcus relaxed. 'You're right. I think we should tell them.'

Joanna turned to Helen. She nodded.

Joanna said, 'This might take some time but I'll give you an abbreviated version if I can.' She started in India where the dying monk had told Marcus to take the Scroll to the Mahathat Temple and that its contents would change the world. She touched on the Great Mysteries it revealed and the Illusions. She told them about the inter-dimensional portals at Stonehenge and Machu Picchu and finished by explaining about the Codes of Power and the crystal ball.

They sat entranced, occasionally nodding, even more rarely asking a question.

'What makes you think I know anything about the crystal piece you're looking for?'

Joanna told Sid about her vision of the apples but not where she had seen the apple in his house. As she finished Sid stood up and began to pace the room. 'My father waited for this all his life,' he began. 'And for some years after he died, I waited too. Then I forgot about it. I don't even know where it is any more.' He looked at the junk in the room in a somewhat defeated manner.

Joanna wanted to jump up and scream, 'I do.' Instead she controlled herself and said, 'If you knew where it was, would you give it to us?'

'Of course,' he replied, surprised. 'I guess our family has been holding it in trust for you for lifetimes.'

Joanna jumped up and threw her arms around him in excitement, to his laughing embarrassment. As he clumsily tried to hold on to her he was unaware of the flush of anger spreading over Freya's face.

'Can I look on top of the tall bookshelf?' asked Joanna, pulling herself free. 'I think it might be there. That's where I saw one of the apples in the vision.'

'Climb on the table,' said Sid. 'I'll do it if you like.'

Joanna did not intend to run her hands through the possibly spider-infested top of the bookcase but she wanted to look herself. Marcus read her dilemma immediately.

'Have you got a ladder?'

Sid fetched a ladder from the garage. After clearing a pile of books from the floor he placed it according to Joanna's directions. He tried to help her up the ladder, letting his hand linger on her bare arm but she shook him off as if he were an irritating fly. Marcus was amused by Freya's tight-lipped expression.

Totally oblivious, Joanna shinned up the ladder, heart thumping with anticipation. What if I'm wrong? she agonised as she peeped along the top of the dusty shelf. But she wasn't. There in the dust lay the crystal. Even in the dark, dirty corner it seemed to shimmer and twinkle at her. She reached out her hand and grabbed it tight.

'But why have you got it?' asked Marcus later. 'You're white. I don't understand.'

'Fair do's,' replied Sid. 'Let me get you a beer and I'll tell you. It's a weird story that's for sure.'

Sid opened the fridge and threw cans of beer and soft drinks to everyone in casual fashion.

'Right,' he announced, pulling off the tab as he perched on a hard chair. 'I'll start with my great-grandfather; maybe it was my great-great-grandfather, I don't know. They were among the pioneers who settled here.

'Well, the story goes that an Abo saved my great-great-grandfather's life. Risked his own doing so. And the old ancestor always felt indebted. He protected them as best he could. This was in the times when Abos were hunted like dogs, you know. They were considered to be sub-human savages.' He took a swig, sniffed and ran his hand across his mouth.

A rather unattractive trait, thought Helen.

'Apparently my ancient relative was ahead of his time. He didn't think Blacks should be treated as game sport.'

He looked round at them assessing their reaction. 'One time he hid an Abo from a white mob. It was a brave thing to do, though the Whites couldn't prove it. But as he refused to join their lynch gangs he was considered suspect.'

'Brave man,' commented Marcus.

'Very! They burned his house down. His wife died in the fire leaving him with two young kids. Apparently he nearly went demented.'

'I'm not surprised,' murmured Helen.

'The Whites burned it down?' asked Joanna, surprised.

'I guess so. He rebuilt the house but after that he became quite reclusive. The local Abo clans were deci-mated, hunted down and finished off, you understand. They couldn't pass on the ancient wisdom any more. He used to say it was terrible. One day an old medicine man came to the house and gave him this crystal. Said he was to look after it, for it held great secrets. It was his sacred duty or something to keep it and make sure his children and children's children looked after it, for one day someone would come to claim it. They said he would know when that time was.'

The same story, thought Marcus in wonder. They'd know when the time was.

'And?' asked Joanna with a smile of expectation.

'It was passed down like an heirloom. Now it's yours. Sorry I didn't look after it better.'

'You did perfectly,' said Helen. 'But did the medicine man say what the piece of crystal represented?'

Sid looked stricken. 'There was something. Oh hell! I can't remember. But I'm sure I've seen it written down somewhere.' He jumped up and rummaged through some piles of paper on the table. 'No. It would never be there.' He ran his hand over his prematurely bald head. 'Sorry, guys, I'll think about it and call you. Look, I feel rude rushing you but I've got to go out in five minutes.'

Disappointed, they all stood up, Joanna still cradling the crystal, and said their thanks and goodbyes.

'And you rest, my dear,' he said, clutching Joanna's shoulder with a proprietary air. 'Your immune system's taken a mighty bashing.'

She wriggled from his touch. 'I will,' she replied cheerfully.

Chapter 41

Marcus's mobile aroused him the following morning. Sid's cheery voice announced without preamble, 'I've got it. The bit of paper with the meaning of the crystal on it.'

Instantly Marcus was wide awake. 'What does it mean?'

'Come round and see for yourself. I've got something to show you. Bring all the pieces of the crystal ball with you. I want to see it.' He sounded very pleased with himself.

'Okay. What time?'

'How about breakfast? Eight o'clock?'

Marcus bargained him to 8.30.

'You're on. You'll smell the coffee as you come in. Cheers.'

'Who was that?' murmured Joanna and promptly fell asleep again. With her long brown hair spread across the pillow and a faintly seraphim-like smile on her lips, she looked like some archetypal princess. He thought how much he loved her. Then, kissing her lightly on the cheek, he crept from the bed to look out of the window at the breathless sight of the rising sun lighting up the red desert.

Some birds sang sweetly. Parrots cawed raucously. Early morning tourists were already cramming into buses, and in the middle distance, as if in a different world, a pair of dingoes ran fleetly through the bush.

Marcus sat quietly, watching the dawn for half an hour before Joanna stirred and he was able to tell her the good news.

They truly could smell the coffee as they drove into Sid's somewhat overgrown driveway.

'Mind the spider's webs across the porch. You're the first through it today,' he called as they were about to step through a tangled and luxurious archway, which led to the front patio and front door.

Marcus looked carefully and indeed at head height an intricate web spanned the porch, a fat huntsman spider sitting in the middle of it, glaring at him. 'Sorry, mate,' he said to the spider and broke the web with a stick so that they could safely pass.

Freya had arrived before them. She had ducked under the web, she told them, which made Marcus feel terrible but Sid said, 'Don't worry, that spider must be used to it. I've been telling it for years to spin its web somewhere safer, but it won't listen.'

They laughed. 'Do they live that long?' asked Helen.

'No! But I've said the same thing to his ancestors. You'd think they'd learn. But be careful. They can put you in hospital.'

'Ugh!' responded Helen.

Either Sid or Freya had cleared room on the table and

a battered, old-fashioned, cloth-bound photograph album graced the clutter-free space.

'Did you bring the crystal pieces?' asked Freya eagerly, her blue eyes alight in anticipation.

They shook their heads. 'Sorry,' said Helen. 'We forgot.'

The truth was she had woken with a clear impression that they should not take the pieces of the ball to Sid's house. She could not think why she had such a strong feeling but, when she told the others, they immediately agreed to follow it. 'We said we would always honour our intuition,' Marcus reassured her.

'But I wanted to show them the crystal ball, so nearly complete,' she protested, arguing against herself.

'No, Mum. We'll leave it here.'

'We'll do better than that,' Marcus said, picking up all the pieces and wrapping them in a clean shirt. 'I'll put it in the hotel safe with the passports and money.' He walked purposefully from the room. 'See you at the car in a minute.'

When they said they'd forgotten it, Sid's head jerked up, showing the puckered piece of skin on his cheek and he eyed them closely with his light, clear eyes. No wonder he anticipates the snakes' every move, thought Joanna with a slight shiver. I have a sense that he knows everything that happens.

Sid smiled and looked into her eyes. She knew and ignored that he fancied her.

'No matter.' He shrugged, but for an instant Freya

looked disconcerted and cross. Then Sid walked across to the table and the tension that had hung in the air evaporated.

'Look.' He opened the cover gently with his disabled hand. They could see that the stump of the finger was still scarred. 'This is my great-great-grandfather.'

They could see a faded sepia photograph of a big bearded man, formally dressed in suit and hat, clothes more suited to Europe than the tropics. He looks a tough man, thought Marcus, but he supposed they all must have been in those days. And to stand up against the customs of the day, he must have been remarkable.

On the facing page was a photo of an elegant young woman in a long dress with a pinched waist, long sleeves and hat. She was evidently his wife and could have stepped from an English Victorian picture.

'Phew, she must have been hot,' commented Joanna.

But her mother was looking at the woman's face. Her eyes were too small to call her beautiful but she had delicate features and full, rather pouting lips, which enabled her to pass for pretty and suggested sensuality.

Sid turned the page. 'These are his children, as adults. The boy died in his thirties and the crystal was passed down through the daughter.'

He indicated with his hand a plump woman in her fifties, again formally dressed. Even the photograph gave the impression of someone uncomfortably hot. Maybe it was the brown-orange colour of the photographs in the album. She had a flat, squashed-looking face, which reminded Helen of a dried apricot. She, too, looked tough. No soft fleshy lips on this one. Her mouth was a tight humourless line.

'She was a Christian,' said Sid. 'Fundamentalist I imagine. Here's the piece of paper I told you about.' Very delicately he opened a piece of brownish, fragile-looking paper, which had been folded in two. On it was written in fading ink:

14th March, 1838

On this date the native medicine man known as Silas gave me, Thomas Jamieson, this crystal, asking me to hold it in trust and pass it to my family to hold in trust for the people of the world. I vowed to do so.

He explained it is part of a sacred Aborigine crystal ball from the heart of this land. As he gave me this crystal he went into a strange trance and said as nearly as I can record in proper English, 'Every thing and every creature expresses a different aspect of Byamee. All is part of the Great Spirit.'

I extend this vow to my children and children's children until this crystal is claimed by the right person and fitted into the original crystal ball.

Signed: Thomas Jamieson

'Byamee is a local word for the Great Spirit, is it?' checked Helen.

'Yes. There are different words in each area.' Sid pointed to the bottom of the page. 'You can see he also drew a picture of the crystal piece in case it ever got lost or separated from the paper.' He indicated a diagram under the statement, complete with measurements and full description. 'You can see he took it very seriously.'

'He certainly did,' agreed Marcus. 'He must have been very impressed with Silas, the medicine man.'

Joanna reached over and turned the page back to look at the photo of the old man who had recorded these words so long ago. Sid's hand moved slightly so that he brushed Joanna's arm. She turned away to break the contact and Marcus watched. Freya noticed too and her eyes narrowed.

'Oh, there's something else,' added Sid, carefully turning more pages. 'Here.' He pointed to another piece of paper, lying loosely in the album. 'This was written by his daughter.'

They leaned over to read the copperplate handwriting of Sid's great-grandmother, the Christian with a face like a dried brown-orange apricot.

3rd January, 1879

In respect to my beloved and revered father and in honour of the sacred vow which he took on behalf of the family I keep this crystal in trust and pass it to my son.

My father has recorded the words of a heathen savage for posterity. They are animals and therefore subhuman. They have no souls and cannot be saved. I wish to record that only we Christians are beloved of God and can enter heaven. In the name of Jesus.

Signed: Elizabeth Smythe née Jamieson

They stared at it.

'I know,' said Sid. 'Say no more.' He closed the album. 'It's a pity you didn't bring the other pieces of the ball.

Now I've read the paper again I feel a bit guilty about handing the crystal over without seeing it.'

'Come over to the hotel later and we'll show you,' said Marcus.

'Right.' Sid looked relieved. 'I'll get the coffee and rustle up the breakfast.'

Chapter 42

That night they had dinner with Tamsin, who told them she had phoned many of her contacts about the lifting of the curse. All had directed her to one particular medicine woman, a karadji much revered and honoured, who was reputed to be particularly powerful, but she turned out to be on walkabout. 'I didn't know what to do,' admitted Tamsin, 'but something told me to go to her house anyway and maybe someone would know where she was. When I got there her family told me she had just returned from her journey!'

'Amazing!' they all agreed with a sigh of relief.

'Could she lift the curse?' asked Helen.

'It was extraordinary,' Tamsin continued. 'She came out of the house and stared at me. Her look seemed to penetrate me and I hardly had to tell her anything. It was as if she already knew about it. She just went into a kind of trance, danced and shrieked for ages and ages, then collapsed on to the floor and her family told me she'd taken the curse to herself but she could release it. She did some weird breathing and a lot of coughing and then she came to and said, "Gone! No more trouble from that one." She refused to take any money and sent blessings to you all.'

They all felt incredibly relieved and thanked Tamsin profusely. Joanna felt as if she could breathe again. She hadn't realised that the fear of the curse had been pressing down on her so much. The headache, which she'd put down to the heat, lifted with Tamsin's words and she found herself smiling.

'I suppose some would think it was luck that she returned from walkabout at that time,' said Marcus, 'but I guess it was universal energy at work to place the right person in the right place at the right time.'

'Of course.' Helen smiled. Then she started to bring Tamsin up to date on the latest piece of the crystal ball.

'It's the eighth piece!' interrupted Joanna excitedly. 'Listen! ' She found her notebook and read aloud: 'Everything and every creature expresses a different aspect of Byamee. All is part of the Great Spirit.'

'We Aborigines have always known that.' Tamsin nodded. 'Metaphysically everything represents a divine energy.'

'Like your totems represent an aspect of God?'

'Well, yes.'

'I think we understood it too. For instance when we saw the crocodile we looked to see what message it was bringing to us.'

'And it is interesting,' said Helen thoughtfully, 'that when society changes the animals change too to reflect it. I suppose they are reflecting a different aspect of the divine to the people.'

'Give us an example, Helen,' suggested Marcus.

'I'm thinking of England. Mothers used to stay at home to create nests for their husbands and children and the birds reflected that. When I was a child every garden was full of tits, wrens, robins and blackbirds and thrushes. Lots of hedgerow birds.

'Then land was gobbled up to build more houses. People wanted consumer goods and mothers went out to work to finance the demand. At the same time small businesses and schools and shops were gobbled up by huge consortiums. This was reflected in nature where predatory magpies came into towns and villages and ousted most of the small home-loving birds.'

'Interesting,' agreed Marcus, nodding.

'And the message would seem to indicate that rocks and plants are all simply aspects of the divine.'

'Yes. And the blueprint did say that everything and everyone is equal. So in the eyes of God a leaf is as important as a person.'

'So much for natives being less beloved of God than Christians, as Sid's great-grandmother seemed to believe.' Helen told Tamsin about the photos of Sid's ancestors and the letters they had left.

'There are still a surprising number of people out there who believe that Christians are not just more special, but that they are *the* special ones.'

'In fairness other fundamentalist religions believe the same thing,' put in Marcus quietly. 'But the energy of the crystal ball seems to indicate that everything is not just connected to the divine but is divine. More importantly that everything can transfer divine energy to something else.'

'Lots of people hug trees and give them healing as well as receiving it,' commented Joanna.

'And I know several dogs that are great healers.'

'Cats are healers too. They carry beautiful energy.'

'Surely rocks hold divine energy. Just imagine how high you feel in some rocky places. It's as if the energy is coming from the rocks and charging you up.'

'Yes and it lasts for some time,' agreed Tamsin.

'But we're saying that everything has that potential?' asked Marcus. 'Even the Black Mountain or a crocodile?'

There was a moment's silence. 'Surely it's part of the duality. God is an impartial observer of duality. Everything has energy but the intention expressed by that energy is different. Rocks hold the energy of humans and nature. The Black Mountain holds certain fear energy and radiates it out but it is still expressing the divine.'

'Just a minute. Let me get this straight.' Marcus wanted to be clear. 'One plant heals humans. Another poisons them. Both are divine because everything is part of the Great Spirit, who impartially observes.'

'That is currently the blueprint for the planet at a third dimensional level,' agreed Helen. 'That's where we are right now,' she emphasised. 'But the Codes of Power are giving us an opportunity to reinstate the original blueprint. In those early Lemurian times the light had fully embraced the darkness and transmuted it. Then everything was accepted as an aspect of the divine, on Earth solely to help everything else grow.'

'I think I've got it.' Marcus smiled.

'I feel it's time to move out of Alice Springs if you're up to it, Joanna,' Helen announced as she finished her coffee. 'I think we should go to Uluru. I'm longing to see it and I've got a gut feeling we need to be there.'

'Yes, I think you're right,' agreed Joanna. 'I'm much better today. I'll be glad to get out of here. There's a kind of brooding feeling everywhere.'

'I know what you mean.' Marcus had been patiently waiting for Joanna to recover fully.

'Do you want to come too, Tamsin? Have you got time?' Helen asked her.

'Yes, go on. Do come,' the others urged.

Tamsin shook her head. 'I'm working in Alice tomorrow but I could come for the weekend. I'd like that.' So by the time they'd settled the bill it was agreed that Tamsin would join them at Uluru resort at the weekend.

When they got back to their rooms, Marcus phoned Sid and told him of their plans to set off in the morning to Uluru. 'I'm sorry you'll miss seeing the pieces of the crystal ball,' he apologised.

'Don't worry, mate. I'm off to Uluru myself the day after tomorrow for a snake demo. I'll look you up.'

'Great,' said Marcus, not altogether honestly as he hung up. Despite his extraordinary great-great-grandfather, he was not altogether certain of Sid. Perhaps it was his strangely puckered face where he had been bitten by a snake. Or maybe it was the snakes themselves. Maybe it was because he was slimy with Joanna. Marcus was not sure of the reason but he was not certain he wanted to see Sid.

Joanna, however, said, 'Oh good,' with perfect indifference when he told her and Helen made no comment at all.

Chapter 43

All good plans are made to be broken. They say humans plan and God laughs. After a tedious journey through red, scrub-veiled desert, they stopped for lunch at one of the dusty, concrete roadside eating places with its seemingly mandatory netted area containing a tame camel and an emu. The heat was impossible. None of them wished to risk being fried in order to see the poor animals, so they sat under a kind of arbour to eat their food at a long table with other tourists.

Marcus got into conversation with a tour guide who told him they must on no account miss Stanley Chasm or the Kings Canyon. Her descriptions enthused him to such an extent that nothing would suffice but they turn off at the next junction. 'You'll be okay in a four-wheel drive,' the guide told him airily.

'Let's do it,' agreed Joanna, so they filled extra water bottles and set off intrepidly down the minor road.

The road twisted and turned through sheer cliffs, which rose by the roadside, grey, pink, orange, buff red, deeply grooved and layered. Where the cliff had fallen, little rock wallabies played on the avalanche of boulders. They watched the miniature creatures as they chased each other from rock to rock like squirrels. A mother wallaby squatted patiently on a flat rock, proudly watching her two tiny kittens engaged in a play boxing match.

A few scrubby trees with olive-coloured leaves dripped with bunches of red mistletoe. Spectacular red- and green-coated hills sheered ahead, sporting the bare white trunks and branches of ghost gums.

At last they turned into Stanley Chasm, which according to Helen's guidebook was named after Ida Stanley, who dedicated her life to looking after half-caste children. 'It was formed nine hundred million years ago,' she read aloud, 'and is seventy metres high and five metres wide at the narrowest point.' They climbed out of the vehicle and gazed at the magnificent formations.

Then Helen spotted the loos. 'I can't believe it. Even out here in the middle of nowhere the loos are beautifully painted with murals. Just look at that!' Indeed, the concrete block was decorated with a glorious view and a picture of a rock wallaby. 'Isn't it fabulous,' she said.

They wandered up the gorge, with its vegetation-covered rocks. Incredibly, occasional tenacious bushes managed to get a hold and grow in some twisted fashion, high up on the rock.

There were budgerigars everywhere. Dozens of bright green and yellow birds clung to one tree. At first glance it gave the illusion of being a tree in luxuriant spring growth. Then it was obviously alive with twittering, happy birds, flying off, fluttering round and resettling. All were singing, a choir of sound in the isolated gorge. The trio sat on a rock in silent enchantment.

At last they clambered higher up the gorge until they

were stopped by deep, ice-cold, clear water, which formed a pool between two sheer walls of rock. It blocked the pass. They found a place to squat, relieved to be in the shade, and stared into the water.

Unexpectedly a bird, quite small, they never knew what kind, with a twig in its beak, fluttered in and perched beside them. It seemed totally unafraid. Then it hovered above the water, slightly disturbing the surface. They watched, intrigued. It squawked and perched beside them again.

'It's trying to tell us something,' exclaimed Joanna. She peered into the water. 'I wonder.'

'What?' Helen and Marcus peered too through the crystal-clear, ice-cold water.

Suddenly Joanna screamed, 'There!' She pointed. The bird flew off in panic.

'What? Where?' called out Helen and Marcus again.

'Look. Can't you see it?'

'No. What are you talking about?'

'The crystal. The one I saw under the water. The bird was showing us. It's there.' Joanna pointed down dramatically.

Helen and Marcus gazed intently. Neither could see anything special.

'Are you sure?' said Helen dubiously.

'Of course I am. It's there.' Joanna's face was flushed as if she had a fever. Her eyes were bright. 'Can't you see?'

Marcus and Helen looked at each other, excited, perplexed and concerned.

'Get a stick. Quick!'

Marcus jumped up and searched. Within moments he brought back a branch, from which he broke off extraneous twigs. 'Here.' He handed it to Joanna, who pushed it into the water and touched the bottom.

'Can't you see now? It's pulsing with light.'

Helen felt increasingly concerned about Joanna's mental state, for she could see nothing. Joanna lay down and reached her arm in as far as it would go. She gasped. 'Ooh. It's ice-cold.' She could not quite reach what she wanted and withdrew her arm. 'It's freezing.'

'Hey, let me get it,' offered Marcus but she brushed him aside.

'No. You can't see it. You don't know which one I mean.'

Suddenly she threw herself down on the edge, took a deep breath and plunged her head into the freezing water. She seemed to push with her knees on the side and thrust herself deeper into the water. It happened so quickly they could not stop her. She emerged clutching a stone in her hand.

'I've got it. I've got it. Oh, I'm frozen.' She was grinning inanely, laughing and shivering all at the same time.

Helen grabbed her in typical motherly fashion. 'Quick, into the sunshine. You'll catch your death.'

Joanna let herself be led away, saying, 'But I've got it.'

Marcus said, 'Show me. Is it from the crystal ball?'

Joanna sat on a rock in the sun, long hair dripping and shivering from the shock of the iced water.

'Yes. Yes. When I saw the pool of water I recognised it

from my vision. Then when the bird flew over it, I knew it was trying to give me a message. I looked in and saw the crystal. I knew it at once. I couldn't get you to understand, so I had to get it myself.' She held it out to them. 'Here it is.'

They examined the stone. 'Yes, this is it,' crowed Marcus. 'Clever you, Joanna,' and he gave her a big kiss.

'Well done, love. You were tremendous.'

'All is transparent,' said Joanna.

They stared at her.

'That's what it means. "All is transparent." As I plunged in to retrieve it the words came into my head clearly. "All is transparent."' She paused as if groping for words to explain. 'The blueprint for Earth presumes that everyone is honest and truthful, totally clear in their auras, in other words transparent.'

They looked at her in some awe. As she sat on the rock drying her hair and warming her body, she was held in a shaft of sunlight, and seemed to shimmer.

Later, when her hair was dry and she was warm again, they walked back to the car. Joanna remarked, 'It's so interesting how we were led here. First I got bitten by the snake, which enabled me to have the vision of the pool with the apple in it. Then we felt it was time to leave Alice Springs for Uluru. After that Marcus had the conversation with the tour guide and we decided that it was right to come here, where the bird tried to give us a message. That made me realise it was the pool I saw in the vision and I could see the crystal so I had to reach into the ice-cold water to retrieve it, and I received the meaning.'

'So you were led here step by step!'

'Amazing, isn't it!'

Helen had a sudden flash of Joanna as a priestess of old, trained in clairvoyance. Maybe the snake bite had re-awakened abilities that she had possessed in former lives, which enabled her to 'see' the crystals. Was the clair-voyance temporary or would it last? she wondered.

When she told Joanna and Marcus of her awareness about the snake bite, Joanna groaned, 'Trust my soul to wake me up the hard way,' but she was so exuberant about finding the crystal that she was laughing as she spoke.

'Only two crystals to go. I hope we find them soon. Then we'll have the crystal ball complete.'

'Does that mean we will have passed our initiation into the Codes of Power?' Marcus asked.

'I hope so,' replied Joanna.

Chapter 44

That night they received a reward from the universe. They were forced to check into the campsite at Kings Canyon as they could find nowhere else to stay. So they spread borrowed blankets on the ground and lay out under a superb black, velvet sky, spangled with diamond stars and a crescent moon. Even the birds sang to them, lulling them into profound slumber. They slept in the cradle of heaven and woke deeply refreshed but very hot.

Early next morning in the pink piccaninny light they walked up the uneven steps cut into the orange-red cliff of the canyon. Early as it was, a stream of tourists were taking advantage of the relative cool of morning.

They followed the walk along the rim of the cliff, with its stupendous views through incredible rock formations across the eternal red desert. In places the giant cliffs looked as if they had been sliced with a serrated knife, leaving different coloured layers, every hue from yellow, through white and orange to red.

'What a start to the day!' marvelled Marcus, as they returned to the car. 'And now, Uluru, here we come.'

They thought they had experienced heat earlier. Now as they drove to Uluru, heat seared into the car, rendering the air-conditioning pathetically inadequate. They felt like overheated tomatoes in a tin can. Outside the earth was baked red. The yellow sun, looking so cheerfully innocuous, was savage. It had no clemency. No droplet of water stood a chance.

'I'm never ever coming here again,' moaned Helen, fanning herself with a book. 'I can hardly breathe.'

They drank water as if it was going out of fashion and Helen constantly sprinkled Joanna who was mercifully asleep in the back.

'Think of that ice-cold pool.' Marcus smiled.

'At this moment it feels too tempting.'

'I wouldn't bank on it. You'd probably have a heart attack if you went into it in your overheated state.'

'I don't know. It'd be like the cold pool after a sauna.'

But when they saw Uluru rising from the flat, motionless desert like a red slumbering dinosaur in the distance, it was worth it. The monolith was breathtakingly huge and bare, brick red against the sapphire sky. As they drew nearer they could see that the seemingly smooth rock was scored with fissures and heavily dented.

'So that's it. The keeper crystal for the planet.'

'It's amazing.'

'Incredible.'

'And the crystal within it is like a huge silicone chip on which is recorded the original blueprint for planet Earth,' said Marcus in awe.

'And the entire history of the planet, going back millions and millions of years is recorded in it.'

'Yes, through all the golden ages, which we no longer know about.'

They stopped the car and stared.

'If we bring together all the pieces of the crystal ball, and pass the initiation to the Codes of Power, perhaps we'll hold that energy, so that we can help the planet to become a place of peace and enlightenment,' remarked Helen reverently.

'What a responsibility!' responded Joanna but her eyes were shining.

Marcus was restless.

'Let's come back later at sunset when it's cooler,' suggested Helen quickly, half fearing that Marcus intended to plunge them into the fiery furnace of the outside world to walk up to the great rock.

He laughed, having correctly gauged her thoughts. 'Good idea, Helen. Let's find the resort and check in.'

Tamsin finished work early on Friday and left Alice Springs in the afternoon. A friend had offered her a lift to Uluru in his light plane and she was checking in at the hotel when Helen, Marcus and Joanna returned from their sunset tour.

She joined them later for dinner. 'Do you know who I've just seen,' she remarked as she sat down. 'Sid and Freya. Apparently he's doing his snake talks here this weekend.'

'He told me he was coming down this weekend,' Marcus said.

'I didn't realise they were an item,' remarked Helen. 'I thought they were friends and neighbours.'

'No, I don't think they're partners,' Tamsin replied. 'But she said she fancied a trip to Uluru so she came with him.'

Joanna shivered suddenly. She felt as if someone had walked over her grave. Later, when the feeling had passed, she leaned her elbows on the table and said, 'You know the vision I had of the apple in the cave is as vivid as ever.'

'Tell me again,' begged Tamsin.

Joanna closed her eyes to picture it. 'There are a huge number of undulating domes in the middle of the red sand. The sun is rising and the rays shine into this low cave. The apple sits under a ledge on the right-hand side of the cave as you enter. Outside there is a bare tree, bleached white. There's a big bird sitting on it. I don't know what it is.' She opened her eyes. 'Wow. I saw more this time.'

'I think that's Kata Tjuta. You call it the Olgas,' exclaimed Tamsin triumphantly. 'It means many heads. There are thirty-six domes. I'm sure that's where your vision is.'

By now they were all very excited. 'Hang on,' said Tamsin prudently. 'It's a vast area.'

'Yes, but we know about the position of the cave. The rising sun strikes it and there's a dead tree outside it.'

'And what about the bird? Perhaps it often perches there.'

'Could do. I don't know.'

'Can you remember anything else, Joanna?' asked Marcus.

But she could not.

'Let's look at a map of Kata Tjuta,' suggested the pragmatic Tamsin.

'There's one in my guidebook,' said Helen. 'I've got it here.' She pulled a battered, well-thumbed book from her bag and looked the Olgas up in the index.

'Here!' She passed the open book to Tamsin, who set it down in front of Joanna. 'The sun would rise here in the east, I think. Yes, that's right.' She turned the book slightly.

Joanna appraised it, her hand with one finger pointed hovering over the page. 'I'm not sure but I'm drawn to here.' She pointed to an area covering three of the hills.

'Good,' said Marcus. 'You've done brilliantly, Joanna. That will narrow it down.'

'We were told to use our intuition. I'm sure the universe will help us find the crystal. Look what's happened already,' Helen declared stoutly. 'If you look for a needle in a haystack, it's impossible. But if you have a dirty great magnet, the needle will jump out to you. In our case we're all magnets and the crystals are coming to us.'

'I like that analogy,' said Marcus. 'Yes, I like it.'

But Joanna said in a worried tone, 'I just hope my intuition was right and that my head didn't get in the way.'

The following morning Joanna felt tired. She still had not fully recovered from the snake bite. 'You go to the Olgas without me,' she suggested to Marcus. But he would not have it.

'No,' he insisted. 'I'll wait for you. We still have a few days before we leave Australia. We can go tomorrow.'

'Thanks.' She smiled and he realised just how much she wanted to be with them when they looked for the tenth crystal and how much she hoped they would find all of them before time ran out.

'It's okay. I'm learning lessons in patience.' He grinned. 'What do you fancy doing today?'

'I know Mum's longing to visit the Aborigine cultural centre and I'd like to see it too.'

'Good idea and then we can always go to Sid's snake show,' he said, poker-faced. She threw a pillow at him and he laughed.

Helen was breakfasting with Tamsin when they reached the dining room. Tamsin said she had been to the cultural centre lots of times and would spend the morning quietly at the resort. They agreed to meet later.

'Let's grab our sunhats and go,' suggested Marcus as they walked back to their rooms after breakfast.

'Won't be a second,' said Helen. 'You did put the things in the safe last night, didn't you, Marcus? I've still got my passport.'

'No. You're right. I forgot and I've been conscious of leaving the pieces of crystal ball in our rooms. Give me your crystals and your passport, Helen and I'll take everything to the safe on the way out.'

She popped into her room to fetch her passport and the pieces of the precious ball.

'Thanks,' said Marcus. 'I'll go to reception with them now. See you two at the car in a minute.'

*

Three hours later they returned to the hotel after a fascinating trip, longing for nothing more than a cool swim followed by a siesta. There was a problem at reception when Helen's door key was missing from the peg.

'I'm sure I didn't take it with me.' She frowned. 'Where is it?'

'Perhaps you popped it into your bag?' suggested the receptionist.

'No. I handed it in.' All the same she tipped everything out of her bag but there was no sign of the door key. The receptionist was very pleasant and gave her a spare.

But when Helen unlocked the door she had a shock. The room had been ransacked. Every drawer was open and the contents tipped out. Her suitcase had been turned upside down on the floor and everything thrown haphazardly as if someone had searched it in a hurry. The pillows and bedclothes had been stripped off and dropped.

She gasped loudly.

Marcus, in the act of opening his door, turned. 'What's the matter?' In an instant he was behind her, looking over her shoulder at the trashed bedroom. His jaw was clenched. 'Call reception, Joanna. I'll check our room.' But no one had been in there.

'They must be after the crystal ball,' said Joanna, as she surveyed the chaos.

Shaken, Helen sat on the edge of the bed.

'Who knew about it and the Codes of Power?' asked Marcus.

'Well, Dirk, Billy and Philip obviously know about the crystal ball. So do Sid and Freya.'

'It can't have been Sid or Freya. They saved my life.'

'Tamsin knew about it.'

'And people like Stephen and Martha but they're in Sydney.'

'Who knew your room number?'

Helen concentrated. 'Tamsin. No one else. But someone only had to ask reception.'

'Hmm.'

Marcus frowned. He didn't know where it came from but a nasty suspicion about Sid came into his mind. He had no rationale for it but it buzzed in his brain until Joanna's voice, shrill with tension, knocked the thought out. 'Is the crystal ball okay in the safe?'

'I'll check it,' Marcus said firmly. He strode out, returning ten minutes later, looking relieved.

The hotel called the police and they wasted all afternoon waiting for someone to come. Eventually a young policeman turned up, who asked if anything had been taken.

Helen said, 'I don't think so. Money and everything was in the safe.'

'Good,' he said and almost shrugged. 'Ground floor. Kids, I expect.'

'But how did they get in?'

'Was the window open?'

'No.'

After a perfunctory glance round the policeman said, 'Someone must have found your key and got in. You were lucky nothing was taken, madam.' And he left, leaving Helen feeling as if she were to blame.

Later, when everything had been picked up and order restored, they went to talk to the receptionist.

Helen said, 'I can remember handing the key in at reception this morning.'

'Yes, you did, Mum.' Joanna supported her. 'We walked out together because Marcus went ahead to the safe.'

The receptionist, pink-faced and defensive, clearly felt she was going to be in trouble. Almost in tears, she re-iterated that she had been at the desk all morning. Suddenly she stopped. 'Except when the man slipped on the steps in front. I ran out to help him. Of course I left the desk then for a few minutes.'

She paused for a moment, thinking. 'No it's nothing.'

'What?' asked Marcus.

'It's just that he swore someone pushed him. He was quite old, a bit tottery, you know. On a tour. Japanese. He was all right. Just a bit shaken.' She frowned. 'I remember. He didn't speak good English but his tour guide kept saying he said that someone pushed him.'

'Can I talk to him?' asked Marcus quickly.

The receptionist shook her head. 'No, they left for Alice.'

'Damn,' said Marcus.

'There's nothing more we can do,' said Helen. 'I'm going for a swim.'

'Me too,' said Marcus.

But Joanna wanted to lie down. 'I'll have a snooze while you swim. If you let me into the room, Marcus, you can take the key. That way you won't disturb me if I'm asleep when you come back.'

So Helen and Marcus swam and lazed and chatted. Then Marcus took himself off to explore while Helen settled back on a lounger with a book. At least we're safe here, she thought, relieved.

Chapter 45

In the room Joanna felt hot and drowsy. She turned the air-conditioning to maximum and lay on the bed. Before she closed her eyes she glanced at her notebook and read:

The crystal ball coded with the blueprint for the planet.

1 Humans are caretakers of Mother Earth.
2 Everything is in balance.
3 Life is a celebration. Celebration is gratitude to Great Spirit and helps us to connect.
4 Humans' task is to maintain harmony between humans and the natural world and revere all life.
5 Everything and everyone are equal.
6 Learn from and honour the differences.
7 All are to share and care for each other. There is enough for all.
8 Everything and every creature expresses a different aspect of the divine.

She picked up a Biro and added:

9 All is transparent.

Then she smiled to herself as she pulled up the sheet and dozed.

*

She was asleep when she heard the key in the lock. Marcus is back already, she thought and turned over. But something about the way the door closed made her open her eyes, suddenly alert. She sat up in bed.

Freya stood there, a sack in her hand and a peculiar expression on her face.

'What's going on? Freya?'

'Yes. It's me.'

'What are you doing here?'

'I want the crystals.'

'You want the crystals,' Joanna repeated stupidly. Her eyes dilated in horror as she saw the sack, which the older woman was holding half hidden behind her back. Instinctively she backed away.

'I want the crystals now! I want the Codes of Power!' hissed Freya, looking satanic. Her lips were bloodless and her eyes pale and hooded. 'Give them to me and I won't let this beauty out.'

Joanna stared at her, white-faced. She didn't say, 'You wouldn't dare,' because one look at Freya's face told her that she would.

'They're in the safe.'

'I don't believe you,' Freya was arrogantly certain. 'Okay, have it your way.' And she moved to open the sack.

'Why do you want the Codes of Power?' asked Joanna, pulling herself together by sheer force of will. 'What can you do with them?'

'I'll have power,' she replied. 'Power to do what you can do without trying. Do you realise,' she snarled, 'that

I have known Sid for thirteen years. Thirteen years! I'm the one who nurses him. Gets his shopping. And he doesn't know I exist as a woman. Once he slept with me when he was drunk. Once. And next day he couldn't remember. And you . . . He undresses you with his eyes. And you don't care. You don't want him.'

The venom in her voice was more dangerous than that of any taipan. Suddenly Joanna understood this was not about the blueprint of the planet.

'You trashed my mother's room.'

Freya nodded. 'Easy to get the key. Pushed the old man over and the receptionist rushed to help him leaving the desk untended. I did the same thing just now. Didn't realise you were in or I needn't have bothered. Just thought I'd wait for you and give you a little surprise.' Evidently she was pleased with herself. She was moving nearer to the bed. 'Give me the crystal ball.'

Joanna forced her voice to stay steady, though she knew it was trembling slightly. 'I've told you. It's in the safe.'

Freya smiled the most horrible twisted smile that Joanna had ever seen.

'Stupid. You're still lying. You'll regret it.'

'I'll get it from the safe,' offered Joanna.

But the woman screeched suddenly, loudly, 'Think I'm stupid.' And with a flick of her wrist she had opened the sack and thrown the slithering and terrified snake on to the bed.

Freya backed very slowly and silently to the door and let herself out.

*

As Marcus was returning from a very satisfactory walk, his mobile rang. It was Tony with news of the Codes of Power. 'Can I phone you on a land line?'

'Sure!' Marcus gave him the hotel number. 'I'll be back there in fifteen minutes. I'll grab Helen from the pool on the way.'

He hurried back into the hotel and found Helen dozing in her chaise-longue with the book on the ground and a frown on her face. He touched her lightly on the shoulder and she started. 'Oh, Marcus! I just had the most horrible dream about snakes.'

'Oh, poor you! Perhaps it's about what happened rather than about what's going to happen.' Marcus's stomach sank but he did not have time to pursue it now. 'There's good news. Tony's just phoned. He's phoning on the land line in fifteen minutes.'

Helen jumped up and gathered together her things with alacrity. She tried to shake off the horrible feeling.

As they hurried into the vestibule, Sid came out looking worried. 'Have you seen Freya?' he called.

'No.' They spoke at once. Something in his tone of voice made them stop.

'She was acting strangely this morning. I can't find her and I've just been to set things up for tonight and one of the snakes is missing. She was the only one with a key to the cages.'

Helen thought she was going to swoon. Things about Freya and Joanna that she had never thought of before instantly became totally clear. She pushed Sid aside, ran along the corridor and hammered on Joanna's door, then shook the handle but there was no sound from inside. Marcus took in at a glance that their door key was not on the rack behind the reception desk. Joanna must be in there. 'Give me the master key! Hurry!' he shouted at the receptionist, who responded immediately. Marcus grabbed it and raced after Helen, reaching their door first. Sid and the receptionist followed, arriving as Marcus got the key in the lock and flung the door open with a crash.

'Oh, my God!' Marcus yelled.

Helen screamed.

Joanna sat immobile and frozen like an ice statue, while the snake, which had been curled up on her leg, was poised and hissing at them. With a fluid movement, Sid pushed past them.

When the door slammed behind Freya, Joanna froze in shock and horror. She knew the snake was frightened and therefore dangerous. She knew snakes can smell fear and that they seek out warmth. Most of all she knew she must not move.

Immobile with dread she didn't dare even to blink. A fly landed on her and for once she did not even feel it. She tried to breathe shallowly so that there was no movement but her heart was thumping so loudly she knew the snake must sense it.

If I move it'll get me, she thought. The snake was on high alert, its tongue flicking, sensing for danger.

I must render myself harmless. Initiates used to keep

snakes at bay with their thoughts. But I'm not an initiate. Her thoughts went round. I'm going to die. No! she screamed at herself silently. Just stay still. Try to meditate. But she dared not close her eyes. Better to see the danger.

Because she had been breathing so shallowly she inadvertently took a bigger breath. The snake felt the minuscule movement and swivelled to face her. I wish I'd gone to the snake show. I might have known what to do. But reason told her there was nothing she could do.

She remembered the fangs of the other snake biting her, the pain, the feeling of the venom being injected, and broke out into a cold sweat. Don't think about it. Remember it's frightened. Send it peace and love.

So this she tried to do. She gathered every ounce of courage and strength and sent the creature love. She imagined it feeling safe and relaxing. Then suddenly she thought, What will happen when Marcus comes? Will he be attacked? And the horrible treacherous thought crept in, If I'm alive. Of Freya she thought nothing at all.

And so minute after elongated minute crept by.

After a long time the reptile relaxed its strike position and moved nearer her. Sensing warmth, it snaked up to her leg and half curled on it. If anything her sense of dread was greater now. She must relax. She must conquer her fear. Her hands were ice-cold and clammy, every inch of her body rigid with tension.

And then she heard rushing footsteps and the sound of a key scraping. There was a crash as the door was flung open. The snake reared instantly into attack position, facing the new danger. Joanna sat still as a statue though she could not control ice-cold shaking.

'Stay still,' Sid said in a low voice filled with urgency. No one needed telling. His eyes searched the room for something, anything he could use as a pronged stick. Nothing.

Helen inched backwards out of the room, pulling the receptionist by the arm. 'A broom,' she whispered. 'We need a broom.' The girl nodded and ran down the corridor to a broom cupboard. She opened it, grabbed a mop and hurried back. Wordlessly Helen grabbed it from her and held it up for Sid to see. He nodded and slowly, slowly she fumbled it to him, her hands slippery with sweat, fearing she would drop it. She found she was holding her breath.

Freya had left the sack on the floor. Evidently she did not care if she was caught. Slowly, carefully, Sid bent and picked it up. He crept towards the bed. Perspiring even in the cool room, very slowly he eased the snake with the mop handle away from Joanna. Eyes huge, she was watching everything in total shock.

He opened the sack and the snake slid effortlessly into it. He pulled the drawstring tight. Joanna held her arms out to Marcus and he leaped across the room and held her. Sid ran from the room in search of Freya but she had disappeared.

When Tony rang Helen answered the phone and was evidently deeply shocked. She explained the horror of what had happened. It all seemed surreal somehow. 'They haven't found Freya. She's disappeared and she's mad. She could do anything.'

Tony listened to her words and heard the panic underneath them. He comforted her as best he could, then said that he would phone back later.

She realised later that she had not even asked if he had finished his book or about the Codes of Power. For that minute she did not even care. She put the phone down and walked over to Joanna and looked tenderly at her pale, thin face.

Joanna looked back at her with big brown eyes. 'It's okay.'

'I know. It's over. The police will find her.'

'Mum, it was the most terrible thing I've ever experienced.' Joanna was shaking and all Helen could do was make a cup of tea.

They let Joanna talk and talk. They all talked. Tamsin heard the rumour and arrived distraught and horrified.

Sid came back to the room and heard with mounting distress what Freya had said to Joanna. Comprehension was beginning to dawn. 'I had no idea. No idea at all.' He looked Joanna in the eyes. 'I'm so sorry.'

She could see his regret. 'It's all right. It's not your fault,' she said and meant it.

'And I owe you an apology too,' Marcus said to Sid. 'I thought you trashed Helen's room looking for the pieces of the crystal ball.'

Sid frowned, puzzled. 'But I gave you one of the bits.'

'Yes, I know. But you didn't know then how powerful it was. And I thought, well, maybe you gave away one to get hold of all the crystal pieces we have so far.'

'The only problem is' – Sid's tone lightened – 'you're the ones who've been chosen to bring it together. I haven't. I don't have your sense of destiny. In fact I was just pleased to be able to help in some way. It felt good.' He nodded. 'Yes, it felt very good to think that my family held the stone in trust.'

Marcus shot out a hand and shook Sid's. 'Thanks.'

The police arrived and Joanna told the story again, without mention of the crystals or the Codes of Power. 'Don't worry, love. We'll get her,' they reassured her.

She was beginning to look better. 'I'm starving,' she announced with a return of her irrepressible grin. 'I need to keep my strength up to go to the Olgas.' She looked at Tamsin. 'Sorry, I mean Kata Tjuta tomorrow. We've got a destiny to meet.'

Chapter 46

They phoned the police before they left at first light for the Olgas but Freya had not been caught.

'Weird.' Helen frowned uneasily. 'Where can she be?'

'I'm sure it'll be fine,' Marcus reassured her, with male confidence. 'Between us we won't let Joanna out of our sight.'

'And Tamsin's coming with us too,' reminded Joanna.

'You're right of course. Everything'll be all right.' Helen wanted to be persuaded.

As they left the hotel the sun was rising, a magnificent red ball of light, illuminating everything it touched. Rock formations became luminous, as if they were alive. A kangaroo glowed orange so that it seemed to be on fire as it bounced through the flat expanse of spinifex, mulga scrub and occasional black skeletal trees. Gradually the sky transformed into a wash of pale blue streaked with apricot and dotted with puffs of pale pink. Already it was furiously hot.

Soon they could see the domes of Kata Tjuta nestling like giant eggs in the distance.

They parked and, on Tamsin's advice, started to follow the track of the Valley of the Winds walk. They looked out for the cave of Joanna's vision, though as many of the escarpments were dotted with them, they soon realised it was an impossible task.

'We've been led so far. We'll be shown, if it's right,' Helen reminded them wisely. She knew Marcus was impatient.

'Only two more,' he kept saying.

'And the tests that go with them,' warned Helen soberly. But he was in ebullient mood.

'Keep your eyes open for a biggish bird, something like a hawk,' suggested Joanna. And so they walked and marvelled at the display of light and shade on the rocks.

'I think this was an initiation site,' said Tamsin quietly as they skirted one of the sleeping domes. Close up they could see that the smooth rock was gouged and pitted. Black streaks proved to be lichen. It was getting hotter and hotter.

Helen fanned irritating bush flies from her flaming cheeks. At last she said apologetically, 'I must sit down. Can we sit in that shade for a little while?'

They all acquiesced gratefully.

'Look, you go on,' Joanna said to Marcus and Tamsin. 'I'll wait with Mum.'

'No, I've walked far enough,' declared Tamsin. 'Marcus, why don't you look round the next dome and we'll wait here.'

'Okay.' Marcus was happy to stride on in the blazing heat. 'Just take care of Joanna, won't you.'

'We'll be all right.' They waved languidly as he strode off.

*

Sid was up early. He had changed the locks so that no one could touch his snakes. He had been more badly shaken by Freya's actions and the revelations accompanying them than he cared to admit. He could not understand it. He felt angry, perplexed and in turmoil. Somewhere deep inside he felt that Freya was not in her right mind and might still harm Joanna. With this in his thoughts he walked round the hotel, keeping his eyes open, but Marcus and the others had left already, so he did not see them.

He wandered down to the car park but could not see their vehicle. That was strange! Deep in thought, he walked into reception and asked after Joanna.

'Oh,' said the receptionist, smiling. 'She was right as rain this morning. Brave girl.' She shuddered. 'They went off to the Olgas. Best thing if you ask me to keep her mind off it. They haven't caught the woman though. If you ask me . . .'

Suddenly like a lightning flash Sid remembered Joanna's vision. The apples. The tenth crystal. He tried to remember what she had said. They were going to the Olgas to seek the cave where the crystal was hidden. And Freya most certainly knew that. In the same instant he clearly knew she was mad. She could do anything.

Sweat poured from him, not just the sweat of heat, the sweat of terror. He turned and ran, leaving the receptionist open-mouthed.

'Rude man,' she muttered.

Sid raced to his truck and sped down the road to the

Olgas. 'Damn!' he kept repeating. 'Damn! Let me get there in time.'

He raced in a cloud of dust, cursing, trying to reach into the mind of this woman he had known for so many years, thought of as a friend and helper. This woman who had loved him in a strange perverted way and had finally flipped. At last he realised he did not have a clue what she might do. He could only try to stop it, whatever it was. Every gut instinct told him that there was danger ahead. Joanna was in deadly danger.

Marcus was soon out of sight of the women. His sharp eyes were scanning the rock sides, looking for anything that might alert him to the cave Joanna had described. He started when he saw a large bird floating over the rocks but it did not perch. Nothing else seemed to be moving. He was frying alive in the sun. Better be careful of sunburn, he thought and walked off the path into a shady gully between two of the rock formations. A lizard scuttled suddenly and made him jump. Then again the uneasy silence.

He glanced up and what he saw made his heart lurch. A large bird of prey seemed moulded to a dead tree. It sat utterly still. Behind it was a cave, fronted by a ledge.

I wonder! Oh, please let this be the one. It was quite high up but there had been a rock fall, so that he could clamber over fallen stones and then pull himself up the face for those few feet. If that tree would hold his weight, he thought he could make it. If not the ledge ran round to the other side of the rock and he could get at it from there.

As he scrambled over loose stone, the bird flew languidly away.

I ought to tell the girls, Marcus thought guiltily. But I'll just have a quick look. Won't take a sec. And if I can't make it, I'll go back.

His heart was pounding with exertion and excitement as he hauled himself up the last three feet to the cave, gripping the prickly and uneven base of the thin tree. His trousers were torn and his hands scraped but he made it.

He expected the cave to be shallow but it was not. The sunlight flooded the entrance and he stooped to enter.

She saw the apple on the right under a ledge, he reminded himself. The cave seemed to go back a long way. He paused to let his eyes become accustomed to the dark and then shuffled in, feeling the left-hand wall.

'Hello,' said a woman's voice. A familiar voice. His blood ran cold. It was Freya, sitting in the dark waiting.

'What are you doing here?' he managed.

'Just stay still. I've got a gun and I know how to use it. And I can see you but you can't see me.' She laughed harshly, manically.

'What do you want?'

'You know what I want. The crystal for the Codes of Power.'

'I don't know where it is.'

'Then what are you doing here?'

He was silent. Then he said, 'Looking for it.'

'It's okay. I've found this one. Thanks to your lady love.' She held up her hand. 'I just want the other ones.' He stared into the gloom towards her. He could make out her shape. 'All of them.'

She was right. He was silhouetted against the mouth of the cave. He was a clear target. *I must talk to her. Get her on my side,* he thought, trying to clear the fog of panic from his mind.

But at that moment a pebble fell at the mouth of the cave and the sound reverberated. She called out, 'All right, lads. He's yours.'

Two dark forms appeared at the mouth of the cave. Dirk and Billy. In an instant Marcus knew he had to fight for his life. Like lightning he twisted and swung a fist at Billy, connecting with his chest. Billy staggered back and glanced his head on the side of the cave.

Ducking instinctively, Marcus only partly avoided Dirk's boot which had been aimed for his head. It caught him in the side and hurt like hell but he could not afford to feel pain. As he kicked out, Dirk had been knocked off balance and Marcus leaped to take advantage of it with a quick punch at Dirk's head. Though the space restricted him he caught the back of the youth's head, where it was already cut, opening the old wound. Blood gushed and blinded him for a second.

Now Billy recovered and jumped on to Marcus's back. Marcus backed him against the side of the cave as hard as he could. He felt Billy slump and let go but Dirk was wiping the blood from his eye with his arm. He was filled with murderous rage.

'That's for killing my Uncle George,' he shouted, punching Marcus in the shoulder.

Marcus kicked him, catching his shin. Dirk fell and Marcus plunged past them on to the ledge. He stood at the side of the cave entrance and kicked the next person to come out. It happened to be Freya. The gun flew into space and she clutched her broken arm, screaming.

Billy lumbered from the cave and grappled with Marcus but Billy was woozy and Marcus pushed him until he slipped and with a tearing scream slid over the edge down the rock face and over the scree, tearing the flesh on the entire front of his body and slumping into a heap.

Dirk charged like a bull out of the cave. Marcus could have tripped him over the ledge but he did not. Dirk realised this and looked at him, puzzled. Then he looked over the ledge and saw his friend lying on the rocks drenched in blood.

Billy called, 'Help! Please, Dirk!' But Dirk had fainted.

Marcus left him and clambered down to Billy, whose skin was scraped raw. He looked a terrible mess and was in a lot of pain. 'Can you move?'

'Yes.'

By the time he was fairly sure that nothing was broken and that Billy's injuries were mainly bruising and massive scrapes and gouges, Dirk had recovered and was standing over them. All the fight had gone out of him.

'Is he all right?'

'Yeah, I think so but he needs medical attention or care of some sort,' he added, thinking of their Aboriginal remedies.

'Why are you helping him?' asked Dirk, puzzled. He paused. 'After what we've done.'

'Because it's got to stop, mate.' He stood up. 'The Whites did terrible, appalling things to your people and you and Billy did awful things to Helen. If we seek revenge on you it just carries on. I can't speak for anyone else but I forgo my revenge.'

He looked full into Dirk's dark eyes and all he could see was the fear and hopelessness of his people. 'It's got to stop now. We've got to work together. This crystal is about loving and supporting each other not power or gold.'

He saw something change in Dirk's eyes.

Then Sid, followed by Joanna and Tamsin, with Helen in the rear, charged round the corner. 'Hang on!' Sid shouted to Marcus. Then he looked up and saw Freya on the ledge in front of the cave holding her arm and whimpering.

'Hell. It's you! What have you done?'

'She had a gun.'

'Where is it?'

Marcus and Dirk together were helping Billy up. Marcus waved towards the scree. 'Down here some-where.'

Joanna shouted, 'Marcus! Are you all right?'

'Just about.' He grinned somewhat lopsidedly as his

mouth was beginning to swell where he'd caught a punch.

'She's got the crystal,' he said and glanced up at Freya.

'Right!' Joanna launched herself at the cliff but could not reach the tree to get enough purchase to pull herself up.

'Be careful!' called Helen.

'Let me go first,' said Sid and hauled himself up. He gave Freya a look more venomous than any viper. 'Up,' he ordered but she shook her head.

'I can't move.' He tried to pull her to her feet but she screamed with pain.

'Sid, help me,' called Joanna and he lay down on the ledge and reached down to pull her up.

She went straight to Freya, whose good fist was clamped around the stone. 'Give it to me,' she ordered.

'No! ' Freya shrank from her.

Joanna stood over her. 'Give it me or I'll kick your arm,' she spat.

Freya took one look at her and opened her palm, with a mew like an injured kitten. Joanna was unmoved. She grabbed the crystal.

'You would have done too!' exclaimed Sid, looking at her with new eyes.

'Oh yes. There are times for compassion and times for firmness.' She folded a tissue round the stone and placed it carefully in her bum bag. 'That's ten. It means love and support each other.' She thought it was strange how 'knowing' kept coming to her since the snake bite.

She glanced at Freya. 'The ambulance is on its way. And the police.'

None of them remembered Philip or wondered what he was up to.

Chapter 47

Joanna was covering Marcus's bruises with arnica and gently cleaning his wounds. Her fingers felt cool and tender.

Tamsin was making them a cup of tea. She said, 'I heard what you said to Dirk, Marcus. You're right. It's time revenge ended. Tit for tat in families. Eye for an eye between countries. Everyone ends up blind.'

'I know,' agreed Joanna. 'It's got to end now, not just when we've had another swipe and we're on top.'

'Are you advocating no more punishment?'

'Not really. I suppose I'm thinking more of justice with mercy or even justice with common sense. Take Freya.' She shivered. 'I have a bad feeling whenever I think of her and I feel she needs to be kept in a safe place for her own protection, so that she doesn't earn more karma and, of course, for the protection of others. I don't think it's a question of punishment, more of treatment. She's mad.'

'In our culture we'd say she'd been taken over by a bad spirit, which needs to be exorcised.'

'I agree but I think the bad spirit is her own jealousy and envy.'

Tamsin nodded. 'We'd say her jealousy and envy called in a bad spirit.'

'I think we're saying the same thing. Either way she needs to be cleansed psychologically and psychically so that a new better spirit lives in her.'

'I don't think prison will do that,' murmured Marcus.

'Do you think she'll go to prison?'

'I expect so,' he replied.

'Is that what you want?' Tamsin asked Joanna, who shrugged. 'It's a strange thing. I feel as if it happened ages ago and I don't really care any more.'

Marcus said, 'I'd forgotten until now. When I was fighting off Dirk, he shouted, "That's for killing my Uncle George."'

Joanna said, 'It's almost laughable, isn't it, how we can't cope with our own darkness.'

'What do you mean?' asked Marcus.

Tamsin explained. 'When someone does something terrible that they can't subsequently accept, they go into denial. Then they project it out and believe that someone else did it.'

'Yes,' agreed Joanna. 'Everyone does it but not usually on such a big scale. We only hate people who exhibit our own denied behaviours or beliefs.'

'Countries do it too. It's the biggest cause of war.'

'I know.'

'Dirk too needs help,' said Tamsin.

In the next room Helen was phoning Tony. She did not care what time it was and he had said, 'Phone any time, day or night.'

He answered the phone.

347

'What time is it?' she asked.

He recognised her voice. 'Early in the morning. Very early. Is everything all right, Helen? How's Joanna?'

'Joanna's okay, but . . .' And she told him what had happened that morning.

He listened in horror. When she had finished he said, 'You need someone to look after you.'

I wish! she thought ruefully but she said, 'At least we got the crystal piece. According to Joanna it means, "Love and support each other." Now there's just one more piece. Only one more. Oh, I do hope it comes to us before we have to leave.'

'So do I,' he said. 'I can't stand the suspense and I'm not even there.'

They laughed and he said, 'It's good to hear you laugh again, Helen.'

'Another bit of good news. Sylvie's son and his girl-friend have offered to fly here and drive the four-wheel drive back to Cairns.'

'That's good of them.'

'I know. Everyone has been unbelievably kind and helpful.

Tony cleared his throat and continued in a hearty voice. 'Did you get my e-mail? I sent it yesterday when I couldn't speak to you.'

'No. We haven't logged on.'

'Okay. Let me read it to you. It's very important. The Lemuria section of the Scroll says that those who seek initiation into the Codes of Power must have demon-strated certain behaviours:

' "Whosoever has passed initiation into the Codes of Power is in service to the planet and carries certain symbols of power within the aura. Initiation confers responsibilities and a higher state of consciousness. These initiates will find themselves placed where they are needed on Earth. They will follow the call of the highest and walk in the footsteps of those Great Ascended Ones who lead the planet forward. This is not an easy path but those who attempt the initiation are serving the universe itself. All will have demonstrated the following:" Just listen to this.'

'Go on, tell me.'

' "All will have demonstrated the following," ' he repeated and continued: ' "The integrity to defend someone or speak out against injustice. Harmlessness towards every thing and creature. The ability to walk alone. The courage to face fear. The power to speak and act with wisdom. Forgiveness. Generosity and compassion." '

Helen swallowed. 'I don't think I've done all that.'

'I'm pretty sure you have. You've been tested enough.'

'Anyway we've tried,' she continued philosophically. 'We were given the opportunity and we've all faced the challenges as well as we could.'

'I think many people now are going through this initiation,' said Tony. 'Look at the chances on offer for forgiveness and courage. Wouldn't it be excellent if everyone realised this and war and fighting ended?'

'It would indeed.'

'Look, Helen, I've got my own challenge of courage and it's to do with you.'

'Me?'

'I've got something to ask you when you come back to England. Something very special.'

She blushed like a teenager and her knees wobbled but not with fear.

While they were saying goodbye to Tamsin, the phone rang. It was Sid who was at the police station. He wanted to update them. They suspected that really he just wanted to talk to them. He sounded quite shaken.

'They want Freya to have psychiatric assessment,' he told Marcus. 'Do you think she's mad?'

'Temporarily out of her right mind, at least,' conceded Marcus.

'I can't believe she's done all that. Trashing Helen's room, the snake and now the gun. I'm so sorry. I feel responsible.'

'It's not your fault.'

'Well, she said she wanted me to notice her. And it's true I never did. She was just a friend who helped out sometimes. I never thought of her like that.'

'I know,' replied Marcus soothingly. 'Look, Sid. It's not your responsibility.'

'I feel bad about it all the same.'

'I think she needs help. And she's helped us to grow.'

'What do you mean?'

'We believe that our soul calls in challenges to test us. Someone has to step forward to present us with those challenges. Say my soul wanted me to deal with a fear of violence, I would have to experience violence. Someone would have to volunteer to fight me, so that I could go through the test.'

'Sounds barmy to me,' said Sid. 'But if you say so.' Unaccountably he felt better and privately he hoped Marcus was not going loopy too.

'How's Joanna?'

'She's fine and so am I.'

'Snakes I can handle. Women I don't have a clue.'

Marcus laughed. 'Good luck, mate.'

'And you.'

Chapter 48

Philip had parked in the car park at the base of Uluru and was shuffling along the wide dusty path, which ran round the great bare rock. He appeared unimpressed by this legacy from the great ancestors and oblivious to the unrelenting heat from the late afternoon sun. He merely scowled in heavy concentration as he scuffed among the loose stones at the edge of the path. From time to time he picked up a stone, then threw it away with a muttered expletive of disgust.

A handful of red-faced tourists watched him covertly as if he were some stray exhibit, while a circling bird of prey observed and ignored him. All inhabited different worlds.

At last he sauntered into the shade of an area marked as sacred to the Aborigines and forbidden to the public. 'I'll find it here,' he muttered and his scowl deepened as he kicked at loose stones. For half an hour he hunted until at last he pounced on one with a shout of triumph. 'Yes,' he exhaled with a jubilant chuckle, examining it from all angles. 'Yes! Yes!'

He plunged it into his pocket, a sly grin twisting his mouth, and wandered slowly back to the path, then to the parking area. He had been so engrossed in his mission that he was unaware of the man in a black car quietly watching him. It was only when Philip had clambered into his battered old vehicle that he glanced up and noticed that the man was gazing intently at him.

The Aborigine paled and a cool, clammy sweat broke out over his body, unlike the perspiration caused by the heat. He realised in a horrible moment that the men from the Elite were following him. It dawned on him that they did not trust him. How dare they! For a second a sense of holy indignation nulled his fear but then even he knew that they were justified in their lack of trust. Well, he'd be careful. He'd got a plan and he'd get the pieces of the crystal ball tonight. Then he'd have the ball and money and power. Those men had told him such stories of what he could do when he'd got it. Complete or incomplete, they'd said, even the pieces of the ball contained power. When he had it they wouldn't be able to touch him. He'd power them out of his life. Then he'd have it all.

So confident was he in his plan that he smiled cockily as he waved to the man in the black car and drove out of the car park. The man, an experienced agent of the Elite, could smell betrayal like dung on a trail. He saw Philip's expression as the smile on the face of the fool on his way to his execution.

At their hotel Joanna was pulling herself out of the swimming pool. 'Let's go to the viewing station and watch the sun going down over Uluru,' she suggested to Marcus and her mother.

'Great idea.'

'And shall we take the pieces of the crystal?' Helen paused to pull the threads of her thoughts together. 'Almost as if . . . if we take it to Uluru, it will call the last piece to us. We've only got another couple of days here to find it.'

'You're right, Mum. Perhaps it would bring in the last piece,' agreed Joanna excitedly. 'It would be a really powerful gesture to the universe. We could assemble all the pieces that we have found and hold it up to the sun as it goes down over Uluru.'

'Yes!' agreed her mother. Joanna's excitement gave her hope.

Marcus, however, was less enthusiastic. 'It's asking for trouble. The Elite are waiting until we complete it before they pounce. You know that. I bet they're watching us right now.'

They all shivered as if the sun had gone in. 'Do you really think so?' Helen felt a flutter of apprehension slide down her back.

'I do,' said Marcus firmly. 'We should leave all the pieces in the hotel safe. If they get hold of it the Elite can use the power to make the rich richer and subjugate the poor. All the policies of darkness like genetic engineering and exploitation of the third world will continue. So will massive corruption and misinformation to people everywhere.'

'That's daft,' Joanna fired back. 'The Elite won't touch us until we get that last piece. Mum's right. We can hold the ball in the light with the intention of calling the last piece to us. Just think how magical that will be. Surely the universe will respond. Then the light can use the power to bring freedom and higher consciousness to all.'

Marcus glanced at Helen, who nodded slowly. 'I think we have to take the risk. Joanna's right. To hold the ball up to the setting sun and call in the last piece would be a powerful signal to the universe. I feel it would respond and that must change the balance of power towards the light.'

'Right!' Marcus accepted their decision but a heavy cloud of misgiving settled on his shoulders and he could not shake it off. They all prayed that the powers of the light would protect them.

Chapter 49

The sunset viewing area was already crowded with cars and coaches when they arrived. Many tourists had set out picnic tables and were drinking wine and cocktails. It was clearly a festive occasion.

Joanna stood between Marcus and her mother in front of their car. She was holding the ball, with one crystal missing, up towards Uluru. Silently they invoked the powers of light to bring them the last piece, so that they could return the crystal ball to Uluru and set the planet back on its true path.

The huge monolith looked sombre in the pinky-orange light, but when the clear bright red disc balanced on top of it and set it on fire they held their breaths in wonder. Then the sun slowly slid away, a truly awesome sight. Helen gasped in amazement.

'Fabulous, isn't it, Mum?' agreed Joanna, now cradling the crystal ball in her arms. Her eyes were alight with excitement.

'Unbelievable.'

Entranced travellers were oohing and aahing all round them. 'That was worth everything,' said Marcus at last.

Gradually the coaches and cars departed until there

were only a couple of other vehicles left in the quiet dark car park.

More and more stars were visible now. It was as if the universe were rolling out a canopy of twinkling lights especially for their delight.

The ball was getting heavy and Joanna reluctantly passed it to her mother. 'I wish we had the last piece,' Helen murmured longingly. 'We could use the power to bring peace everywhere.'

'Or perhaps the power could be used to create more equality in the world and that would prevent starvation,' suggested Joanna.

'And women everywhere could be educated. That would help them and end the power struggle between men and women,' added Helen.

'But we don't know what powers the ball confers,' Marcus reminded them. 'We really have no idea! It's all wishful thinking.'

'True,' agreed Joanna. 'But it's nice to conjecture what we could do to change the planet.' She paused for a moment. 'I'd like to help the animals too. We need to value them.'

'Well, I'd like to be able to heal people in pain,' continued her mother.

Marcus didn't want their expectations to be disappointed. 'We've done our best. I hope the last piece comes to us before we have to leave Australia.'

'Apart from all else I'd like to complete the ball for Uncle George's sake.' Helen sighed. 'He was such a wonderful man.' They slipped into their own reveries and none noticed the door of one of the parked cars opening and a figure flit from it towards them.

'Hi,' said Philip, making them jump.

'Philip!' exclaimed Helen, backing away in horror, trying to hide the ball she was holding. 'What are you doing here?'

Seeing her shock and, in an ecstatic moment realising what she held in her hands, he grinned evilly. 'I've got something you want.'

'How dare you come near us!' Marcus's voice was harsh with anger as he stepped in front of Helen. 'Get into the car, Helen,' he whispered. Immediately she climbed into the back, protecting the ball with her body.

Philip, cocky with confidence in his plan, repeated, 'I've got something you want.'

'What?'

'Guess,' replied Philip provocatively and suddenly they all felt sick, numb, cold. They could all guess what he was about to say and no one wanted to give him the satisfaction of hearing him say it. As it happened he couldn't wait. 'The ball. I've got the last piece of stone, so let's do a deal!'

Marcus glowered. Philip could not see his face but he could hear the fury in his voice. 'No deal!'

Marcus motioned to Joanna to get into the car and she slid into the driving seat behind the wheel. A tiny voice in her head was whispering, 'A deal? Why not?' but she pushed the thought away.

'Hey, listen,' Philip blustered, alarmed at their unexpected response. He had anticipated grovelling agreement. 'I've got the stone. You want it. How about we share the ball?'

'No!'

'Hey, you don't get me. Just think. We can have anything we want – money, houses, cars.' He lowered his voice and whispered to Marcus, 'Women. Go on, let me hold it. Tell her to give it to me.' He nodded towards Helen who had hidden the ball under her bag. 'It's okay. You can trust me!'

Marcus itched to hit Philip and grab the piece of crystal he was holding but discipline and integrity stayed him.

Helen opened the window and called out, 'Show us the crystal!'

Joanna switched on the headlights, which cut through the darkness so that everything beyond the beam looked weird and eerie and Philip opened his hand for a second. Helen, with her head out of the window glimpsed a triangular piece of red stone, before he closed his fingers firmly over it. Helen's heart sank but she said firmly, 'The power's for helping humanity. You wouldn't understand.'

Suddenly Philip cottoned on to their wavelength and in one stride was by Helen's window. Marcus climbed in beside Joanna. Philip spoke to Helen in a wheedling voice, as if he were offering a bargain from a market stall. 'Hey, with this stone the ball is complete. Think what you could do. Make money to help starving children, build a school. You could rule the world your way!'

Helen paused for a lingering moment. Every bit of her

longed for the crystal. Would it really give them power to heal the world? Then she shook her head. 'No, you can't make something pure when it's been tainted. No!'

Philip saw her face. He was feeling desperate now and ready to bargain at a lower level. He moved to Joanna's window. 'How much will you give me for it? Ten thousand dollars. Nothing to you guys, but I'd be satisfied.'

In her mind's eye Joanna saw the crystal ball whole and the initiation complete. But you can't buy initiation. With a sigh, she shook her head.

'Five thousand dollars.' Philip shouted.

'No!' they replied together.

Joanna started the engine and began to reverse from where they had parked. 'Five hundred dollars!' yelled Philip but they ignored him. In rage he flung his fist at the car and threw the stone through the open window.

Suddenly a black car, which had been parked some distance from them, revved into life. Without its lights on the car roared straight at them. Joanna accelerated backwards from their parking space and the four-wheel drive shot back. The black car screeched to a stop, missing them by a hair's-breadth. As two men jumped out, Philip screeched and disappeared into the safety of the darkness.

Joanna threw the gears into first as a shot rang out. The next moments were chaotic. A battered truck appeared from nowhere and swung into the spot their four-wheel drive had just moved from. The karadji leaned out of the window and a beam of light emanating from his solar plexus, the power centre, seemed to knock over the two men, who lay, apparently winded, on the ground. Their weapons, still in their hands, had become unusable lumps of twisted metal.

'Follow me,' the karadji called and, trembling with shock, Joanna forced herself to drive after him.

Scrabbling for the piece of crystal that Philip had thrown into the car, Helen found it at last on the floor. Her hands were slippery with shock at what had just happened and anticipation. But the piece did not fit. Philip had tried to trick them. To think that for one second she'd entertained the thought of doing a deal. 'The bastard!' she exclaimed, telling Joanna and Marcus that the stone was false.

They both gasped. None had suspected that. 'What on earth did he do it for? What was he expecting?' exploded Joanna. 'Did he think we'd hand him the pieces we'd found so far?'

'Maybe. Perhaps he thought he'd do a runner with the ball and give it to the Elite.'

'But it wasn't complete. It was no use to him.'

'I guess he didn't know that. I bet the Elite gave him a big build-up about the power he'd have if he got the pieces from us.'

'Perhaps he thought he'd have most of the power if he had most of the ball.'

'It's weird. I don't understand.'

'He thought he'd have power just by touching the crystals!'

'I guess so. But he was trying to double-cross the Elite. He must be mad!'

361

'He must have thought the power would be his and he'd be invincible.'

'Yes, I bet he thought they couldn't harm him if he had touched the ball.'

'Perhaps he knows where the last crystal is?' Helen's suggestion burst like a bomb in their midst.

'No!'

'How could he?'

'I don't believe it.' All the same their spirits were dampened by the thought. Marcus's jaw tightened. The noble ideals he had voiced previously evaporated. If it was true, he'd get it, he vowed.

'If he's double-crossed the Elite I wouldn't want to be in his shoes right now,' said Joanna.

'And what about those men,' continued Helen. 'I'd give a lot to see their faces when they wake up and try to figure out what happened!'

'And the guns are melted metal in their hands!' added Joanna and suddenly they were laughing, partly with hilarity and partly hysteria.

Whatever would happen next?

Chapter 50

They followed the battered truck driven by the karadji along the road that circuited Uluru. The karadji's truck pulled off the road on to the hard stony ground. He stopped and climbed out.

'Come!'

They did so, silent with anticipation and excitement. Marcus carried the pieces of the precious crystal ball. Five minutes later they were told to sit and wait while the karadji disappeared into the night. They sat for a very long time under the clear starlit sky. They could smell smoke and hear people talking and laughing somewhere out of sight.

'I'm being eaten alive by flies,' complained Helen.

'Me too.'

'They didn't put patience on the list,' giggled Joanna suddenly.

'I suppose when time is immaterial like it is to the Aborigines patience isn't needed. That's why they call the Whites "the clock people".'

At last two Aborigine youths came to fetch them and motioned for them to follow. The youths seemed to be able to see like cats in the dark but Helen, who had poor night vision, held on to Marcus's less bruised arm and still managed to stumble several times on the stony path.

As they rounded a corner they could see half a dozen bonfires, lighting a large flat area. Several men, fully painted, were sitting on the ground and the karadji was one of them. Around them were several groups of people forming a circle. The young men motioned them to sit on the ground and they obeyed, settling themselves to wait.

Suddenly, shockingly there was a loud noise, calls, cries and stamping of feet as a group of intricately painted warriors danced in and performed a ceremonial dance in the space between them and the elders. They disappeared into the darkness and more men appeared and danced. The Westerners felt awed, honoured and elated to be given the opportunity to witness this incredible ceremony.

Then the warriors brought three Aborigines into the circle. Dirk and a heavily bandaged Billy walked but behind them a cowering Philip was dragged in.

'My God, that's Philip. How did they find him?' exclaimed Joanna, startled.

'Shh!'

'What are we doing here?' whispered Helen. 'I don't understand what's going on.'

No sooner had she spoken than the karadji stood up. He gazed directly at the three of them. Immediately they knew what it was about. The trial was to take place. The karadji was telepathically communicating with them.

Philip, Dirk and Billy were invited to speak. They all lied.

Helen, Joanna and Marcus felt they were rising above the trial to a place beyond. A place of higher understanding. Part of them was on the ground listening to the fabrications, contradictions, justifications and pleas of the three frightened men. Another part was beyond it all, where everything is in its right place, where everything serves the whole. New understandings, higher comprehensions dawned.

They could feel the collective pain of the men's race and culture and the personal challenges of their lives. They understood how years of abuse had rendered them vulnerable to influence by men of evil intent.

They all realised that Philip was doomed for this life. His fate was sealed the moment he tried to double-cross the Elite. But Dirk and Billy, weak and greedy though they were, would benefit from clemency and re-education.

It was time for judgement.

There was a moment of intense silence. Not one person moved, not a flame crackled, not a mouse scuttled nor a bat squeaked. Silence.

Simultaneously Marcus, Joanna and Helen stood.

'We plea for mercy with justice,' said Joanna.

'I waive all right to revenge.' Helen's voice, if not clear was at least audible.

'Without them we could not have undertaken the initiation to seek the Codes of Power,' spoke Marcus in a deep voice. 'We ask for clemency.'

The silence deepened. Undaunted, Marcus held up the crystal ball, slotted together with one piece missing and continued. 'We could not complete the crystal ball containing the Codes of Power, but we offer these ten pieces to you. We return it to Uluru where it came from.'

Silence greeted his words. Waves of silence. Were the Aborigines shocked because they had broken the law by speaking as outsiders? Were they evaluating the position? Were they surprised at the return of the crystal ball? The three foreigners could hear their own hearts thumping.

But then the seven karadjis consulted among themselves in low voices and a velvet quality filled the air. The English trio had by now realised that these were the most powerful medicine men in all Australia, gathered for this occasion. At last one announced that the plea had been accepted but the lies of the accused had been noted and for this they would receive punishment.

Unexpectedly, Dirk stood. He both looked and sounded terrified. To their surprise he apologised to Helen, Joanna and Marcus. 'I've learned a lot from you guys,' he added. 'It is time to stop. I too wish to work for reconciliation like Uncle George.'

Marcus felt his heart expand with gratitude and relief. Perhaps it had all been worth it.

The three men were taken out of sight and the elders left too. Only the seven karadjis remained, the wisest of the wise, the most powerful ones. One of the Wise Ones called them forward and they recognised him, of course. His eyes were smiling warmly as he answered their unspoken question, 'Who are you?'

'I am the leader of the Light Ones in Australia. I watch over the Wise Ones and the pure of heart and help them to develop. Shamans and karadjis can work for the dark or the light. Those who were called to attend this ceremony tonight are working with the light to raise the consciousness of our beautiful Earth.

'I have been watching your progress in your selfless quest for the Codes of Power with interest and with pride at your achievement. Your discipline and integrity has helped the planet.'

The already hot cheeks of the outsiders flushed with embarrassment and pleasure. Each was thinking, Why me? Why us? Why Australia?

Again he responded to their thoughts. 'You know the answers already. You were all trained before this life to help the planet and you were ready.

'Your souls called in tests to check that you were indeed prepared to undertake the initiation into the Codes of Power.'

He addressed Helen directly: 'Helen, when you were kidnapped your soul was testing your courage, resourcefulness, compassion and many other qualities. You passed the tests.'

He turned to Marcus and Joanna. 'Your strength of mind was tested by the crocodile and the events in the Black Mountain. And Joanna, you wish to know why you called in the challenge of the snake bite?'

The girl nodded.

'On one level your soul wished to check your ability to forgive but there was more. During an Egyptian incarnation as a priestess you worked with poisonous snakes where you learned that certain venoms, used in controlled circumstances, could open the third eye. Your soul remembered and knew that the only way to gather the remaining crystals was for you to "see" where they were. So you offered to undergo that experience to help all. That was the higher purpose of that particular challenge. We are grateful and you will be rewarded.'

Joanna gasped inaudibly.

'Finally, Philip came in to offer you all a test in integrity. Remember the darkness always serves the light. None of you succumbed to temptation to do a deal with him for the Codes of Power. You turned down what you thought was an opportunity to receive the last crystal because it might give power to the darkness.' He paused. 'Though some of you hesitated.' Immediately they all felt guilty but he smiled.

Unexpectedly he held up a piece of red crystal, saying, 'This crystal contains the message "On earth we all grow through service."'

Marcus took a second to realise what it was. The last piece! Then he held up the ball and the magic man slotted it in. At last the crystal ball containing the Codes of Power was whole. It was the end of their quest and Marcus, Joanna and Helen wanted to shout with joy and delight.

Instead they murmured a polite English, 'Thank you.' But the Wise Ones could see that their hearts were bursting with delight.

The karadji handed the completed crystal ball to Helen. She held it reverently for a minute before passing it to Joanna who did the same before she gave it to Marcus. Then the seven karadjis passed it from one to another. Each held it and gave thanks.

The Wise One spoke slowly and clearly, 'You have demonstrated that you are worthy to carry the power of the light. Henceforth all that you do will be dedicated to the good of the whole.

'I will place in your auras the symbol for the Codes of Power. You will do your part in bringing the consciousness of all on Earth to a higher level until we all once again live in heaven on Earth.

'Your initiation has now made it easier for others to follow in this path which will return our sacred planet to its rightful place in the universe.'

The karadji's voice seemed to boom suddenly as if he had moved into an expanded space. 'The initiation into the Codes of Power unlocks certain powers. Power is a double-edged sword, because it can be used for or against the light. If it is used for personal aggrandisement it will corrupt you, and this will spiral you back into lifetimes ruled by ego and selfish motives. Only use these powers when your heart and mind are balanced and when you are connected to your intuition, your inner wisdom.' He emphasised, 'Only use these powers for the highest good.'

They stood immobile. Awed. Shaken. Proud. And a little apprehensive. 'Helen, I grant you the gift to see into people's hearts and the power to pull out pain.'

Helen's eyes shone but she was aware too of the awesome responsibility this entailed. She even wondered fleetingly if she wanted such power, but that thought evaporated as her heart opened with a flood of joy.

'Look!' indicated the karadji, inclining his head towards a young man who was approaching. Helen saw in the distance that Dirk had been brought to the outer edge of the light from the bonfire and was standing there, looking at her. All at once she saw in the centre of his chest hard black lumps of pain, where hurts had solidified, blocking his heart centre. Behind them layers of hurt, bitterness and feelings of rejection filled his heart. Between the knots of pain and hurt, lights flickered, pink and green, then a flash of gold, followed by a hint of white. She saw that there were lifetimes of pain compressed in his heart centre but also that there was hope.

She longed to help him and she had the power to lift out the pain but she knew that if she did so Dirk would have a massive heart attack. It would be too sudden. She took a breath and balanced her heart and head. Then she sent a small pink flame from her heart to one of the black clots of unresolved pain. Something small in his heart shifted and she had a sense that he smiled. It would be a slow task to open his heart. She realised that a black heart was really a heart full of pain.

She felt very tired. The karadji was watching her. He nodded gravely. 'Good. You will use your power with wisdom. It is not an easy path.'

No, thought Helen. I've got a lot to learn.

'Learn to switch this ability on and off,' he warned, 'or you will be overwhelmed both by the darkness in hearts and by the light.'

The Wise One gave Joanna the gift of understanding animals and the power to communicate with and help them. She was overjoyed but also wary. Instantly she could 'hear' a babble of talking, only she was not sure if it was aloud or telepathic. A frog croaked pathetically, 'This is our home and we are being pushed out. Help us please.' A dingo transmitted telepathically, 'I like being here in the desert. These people are my friends and we work and live together. We love each other and are helping each other to grow. Don't let them put us in compounds.' Joanna put her hands to her ears.

The karadji said, 'You too must learn to turn off this power and use discernment and discrimination at all times. Only help when it is wise to do so.'

She felt her knees turn to water. Whatever had she been given? It felt overpowering. Like her mother she was not really sure if she wanted the power now that she had it.

The karadji turned to Marcus. 'Over many lifetimes on this planet and others, you have shown wisdom and discernment. I give you the gift of being able to see into people's souls and the power to guide them.'

'Wow! ' mouthed Marcus, overwhelmed. What did it mean?

The karadji pointed to Philip who now stood by Dirk, 'See.'

Instantly Marcus became aware of a 'knowing'. He did not understand where it came from but he 'knew' Philip's soul journey. He 'knew' that he had incarnated as an Aborigine many times, often as a hunter fending for his family but there was a thread of anger and frustration running through his lives. He had once been in a position of power in a Lemurian life but he had abused that power, through greed and lust. Then he was aware of a life where Philip had been a caring and responsible woman. It was a lifetime of love and warmth, surrounded by family and friends who supported her.

Marcus felt that it was a tremendous responsibility to be given this information and did not quite know what to do with it. He consciously aligned himself to Philip's Higher Self and then knew that there was little he could do to help Philip in this life. The Elite would kill him soon. He could not alter that destiny. So he sent up a prayer for Philip's soul and beamed into his mind a memory of the lifetime of warmth and love. It was all he could do and he hoped it would help the man.

Feeling frustrated, he looked at the karadji, who nodded, understanding. 'You must learn that sometimes there is nothing you can do but there will be many times you can influence people's destiny. It is a great responsibility.'

'It is,' agreed Marcus.

They stood proudly in front of him as he made movements with his hand in their auras, and they knew he was placing the symbols for the Codes of Power into their energy fields.

Helen's heart sang. Thank you, she thought. Thank you all of you who tested me, for you made it possible for me to pass this initiation. You've enabled me to help people in a way I couldn't before.

At last Joanna, Marcus and Helen were able to look at each other. Tears rolled down Joanna's cheeks. She took Marcus and Helen by their hands and squeezed tight.

They all knew their lives had been changed for ever. They just did not know how much.

The karadji held up the crystal ball, which was to be returned to the heart of Uluru now that it had been made whole.

Then he leaped up the escarpment, nimbly like a rock kangaroo until he disappeared from sight. Soon he appeared high above them silhouetted against the pre-dawn sky holding the crystal ball aloft.

They could hear him call out or perhaps he only did so telepathically.

'We dedicate ourselves to bring about the blueprint for planet Earth. We accept our responsibility as caretakers of Mother Earth. We accept that everyone and everything expresses a different aspect of Great Spirit. We will celebrate life and serve all.

'We accept and pledge ourselves to maintain that: All is balanced. All are equal. There is enough for all and we will share it and care for each other.

'We dedicate ourselves to: Maintaining harmony between ourselves and the natural world. Loving and supporting each other.

'We pledge to: Honour the differences in all creation. Honour and learn from every creature and every culture. Remain transparent in our thoughts and words.'

As the orange red sun rose to herald a new day, he threw the crystal ball high into the air. It dropped into a deep crevice and returned to the heart of Uluru.

Bibliography

Cowan, James G., *The Elements of the Aborigine Tradition* (Element Books)

Hananson, Donni, *Oracle of the Dreamtime* (Connections Books)

Lambert, Johanna (ed.), *Wise Women of the Dreamtime* (Inner Traditions International)

The Little Red, Yellow and Black Book (Australian Institute for Aboriginal and Torres Strait Islanders Studies)

Lockwood, Douglas, *I, The Aboriginal* (Lansdowne)

Neidjie, Bill, *Story about Feeling* (Magabala Books)

Power, Phyllis, *Legends from the Outback* (J.M. Dent)

Reynolds, Henry, *Why Weren't We Told? (Penguin Books)*